Karen Hayes is the author of four previous novels and a volume of poetry, *Between Mornings*. Her most recent novel, *Still Life on Sand*, is also published by Black Swan. She lives in Devon with her husband and children.

D1396183

Also by Karen Hayes

STILL LIFE ON SAND

and published by Black Swan

CLOUD MUSIC

Karen Hayes

BLACK SWAN

CLOUD MUSIC
A BLACK SWAN BOOK : 0 552 99754 4

First publication in Great Britain

PRINTING HISTORY
Black Swan edition published 1997

Copyright © Karen Hayes 1997

The right of Karen Hayes to be identified as the author of
this work has been asserted in accordance with sections 77 and 78
of the Copyright Designs and Patents Act 1988.

All the characters in this book are fictitious,
and any resemblance to actual persons, living or dead,
is purely coincidental.

Condition of Sale
This book is sold subject to the condition that it shall not,
by way of trade or otherwise, be lent, re-sold, hired out or
otherwise circulated in any form of binding or cover other than
that in which it is published and without a similar condition
including this condition being imposed on the subsequent purchaser.

Set in 11/13pt Linotype Melior by
County Typesetters, Margate, Kent.

Black Swan Books are published by Transworld Publishers Ltd,
61–63 Uxbridge Road, Ealing, London W5 5SA,
in Australia by Transworld Publishers (Australia) Pty Ltd,
15–25 Helles Avenue, Moorebank, NSW 2170
and in New Zealand by Transworld Publishers (NZ) Ltd,
3 William Pickering Drive, Albany, Auckland.

Reproduced, printed and bound in Great Britain by
Cox & Wyman Ltd, Reading, Berks.

For Jules

Acknowledgements

For inspiration and information, special thanks to Piers Adams and Adam Swainson.

I would also like to warmly thank my agent Serafina Clarke and my editor Francesca Liversidge, as well as Joanna Goldsworthy, Sally Wray, and the many others at Transworld who have been so helpful. And last but never least, a big thank you to Adrian Boreham.

Chapter One

Lightning corrodes the night sky. Fragments of black disintegrate with each flash, until it seems as if the entire universe is crumbling.

Ivo stands on the flimsy wooden pier leading precariously into the swamp, exulting. At times like this he knows he is a god, knows that he is invulnerable.

The storm moves directly overhead. Ivo laughs aloud as the rain axes him, the wind knifes him. Lightning strikes dangerously close to the giant pine trees nearby, but Ivo ignores it as he takes photo after photo.

The storm diminishes, as turbulence in nature and in the emotions eventually does. The thunder becomes no more threatening than the purr of a cat. As usual, Ivo feels a moment of desolation, not unlike post-coital despair. This says more about Ivo's many sexual relationships than about the thunderstorm.

Now Ivo feels only wet and cold and deflated. Gathering his cameras, his photographic equipment, he places them back into his rented motor boat and slowly chugs away from the soggy island and down the narrow inlets of the vast Georgia swamp. The wind has dropped, and the air is damp and still. Sodden Spanish moss hangs off the cyprus trees growing in the water and the excess moisture drips into the boat, down Ivo's neck, but he hardly notices. The swamps of Okefenokee – the Land of the Trembling Earth – are now flat and uninspiring after the discord of the storm, as is Ivo's state of mind.

Luckily there will be another day, another night, another storm. Consoling himself with this thought, Ivo accelerates, anxious now to disembark, find his car and begin the long drive back to Miami.

Across the sea, Ireland is uniquely blanketed in sunshine. Troy O'Donnell surveys his landscape and his life and finds them both satisfactory.

The calm sea beyond the hidden cove reflects this harmony. A small solitary fishing boat idles near the wooden pier. A heron stands motionless in the shallows. On the shore, crumpled and looking ready to fall into the water, is Troy's home, known for years as Heron's Cove House. The roof of the once imposing Georgian building is wobbly with loose slates, the wooden frames of the grand windows are rotten. Troy isn't fussed. He inherited Heron's Cove from his father's older sister only a year ago, and to him it is no less than paradise, sagging ceilings and all.

Two swans swim in close to Troy, who feeds them with cold toast left over from his breakfast. From an open window in the music room, the silver sounds of a harpsichord filter through the sunlight: Bach. The notes tinkle across the water and evaporate in the sunlight. Troy listens, not so much with his heart but with his head. His passion is music, but it is an intellectual passion, a reasoned cerebral one. He likes the late string quartets of Beethoven, Handel's more rarefied, mythical operas; Bach, which he is listening to now, is a deep favourite. Troy finds an intellectual, almost impersonal style of music entirely to his liking; it is much more to his taste than the rampant emotionalism of some of the later Romantics.

Troy goes inside, stands behind the harpsichordist. Something about her white fingers, fluttering over the keyboard like little seabirds, touches some ancestral memory inside him. He thinks of Irish princesses, slim fingers caressing ancient harps: Isolde playing for Tristan while outside the castle walls mist filters over ancient hills. 'You look like Isolde,' he says without thinking.

The woman smiles without looking up. Troy puts his hand on the woman's shoulder. 'You'll be fine,' he says softly. 'You know that now, I hope.'

She stops playing and places her own hands carefully in her lap; she looks at them perplexedly, as if they were strange sea anemones crawled out from the water and onto her sea-green skirt.

'No,' she says. 'I'm not sure. All I am sure of is that if you hadn't come along there would not even have been the possibility.'

This makes Troy inordinately happy, for reasons he doesn't care to delve into. Probably pure macho pride, he thinks fleetingly: man the hero, come to the rescue of the suffering princess in distress, the stuff of myth and legends. Shaking his head ruefully, he decides it must be Ireland doing this to him. He'll be looking for leprechauns next.

The woman motions Troy to sit next to her. She opens a page of music and the two begin to play a Couperin duet. Troy, as he plays, feels his life calm, ordered, just as he likes it. The upheavals of the past few years are over; he is settled, unstressed, contented.

Outside, the cove reflects the harmony of the music. The swans, sated, are cruising contentedly, the heron remains contemplative. There is not a single cloud in the spring sky. Nature is as tranquil today as the two musicians playing within.

11

On a plane which has just taken off from Miami, Steffie
O'Donnell is also listening to harpsichord music on the
airline earphones. By one of those coincidences that
make Steffie's spine tingle, the FM station is playing a
recording made by her brother, Troy, something by
Pachelbel.

After a time the earphones begin to pinch her ears,
so she takes them off, shaking loose her pale ginger
hair. Steffie is proud of her hair. It is shiny and fine and
without any trace of grey, unlike Troy's who, though
younger, has streaks of white highlighting his deeper
carroty colour. Ivo too, the youngest O'Donnell and
still in his thirties, is losing his marmalade tinge: both
his unkempt beard and thicket hair look now as if they
have been lightly whitewashed, like a ginger tom-cat
in a snowstorm. Steffie smiles to herself as she thinks
of the pain the O'Donnell hair colour caused when the
family relocated for a few years to Georgia, then
Florida. The Ginger Snaps, they were called, after an
American cookie. It was worse when they moved back
to England. In Kent, where they finished their school-
ing, they were referred to mockingly as the Ginger
Nuts.

Steffie, looking out over soft cloud, wonders why
she is thinking of their childhood now. Perhaps it is
because she is about to surprise Troy with an unexpected visit, and because Ivo will be meeting her at
Heron's Cove some time this summer. Ivo has never
photographed lightning in Ireland, and has been
tempted by Troy's account of the electrical storms he
witnessed last summer over the sea. It will be the first
time the three of them have been together for years.

Or perhaps she is reminiscing about her childhood
because she is about to have her own baby. Steffie

glows at the thought; her pale translucent skin, her freckles, her green eyes, all light up like fireflies at the thought of the imminent birth.

Steffie is obsessed with her baby. She is unmarried, she is forty-two years old, she has never had a baby before. She isn't even pregnant. But not a minute of her life goes by without the image of her own baby printed like batik on the cloth of her heart.

It's raining at Shannon airport, but Steffie gets a lift quickly from an Anglo-Irish priest off to Tralee to see his aged auntie before she pops off, as he succinctly puts it. Luckily, he rambles on amiably about dulcet Irish childhood summers while Steffie dreams sweet dreams about her baby. Perhaps she'll bring her up in Ireland, raise her in Troy's new home, Heron's Cove. Steffie was there once, last year when Troy first took it over. She liked the mountains grandly wading into the clear sea, liked the way the house nestled like a turtledove in the mouth of the cove and the way the narrow river ran behind it, like a ribbon wrapping a special parcel.

'We're nearing Tralee,' the priest says heartily, startling Steffie from her reverie. 'What'll you do now? A pretty young thing like you shouldn't be hitch-hiking, y'know. Not in these times.' He shakes his head mournfully.

Steffie, not a Catholic herself, isn't sure whether a priest should notice a woman's prettiness, but she is flattered by the 'young'. Though since he is about seventy himself, maybe it isn't such a compliment. Nonetheless she needs reassuring about her relative youth these days, with a baby on the way. She had one or two barbs from her mother about being the only mother in the Parent–Teachers Association with a

13

zimmer frame and senile dementia; the sort of thing which struck her as particularly unfunny and unhelpful.

'It's quite safe to hitch around Ireland,' Steffie reassures the priest. 'I did a lot of it in the past.'

This is quite true. Steffie is a journalist, a travel writer who made her name discovering hidden but entrancing parts of the world, thus spoiling them for both the natives and the few discerning travellers who had visited the places previously. She sometimes feels guilty about this.

But it has been several years since Steffie has been to Ireland. Since she settled in Miami, she has written mostly about America, primarily for a weekly column in one of the Sunday supplements back in England, and occasionally for a prestigious monthly magazine based in New York. She tops her income with copious articles on disparate subjects, whatever takes her fancy, and has become well known in certain circles for the perception and astringency of her writing.

Now, however, Steffie's mind is far from her work; other things have overcrowded it lately. 'Is this all right?' the priest is saying, dropping her off in Tralee.

Steffie, who had been thinking once again of her baby, assures him it is fine, and thanks him profusely. She finds an amicable pub that does a hearty home-made fish soup, which she eats ravenously with great slices of brown bread, the Irish soda bread she loves. She feels tired now, jet-lagged. She wonders if she's getting too old for this hitch-hiking lark, wonders if she's trying to cling to some worn-out youth in persisting to hitch whenever she's in Europe, just as she did in her earlier travelling days. Growing older has only recently begun bothering Steffie, when the

14

passion for motherhood, long dormant, mushroomed in her almost overnight. She suspects this insistence on hitch-hiking is just another way of proving to herself that she is still young enough, fit enough and fearless enough to cope with the demands of an infant.

Steffie, luckily, is also level-headed enough to realize this, and asks the sweet-faced blonde behind the counter if there is a bus from Tralee to Dingle, the nearest town to Heron's Cove. The barmaid smiles even wider and says to the man sitting on a stool drinking coffee, 'Jack, your prayers are answered, now.' Turning to Steffie she says accommodatingly, 'Jack here lives just outside Dingle; and would you believe, is on his way home this very minute. He hates travelling alone, so he tells me.'

Steffie and the man exchange somewhat embarrassed words, being thrust upon each other so firmly and irrevocably. But Jack, good-humouredly, insists on giving Steffie a lift, after warning her it will be in his dilapidated farm van. Steffie appraises him with an experienced hitch-hiker's eye and decides to accept. They leave the pub together shortly afterwards; the blonde, to Jack's obvious discomfiture, clinging to him for a moment as they say goodbye, asking him rather forlornly not to leave it so long before visiting Tralee again.

The blue van is indeed as wheezy and rusty as Jack has warned, but it's sound and covers the miles. 'What a beautiful day,' Jack says. 'The first for weeks. We've had a nasty spring so far, cold, frost. Everything will be late this year. I've only just put the cows out.'

Jack is a farmer, working on his father's farm. 'I'm the only one left now, other than my parents. My brothers are all in London, would you believe. One's a teacher, one drives a taxi, the other's a bookseller. I

15

was there, for a time, to see what the attraction was. Couldn't find a single thing.'

'So you came back to your roots,' Steffie says lightly. She wonders what it would be like, having roots to go back to.

Jack grins. 'You could say that. My dad took the farm over from his own father, built it up from nine milking cows to a herd of thirty. I'm increasing the herd bit by bit, and we do contracting work too for other farms. With that plus the sheep, we get by, though it's always a struggle. I'd rather be doing it than anything else though.'

Jack talks about farming knowledgeably. He has plans, he has dreams. Having sown his wild oats in England, he tells her, he's ready to settle down in this rural part of Ireland.

After a time, Jack turns the conversation to Steffie. 'Can't quite place your accent. It's not totally unlike Irish, you know. English, liberally tempered with American, right? And what else? There's something of your very own mixed up there.'

Steffie laughs. She likes this young man, feels perkier, her tiredness gone, as they rattle along in the blue van, the mountains looming green and promising around them. Signs of spring are only just emerging: buds unfurling, a tentative scattering of blossom here and there. There's the smell of spring too: earthy, pungent.

'My brothers and I were born in England, but raised all over. Dad is American with Irish parents, Mum's English with a mixture of French and Italian. Dad was a journalist, a foreign correspondent. I think my brothers and I went to school in just about every country in Europe, if only for a few months.'

Jack, growing up under the solid shadow of the

16

mountain behind the farm, in the sturdy turf of family, cousins and aunts and uncles that comprise his earliest memories, can't imagine this, but he says, 'Sounds interesting.'

'I suppose it was.' Steffie's voice is so wistful that Jack takes his eyes off the road for a moment to look at her.

'You don't sound very enthusiastic.'

She shrugs. She would have liked to have seen less of the world and more of her parents when she was growing up. Listening to Jack talk about his parents, the farm which has been in the family for as long as he can remember, has saddened her, and she vows to give her child at least one stable parent, something she and Ivo and Troy never had.

'And now?'

It takes her a moment to realize that Jack is asking her where she lives now.

'The States,' she replies. 'I settled in England until a couple of years ago, now I'm in Miami. One of my brothers is too. The other, Troy, lived in London until a year ago, now he lives in Ireland, a place called Heron's Cove. It's near a tiny village called Ballycaveen. That's where I'm headed now. Do you know it?'

'Sure I know Ballycaveen. And is he liking Ireland, your brother?'

'Oh, yes. He was unhappy in England the past few years. Got a divorce after a brief five-year marriage, gave up being a concert musician to make harpsichords, found working in London stressful and expensive. He's set up his workshop at Heron's Cove and seems blissfully content now. At least he sounds so on the phone; I've not seen him for nearly a year.'

Jack and Steffie talk easily, both surprised at how

17

swiftly the time goes. Jack's a talker, but he's also a good listener. Steffie nearly tells him about her baby, but they're suddenly in Dingle and the ride is almost over. Jack insists on driving through the town and taking her straight to her brother's house, even though it is another twenty minutes or so. Steffie, relieved, doesn't protest too much. It's been a long sleepless journey; she knows she is not very far off exhaustion.

Jack sees this, and says kindly, 'You'll be wanting to go right to sleep when you get there.'

She agrees. 'It's been a long day.' They lapse into a friendly silence the last few miles. Steffie likes this young Irishman, likes his warmth, his openness. She studies his profile as he drives: good chin, long thin nose, full lips, a mass of curly dark auburn hair. He must be around thirty, she decides, perhaps a year or two older.

Jack, directed by Steffie, drives through the small harbour village of Ballycaveen and down a pitted road towards the cove. The road, tarmac splitting with odd pockets of grass and weeds, looks as if it's going to go right into the sea, but instead makes a sharp turn to end up rather abruptly at a large white house nearly obscured by vines, overgrown rhododendrons and fuchsia bushes running riot.

Steffie asks Jack to stop and have a cup of tea, but Jack tactfully declines, knowing she will want space to greet her brother alone. He jumps out of the van to hand her her capacious canvas travelling bag, shakes her hand heartily, and tells her to be sure and visit his farm some day, when she's in Dingle. 'Ask any of the locals where Jack Murphy lives,' he says, waving to her as his van chunters back up the road.

Steffie waves him out of sight and turns to the house which looks sad, neglected, the outside flaky and peeling; the inside, from what she can see through the downstairs windows, dusty and grim. It's not a scrap different from the way it looked when Troy took it over, Steffie decides. She knocks on the door, which is splintered and beginning to rot. A rusty brass knocker hangs broken at eye level. Behind the house Steffie can hear the cry of gulls, smell the sea seeping its salty perfume over the hills.

Steffie knocks again, then pushes the front door open. It is either locked or stuck, probably the latter. She leaves her bag where it is and walks around the house on an overgrown path to the back, the sea smell growing stronger. The fine day has suddenly altered; clouds have come down from the mountains in front of the house and a fine rain, as natural to this place as cobwebs in an old house, is moistening the air. The cove is delicately being sprinkled with this mist, and the swans shake themselves slightly as they drift in the water. The tide is in, lapping politely at the muddy shore behind the house and nearly reaching the new terrace Troy has had built.

Steffie notices that here is where all the changes are. The broken windows in the massive conservatory have been replaced with new glass, and a fine oak door with a stained-glass window has replaced the old one. The door is slightly open, and Steffie can now hear music coming from somewhere beyond the conservatory. She goes inside, making her way through a jumble of plants, a mixture of bamboo furniture, some of it faded and wobbly, other pieces new and barely used. Tables of various sizes seemed to be scattered at random, covered with a profusion of music scores, old magazines, books and newspapers. As usual, Troy's clear uncluttered mind is apparently able to live in harmony with the disarray of his household, Steffie observes.

She looks into the first door she comes to and sees a kitchen; there is no-one there, so she moves on towards the music. There is a new archway at the far end of the conservatory, covered with a beaded curtain, and from here Steffie can hear the sounds of a violin and a harpsichord. The sunny music confronts the drizzle outside, seems to blow the rain away from her face. Smiling with anticipation, she pushes open the door and goes inside.

She is able to watch the musicians before they are aware of her. Her brother Troy is playing the violin, his body rolling and swaying with the music like a ship on a swell. Troy's hair is longer than Steffie remembers and flops about as he plays. The white streaks are more pronounced, although he is barely forty; oddly, the copper hair remaining has grown darker, the colour like an angry sunset. He looks too tall, too lanky, for the small violin, and seems to be fighting it rather than playing on it, though the music is divine. Steffie decides he is far better suited for the harpsichord; he becomes elegant when he plays, like the instrument itself.

She turns her attention to the woman at the harpsichord, noting the instrument first. It is exquisite, no doubt one of Troy's. It is a copy of an eighteenth-century Flemish harpsichord, in pale-green lacquer with gold leaf banding. Steffie stands entranced, and even her baby is forgotten for this one moment.

'My God! Steffie!'

The music suddenly breaks off, filling the air with silent discord, something brutally unfinished. Steffie is engulfed in long spider arms and legs and a spindly body as her brother welcomes her to Heron's Cove. Troy doesn't seem at all surprised to see her. The O'Donnell siblings lost their faculty for surprise years ago, as they were towed as children around America and Europe by their wayward parents.

'Hey, you're looking great, Troy,' Steffie says, assessing her brother. Troy's eyes are clear, his skin unlined. He looks happy.

The harpsichordist is standing by her instrument waiting patiently for brother and sister to finish their reunion. She is tall, thin and pale – fragile. Despite this, Steffie sees a translucent beauty in the harmony of her features, the perfection of her oval face. She is dressed in something sea green and flowing which makes the other woman feel slightly grubby in her travel-worn linen trouser suit. 'Steffie, this is Alina Montgomery, from Dublin. Alina, my sister Steffie.'

Troy beams at both women as they eye each other with a wary caution, as people do who know they are going to have to see a lot of each other, like it or not. Steffie can tell immediately, from the look of pride on Troy's face, that she must take this woman seriously. In this she is more perceptive than her brother Troy, who has not yet realized this.

'Lovely to meet you at last,' Alina says with a slight smile. Her voice has only the slightest trace of an Irish accent. 'I've read your column in the English newspaper, and of course Troy has told me all about you. He's quite proud of his famous sister.'

'Hardly famous,' Steffie smiles in return. 'I'm just lucky to make a decent living from something I love doing.'

Alina looks pained as Steffie says this, and turns as if for help to Troy. He touches her shoulder gently, and Steffie is aware of the grace of his movement, of the contrast between it and his apparent awkwardness on the violin.

'Would you like tea?' Alina asks as Troy and Steffie

21

beam at each other affectionately. Troy is fond of his sister, is not at all disconcerted to find her here at Heron's Cove. He knows she will not disrupt the order of his life, will go with the flow, as it were. Steffie has always been the most adaptable of the O'Donnells.

'Tea would be great,' Steffie stays, noting that Alina is at home enough in Troy's house to play hostess. The last time Steffie spoke to him on the telephone was a month ago; there was no mention of a woman living here then. But then Troy has always been secretive about his private life, believing people to be totally uninterested, as he himself is uninterested in the emotional entanglements of others.

As Alina turns to leave the room Steffie notices a red scar across her throat, as if she had tried to slash it. It had been partially hidden by a thick blond plait, pulled around in front of Alina's neck and snaking down her full bosom.

'That's rather nasty,' Steffie says after Alina has gone. 'The scar.'

'It's not what it looks like,' Troy says softly. 'Not a suicide attempt. On the contrary. Alina, more than anyone I know, wants life.'

Steffie looks at him and waits for more. Troy is always more forthcoming when not questioned. 'A car accident,' he finally goes on. 'Broken neck, fractured spine. Nearly died, then partially paralysed for a time. Her hands are the last things that came to life again.'

Steffie understands. The woman is a musician, of course, a harpsichordist like Troy. She recognizes the name now; she remembers a concert that Troy and Alina gave together in London, several years ago.

'She's lucky she can play again,' Steffie says, feeling inadequate.

'She can't. Or, more importantly, she thinks she can't.'

'And you disagree.'

'Yes. Her playing is almost as fine as before the accident. Almost.' Troy's angled face hardens as he says this. With anger? Pity? Despair? Steffie is not sure.

'And that "almost" isn't enough,' Steffie finishes for him.

'Not for Alina. Though she's still better than any other harpsichordist on the circuit right now. And she gets better every day. But no. It's *not* enough for her.'

Troy walks away from Steffie abruptly, terminating the conversation. She has time to look around the music room, which is a new addition to the house. The ceiling is high, rounded; the windows small enough to protect the harpsichord and Troy's piano which is also in the room, but adequate enough to let in decent light. The floors are polished wood covered in soft Turkish rugs. A huge chandelier hangs from the ceiling, which is new and ornate and rather splendid in a grand baroque manner.

'A beautiful room,' she says.

Troy looks around with satisfaction. 'I've spent all my money on this, I'm afraid. And on my workshop, of course. You must come and have a look later; I had the old stables converted. Unfortunately I have nothing left with which to do the rest of the house, but there's no hurry. The workshop and music room were my first priorities.'

Alina comes in with a laden tea tray. There is a small scuffle as Troy tries to take the tray from her. He is treating her like an invalid still, Steffie thinks, and Alina doesn't like it.

'I was saying how lovely this music room is,' Steffie

23

says, to distil some of the tension she feels coming from Alina as Troy, having won the tussle over the tea tray, hands out cups and pours from a large brown teapot.

'Troy has done a wonderful job,' Alina agrees. 'He had builders in, of course, but he designed it all himself. He even added a couple of bedrooms and a bathroom, over there—' she indicates another door at the back of the music room.

'Handy for visiting musicians,' Troy adds. 'We have concerts here every month now. The locals are very supportive, and of course there is the tourist crowd in the season. Alina is going to do a concert very soon, I hope.'

Again that pained look, then Alina turns her back to straighten some music that has fallen off a table behind her. They are sitting in armchairs at the far end of the music room, around a small marble fireplace which has a blowzy house plant sitting in it. The plant is slightly singed, as if it hadn't been properly moved away when a fire was lit. As Alina fusses with the music, Steffie notices another scar, going down the back of her neck. Though still angry, it is neat and almost dainty, like a cake sliced down the middle for afternoon tea.

Troy fusses over them both, worrying whether the tea is too strong, too weak, over the fact that there seems to be no sugar in the house and perhaps Steffie would like some in her tea. When he finally settles, they talk about Steffie's flight, their brother Ivo whom Steffie saw briefly in Florida before coming to Ireland, their father Ronald who is planning to return to New York after wintering in Palm Beach.

'He's become demented over his health,' Steffie says. 'Not a thing wrong with him, but he broods over his heart, his blood pressure, his muscle tone – everything. He hardly realized I was there.'

'So what's new,' Troy mutters. 'He never knew any of us were there when we were growing up. Nor did our sainted mother.'

Steffie agrees. 'I'm surprised they carted us about on so many of their travels, rather than sticking us in an obscure boarding school for the duration of our childhood.'

'To show us off, of course. You were the precocious young writer, I the budding musician. And Ivo—' He breaks off and exchanges a smile with Steffie.

'Ivo was just real darling,' she says, lapsing into broad American. 'Cute, adorable, cuddly – a definite plus for the parents, when bundled out by the nanny to impress visitors before cocktail parties.'

Troy and Steffie are silent for a moment, brooding on their parents. *I will not be like either of them,* Steffie promises herself, not for the first time. Whatever kind of a parent I turn out to be, it will not be anything like them, which will be at least one advantage my child will have over me.

Troy doesn't ask why Steffie is here, how long she plans to stay. It is one of the most maddening things about Troy, how he refuses to either ask questions or respond to them.

There are raisin scones, bought from the village shop in Ballycaveen, with the tea, and Troy and Steffie eat two each. Alina picks at her scone and Troy admonishes her, urges her to have more, tells her she must regain the weight she lost in hospital. Alina listens, smiles distractedly and continues picking. Troy looks at her worriedly. Again, sensing some tension, Steffie says to Troy, 'I'd like to stay with you for a few weeks, maybe longer.'

'Of course, Heron's Cove is your home too; you're welcome to stay as long as you like.'

'The thing is,' Steffie continues, 'the thing is, I'm going to have a baby.' She'd have liked to have said this to her brother alone, but this new woman appears part of Troy now, sitting near him completely self-contained yet like the same entity, like Siamese twins attached at some spirit level. It unnerves Steffie. She is not quite sure what their relationship is.

Alina exclaims, offers congratulations, asks Steffie politely when the baby is due. Troy looks stunned and, in place of the thousand questions rattling in his brain, pours them all another cup of tea.

'I'm not pregnant,' Steffie smiles, amused at her brother's discomfiture.

Troy thinks of Steffie's ex-lovers and sighs inwardly with relief. 'I don't understand,' he says cautiously.

'I'm adopting,' Steffie explains. 'A baby from South America. Peru. I've been negotiating for months, almost a year.' To his unasked question, she adds, 'I didn't tell you or Ivo, or the parents, because you'd all have dissuaded me.'

Troy thinks carefully about this and decides it is true. Ivo would have called her barmy, and though he himself would have been more circumspect, he wouldn't have encouraged her. She is middle-aged after all, and slightly scatty, he believes. What does she want with a baby, skipping around the world as she does?

'I went up to Dad's condominium in Palm Beach for the day, told him just before I came here. He cautiously sounded me out on my finances, lectured me on how expensive children are, and then drummed into me that *his* money is carefully invested for his old age and he hoped I wasn't planning on asking for his help

26

to support my child. As if I would, for God's sake. Then he said he was too tired and ill to be a grandparent.'

This makes Troy laugh. Ronald is a young seventy, and fitter than most men half his age, despite his constant worries over his health.

'Then there was Ivo. I saw him in Miami. He had just returned from the Okefenokee swamp in Georgia, remember we used to camp there as children? He was plastered in dried caked mud, feeling anti-climactic as he always does after a storm. When I told him about the baby, he looked shocked, then hurt.'

Troy laughs again. 'A touch of jealousy there, I think. You've always mothered him. He's probably surprised that you need another baby after him.'

'I'm only six years older than Ivo,' Steffie says, prickly. 'Anyway, after his initial reaction he was fine. He hugged me profusely, said I'd be a great mother and disappeared into his darkroom, adding rather as an afterthought that I must be completely off my head.'

Troy nods to this. He *knows* they are all slightly mad, the whole family, but he doesn't see this as a problem. He feels that his own peculiarities are at least ordered, under control. His obsession for music, his need to be constantly immersed in it; his detached and slightly cynical wariness of emotion, which defeated his wife in the end; his compulsive need for harmony both in music and in his personal life: these are things he understands about himself, has come to accept, however odd they may seem to others.

'Then I saw our mother in London, stopped over briefly on the way from Miami,' Steffie goes on. 'She warned me that I'd have the menopause and a young child at the same time, and added that she was so frightfully busy with her hectic social life, that I mustn't count on her for babysitting. As if there were any chance, with her in London and me in the States. As if I'd allow her near an innocent baby anyway—'

A crash of thunder breaks off her sentence, suddenly and without warning. The music room is filled with a pale yellow light tinged with opalescence. Then the light fades and the room goes uncannily dark as the storm breaks over them, the day's drizzle turning into heavy rain.

A shaft of lightning illuminates their faces briefly, reflects on the chandelier, turning it into a golden kaleidoscope. More thunder follows close at its heels, like a mad growling dog.

Steffie and Troy look at each other and grin. 'Wouldn't Ivo love this,' Troy exlaims.

'He's looking forward to coming here. I promised him spectacular storms out at sea and over the mountains.'

Troy looks slightly dismayed. 'Ivo . . . here?' It's not quite a question, but as near as Troy can get. He's as fond of his brother as he is of Steffie, but finds him more disruptive. The air seems charged with discord when Ivo is around, like the air before one of his more spectacular storms.

'I thought he told you he was coming. He must have forgotten. I know he meant to.'

Alina looks from one to the other. Her eyes are violet, stark in her pale face like heather in a snow bank. 'How lovely,' she says, 'I'll meet all the Ginger Nuts at last.'

Steffie feels slightly hurt. The awful nickname was a secret she and her brothers bore stoically; Troy had no right to reveal it to an outsider. She knows this is childish and ridiculous, but still she feels niggled.

Troy has, so far, not given her any reaction about her

28

momentous news, about the baby. Risking a question, she asks point blank, 'So what do you think of my adopting, Troy?'

Troy ponders this, then smiles. 'I hope it doesn't have red hair,' is all he will commit himself to.

Steffie has to laugh. She knows her brother, knows he will support her decision, however doubtful he may feel about it. She is immensely relieved about this. The reaction of her parents, though predictable, was nonetheless painful. Though she can laugh at it now with Troy, she brooded about it for much of the plane journey. She is surprised at how her sensitivities sit on her skin like naked nerves, exposed and vulnerable where her baby is concerned.

More thunder rattles in the distance. Steffie is suddenly exhausted and it is Alina who notices, who takes her upstairs to the bedroom after Troy brings her bag from around the front. Troy has remembered that it is time for the swans to come looking for food, and he doesn't want to disappoint them.

'Do you want a room facing inland and the mountains or the cove and the sea?' Alina asks politely as she leads Steffie out of the music room, through the kitchen and up the wide bare wooden stairs to the next floor.

'I don't mind.'

She takes Steffie into a spacious bedroom overlooking the small cove. It is the same room she stayed in the only other time she was here, when Troy had first taken over the place. It hasn't changed much; the same scruffy floral carpet, a new double bed, but the old unwieldy wardrobe and dresser. The wallpaper, pale-pink flowers on a cream background, is still the same, fading slightly and tearing a bit in the corners.

'Troy hasn't been able to do much with the house,

after all that effort on his workshop and the music room,' Alina says, looking out the tall generous windows at Troy, who is enticing the two swans out of the water, trying to coax them into taking food first on the shore, then from his hand. *Like he enticed me*, she thinks whimsically, enticed me back to my music, coaxed me to play again, forced me to make my stiff fingers move, make contact with the keys, make harmony out of the discord my life had become since the accident.

'He has dozens of plans for the rest of the house, but the music room had to come first,' Alina persists. 'The house must have been quite magnificent in its heyday, and of course eventually he plans to restore it.' Steffie notes the singular pronoun and wonders where this woman fits into Troy's life.

She is now tired and wants to sleep for a few hours. But Alina is lingering in the room, still watching Troy and the swans through the partially opened window. Her full skirt billows slightly in the soft breeze from the sea; it is made of some flimsy cotton. Celtic earrings, heavy, bronze, seem to emphasize the angry scar which looks quite naked now, making her neck and throat seem especially defenceless. She moves away from the window; there is a slight stiffness in her movements, which Steffie would have interpreted as haughty, improbably regal, if she had not known about the accident. With that thick plait, her golden hair smoothed straight back off her white forehead, and those eyes the colour of a stormy autumn sky, she looks like a creature from some Irish folk tale.

Alina faces the other woman and says, 'You don't seem to mind. About me and Troy.'

Steffie is taken aback. 'Mind? Why should I?' Something in Alina's manner stops her from asking

30

what exactly there is to mind about. Are they lovers, is Alina living here permanently? Are they secretly married or planning to be? If so, why should anyone object? Steffie needs to know what it is she should be minding about.

She stifles her questions and only repeats, 'Why should I mind?'

Alina hesitates and takes a deep breath. She obviously wants to talk, but is finding it difficult. Despite her awkwardness at this moment, there is a calm grace about her that Steffie finds appealing.

'*My* family mind,' Alina says. 'Well, not so much my daughter Kate. She's at university in Dublin now and leads an entirely separate life, but we talk regularly on the phone since I've been here, and she's been to visit me. She's beginning to understand why it is necess-ary.'

Steffie is surprised; she has assumed Alina was without family, so wholly has Troy seemed to monop-olize her.

'David, too. He minds,' Alina goes on.

'David?'

'My husband, David Montgomery. You may have heard of him? He's a conductor. He used to teach music – Troy was his pupil, many years ago. So was I.'

Steffie seems to remember the name, but cannot place him. If she were this woman's husband, she too would mind Alina holing up in some kind of mutual adoration pact with Troy, for what seems like an indefinite time.

'We're not lovers,' Alina states. But she says this almost sadly.

'Whether you are or not, it's not for me to mind, one way or the other,' Steffie says lightly.

'David doesn't quite believe that after all the weeks I

31

have been here, I have not succumbed to Troy's . . . advances, as he puts it. David is, of course, judging other men by himself. Troy has never . . .' She trails off. 'David worries a great deal about what other people think,' she says finally.

'Well, I don't,' Steffie says. 'And I can't imagine what business your living arrangements would be to anyone other than you and your family, and Troy.'

Alina appears to be thinking this over, then nods. 'I wanted you to know how things are between Troy and me, because I know he'd never say, would never think to enlighten you.' They both smile complicitly, knowing Troy.

'He helped me enormously after my accident, taught me to play again, restored some of my confidence. He is a dear friend.' Again that wistful note.

Steffie is silent. Alina continues, 'I'm glad you've come. I'm afraid I've been relying too much on your brother.'

'He seems to be in his element.'

'He's very caring. Too much perhaps. I have to be careful not to become dependent on him.'

As if suddenly deciding she has said too much, Alina leaves. Steffie, taking off her shoes and her jacket, falls on top of the duvet and is asleep within minutes.

Alina walks slowly down the corridor to her own room, this one facing the mountain behind the house, or rather the front of the house which is never used. The mountain is violet today after the storm, a deep purple hue like her own eyes, if she had looked into a mirror. Alina doesn't look into mirrors much; she never has, and now, after the accident, finds herself deliberately shunning them. The person she sees reflected is a stranger, a thinner, paler version of herself both physically and, she fears, emotionally, creatively. It is both disturbing and terrifying.

Alina stares at the mountain for a long time. Behind it, the other hills are obscured by a mist which hovers above them, sometimes dipping into a curve or a valley. In gaps in the mist appear sparkles of water, the river edging purposefully down the mountain. Alina marvels at how she has ended up back in County Kerry after all her years of travelling. It wasn't very far from here where she first met David, come to the town to audition her and other promising music students for his school in Dublin.

Her parents, now retired and living in England to be near relocated relatives, forced him to marry her to prevent a scandal, for this was twenty years ago in rural Ireland. Alina went along with it. She felt David owed her marriage: he had seduced her in her first year as a music student, and as a much older man he should have known better – or at the very least, known something about contraception.

David, because of his involvement with a student, was nearly forced to quit teaching, but because he made the relationship legitimate, he was kept on. But he was no longer quite the golden boy, and knew his days as a teacher were numbered. He had done some conducting and had been good at it. He took on more, and soon his professional life soared as he conducted orchestras all over the world. In the end, the marriage was not the detriment to his career he had feared, especially when, later, Alina became acclaimed as a concert musician. David felt no jealousy; on the contrary, he felt it enhanced his own reputation, for he had not only discovered Alina, he had also married her, made her part of himself.

If she closes her eyes, Alina finds that the soothing

sound of the river not far away plays in her head like a Brahms lullaby. She listens for a moment, then lies down on the bed. She still gets very tired, though she is supposed to have made a 100 per cent recovery. The doctors say this exhaustion will pass, though Alina doesn't believe it. She thinks it is more than physical, more like a surrender of the spirit.

Troy doesn't allow her to have such thoughts. He is engaged in a battle with her spirit, trying to convince it that she is undamaged, unscathed. Alina loves him for this. Among many other things.

Troy has come back into the house and is playing the harpischord. His lanky frame sits with dignity at the instrument, moving gracefully with the music, Handel now.

The melody fills the house, creeping up the stairs and into the rooms like the mountain mist sneaking into every crevice. Steffie, asleep, dreams of her baby.

Alina, awake, lies motionless on the bed as tears fall wearily down her face. She hardly notices them. She listens to the music and knows she is as good a harpsichordist, better even, than Troy, but not as good as she once was, whatever he says. She knows she should be grateful for survival, for the use of her hands, but it is not enough. She wants, selfishly perhaps, to have what she had before: the ability to make music soar, to have the confidence to do so.

And she wants more. She has grown greedy at Heron's Cove, she will have to go soon. She doesn't know how she will make herself do this, but she knows she must. It will be as difficult as learning how to play again, and it will have to be handled alone, without Troy's help.

She doesn't need this, she thinks angrily. The accident was enough to cope with, without *this*.

34

She allows herself a few moments of uncharacteristic self-pity. She has coped with pain, with the loss of music, with the terror of near death, of partial paralysis; so this is nothing, she tells herself.

Loss. So much of it.

And more to come.

Chapter Two

Alina wakes to the music of a harpsichord and in her half-dreaming state thinks it is herself playing, creating the music which used to stun a packed concert hall into appreciative silence. After a moment she realizes where she is, who she is now, and she cannot get up, cannot stop the thoughts scrambling her brain like tiny electrical jolts.

She is in the hospital in Dublin, after the accident. She is unable to move, unable to turn her head, her limbs. People hovering, doing things to her, cutting off her clothes, adjusting machines. 'My hands,' she whispers to the doctor checking her blood pressure. 'I can't move them.'

Through her cloud of shock and pain she can see clearly the look on his face. That's the least of your worries, his eyes say, as the nurse tells him her blood pressure is falling, falling . . .

Alina wrenches her mind away from the past, but the harpsichord music is still haunting her. She wants to shriek downstairs for Troy to stop playing. Her forehead glistens with sweat, brought on by fear, by terror.

'You have nothing to be afraid of,' says the voice in her head. It is the consultant, now, after the first operation. 'We've wired up the broken vertebrae in your neck from the back; in a few weeks we'll operate again to reinforce it from the front. You were lucky, you'll be able to walk again one day.'

'My hands,' Alina says, her voice fuzzy from the anaesthetic, the morphine they've given her to ease the pain.

'You've got your life back,' he says gently. 'We'll worry about your hands later.'

'No, please, listen,' she says, struggling with the words because fear and the drugs make talking an ordeal. 'My life is my hands.'

The consultant, misunderstanding, thinking she has told him that her life is in *his* hands, nods sombrely. 'You'll live,' he assures her. 'And you'll walk.'

He looks serene, confident. Alina wants to shout out at him to make him understand, but something thick and vaporous is dragging her under, and she tumbles into a fitful despairing sleep . . .

Like the sleep she is in now. No, this is different, she's in Heron's Cove, merely groggy from waking up too suddenly. Downstairs Troy is playing joyously, oblivious to the effect it is having on Alina. He thinks the music will inspire her, remind her that she, too, is a musician still. She is becoming reliant on his will, on his stubborn refusal to believe she is less than what she was.

Forcing herself out of bed, struggling to come to terms with herself again, the damaged body, the scars, the fragility of her spirit – as she has done every day since the accident – Alina dresses herself and prepares to go downstairs.

Steffie wakes, too, to music and cloud. Someone is playing a lively bit of Handel, contrasting sharply with the deep gloom of the sky: black and threatening. She peeps out of the duvet to look through her un-curtained window at the dark morning and closes her eyes again, strains to hear the faint music coming from the other part of the house through the open door of her bedroom. It is reminiscent of the more pleasant aspects of her childhood. Troy, overcome by music at an early age, had toyed with the flute, the violin and the piano as he was growing up, and as far back as Steffie could remember, started the day with his instrument of the month. After many trials and experiments over the years, he finally decided on the harpsichord, playing professionally as an adult for several years, until the stress and uncertainty of the concert circuit threatened to break him. For relaxation, he began tinkering with harpsichords in a garage in South London belonging to a cellist friend of his, and found the life of a craftsman suited him.

The legacy of the house in Ireland was a gift from the gods, and Troy still can't believe his luck. He has never liked cities, despite – or perhaps because of – living in many of the cities of Europe and America with his parents. Heron's Cove had belonged to his father's aunt, a spinster who had lived in it all her life. The two, house and woman, had deteriorated together, but the daunting property did not curb Troy's elation, despite the crumbling walls and rotted window frames and the fact that he was wracked, at first, by guilt that neither Ivo nor Steffie were mentioned in the old lady's will. Some whim had made her favour Troy, to the exclusion of the others.

He had honourably offered to sell the house and split the inheritance three ways, but neither Ivo nor Steffie thought this necessary. 'Then you must consider Heron's Cove your home,' Troy told them. 'Come and go as you like, live here if you like. The house is certainly massive enough.' This idea of a family homestead appealed to all three of them, having never had a base while they were growing up. It looked like

38

none of them would ever have a permanent partner, so the idea of sharing the house with each other in some distant old age was rather comforting.

'But for now, what will you do with the place?' Steffie asked over long distance.

'Organize concerts. Build a workroom. My harpsichords are selling well all over the world, Stef. I can just about name my own price now, and I still have a waiting list.' His voice was throaty with excitement, or that agitation of the spirit which passed for excitement with Troy.

'But the concerts,' he went on. 'I've always dreamed of having a place large enough to accommodate them.'

Steffie understands this. Live music is as necessary to him as air and water, and for this reason, Troy needs musicians. He loves the instruments that make music as much as the music itself; when he sees a finely restored nineteenth-century Erard piano, or a sixteenth-century Venetian harpsichord, he trembles like a lover at the first sight of his beloved naked.

At first the musicians came as a favour to Troy, for he had been well liked on the concert circuit. Then they came again, enjoying the eccentric ambiance of the place: the ruined old house, the splendid music room with its expensive wooden floors and rich lighting, the marvellous acoustics. Often they stayed several days, using the concert as a short holiday, a break from the demands of their profession.

All this Steffie knows, from her transatlantic telephone conversations with her brother. What she didn't know was about Alina, who was never mentioned despite the fact that she has been here for over two months. Typical Troy, Steffie thinks. If he doesn't quite know how to explain something, he ignores it.

Steffie gets out of bed and stares out of the window. The room is damp and chilly. The swans are nowhere to be seen. She had surfaced for a few hours last night, long enough to eat some cold chicken with Troy and Alina, then gone back to bed. Now she feels rested, contented. She lays a hand on her stomach, feeling it plump and motherly under the thin cotton of her nightshirt. Steffie has gained weight lately. She doesn't mind in the slightest; she feels as if it is some kind of a spiritual pregnancy, something that links her to her own forthcoming baby who even now may be in the womb of her birth mother preparing to be born. The thought is so awesome it makes her shiver.

The noise of a vehicle screeching up to the front of the house filters through the open window. A few moments later, a figure comes around the overgrown path leading around to the cove and the back of the house. 'Jack!' Steffie shouts down.

Jack looks up and grins. 'Am I too early? You city folk are all the same. I've done a full day's work already.' This is only partially true. After Jack had milked the cows and taken them down again into their patch, he took a break before joining his parents for breakfast. The air smelled of wet, of the turf fire burning in the house and of cows. Passing the house Jack could see, through the window, his mother and father sitting at the kitchen table, the brown teapot and a loaf of bread between them. The house sat squat at the foot of the mountain, its grey stone blending in with the sodden earth and the steel sky.

'Where you off to, lad?' Jack turned to see his father, Paudie, leaning out the window.

'Thought I'd check the fence where the heifer got out the other day.'

Paudie grinned. 'I'm way ahead of you, boy. I fixed it

40

yesterday, when you were lolling about Tralee charming the ladies.'

'I should be so lucky,' Jack called back as he headed towards the back field at the foot of the mountain. 'I'll check the fence, see if you did a decent job of it.'

Paudie swore good-naturedly, and hollered at Jack to hurry back or he'd miss his bacon and eggs. Jack jumped over the bank of stone and sod separating his mother's garden from the field and ambled up the slope, forgetting the fence. A wren, perched in an earthen bank of gorse bushes and fuchsia, suddenly, stridently, attacked the steely sky with an outburst of song. As if shocked into action, a thin sliver of sunlight edged its way through the clouds. Jack walked aimlessly, enjoying the unexpected burst of warmth from the sun, watching the mist clear from the mountain, seeing how the cows shook themselves with pleasure. 'I know how you feel,' Jack murmured to them, only it wasn't the long-awaited seeping of spring in the air making him so oddly happy, but thoughts of Steffie.

It's been a long time since he's met a woman like this one, who's affected him like this one. 'You're dreaming, Jack,' his mother scolded him later when he let his breakfast grow cold.

He thinks he's dreaming now, watching Steffie from the terrace. She looks as good now as she did yesterday. He had to come out, see for himself, even though it's turning out to be a busy day. Paudie has decided to take some beef cows to market and needs Jack to help sort them, load them up.

'Go on in,' Steffie is shouting down to him. 'I'm sure the door's not locked, it never is. I'll throw on some clothes and join you in a minute.'

'Don't bother, I can't stop now. Off to pick up some feed from a farmer nearby, got to get back. I brought

41

you some fresh milk from the farm, and a loaf of my ma's bread, fresh baked this morning. You were on about Irish soda bread at the pub yesterday, and my mother bakes the best you'll get anywhere.'

He puts down a large loaf wrapped in a clean tea towel, and a Paddy's whisky bottle full of milk, on the table on the terrace.

'Well hey, thanks,' Steffie calls down. 'Are you sure you can't stop for a cup of coffee or something?'

'Not this time. I'll be back, so.' He grins at her in such a suggestive manner that she says, 'And that sweet girl in Tralee, who was nearly in tears when you said goodbye to her? Will you be going back there, so?' she teases him in his own accent.

At this he laughs out loud. She likes his laugh, likes flirting so outrageously in this delightful place with someone she has only just met. It lifts her spirits enormously.

A sudden downpour ends the conversation. The brief morning sun has vanished. Jack waves and is gone. Steffie, pleased with herself, with her new young admirer, puts on a towelling robe over her nightshirt and heads down the wooden stairs and into the kitchen.

This is vast, cavernous, and in some disarray. Old white tiles line the wall behind an ancient wood-burning stove, and rickety wooden shelves, open and filled with packets of tea, rice, pasta, barley, lentils and oatmeal, line the opposite side. There is a stone sink, which is quite magnificent, and horrid shiny green tiles behind it. A fine mahogany table sits imperiously in the middle of the room, but the chairs around it are cheap and ill-assorted. Writing paper, correspondence, bills, invoices and more musical scores are stacked on one side of the table, but the other is cleared and clean and is neatly set out for breakfast, with fine Italian bowls, plates and coffee cups.

Alina is at the kitchen sink, filling the coffee pot. Her sunny hair hangs loose to her waist and her face looks clean and soft. She is wearing a Japanese kimono, white with prints of pale-blue birds.

Troy is still playing the harpsichord, Vivaldi now, a sharp sunny piece which reflects Alina's shining hair. The day seems to brighten, and even the stone tiled floor begins to feel warm under Steffie's bare feet.

'Coffee?' Alina asks.

'Yes, please.'

Alina takes the red enamel coffee pot over to the table. Suddenly there is a loud clatter as the pot and its full contents spill onto the floor. Alina involuntarily cries out.

'Oh God,' Steffie says. 'Are you burned?'

'No, no, it didn't touch me. I'm fine, it just took me by surprise. What a mess.'

Troy runs in, concerned. He sees Alina crouching by the spilled coffee and goes to her, cradles her in his arms. They stay this way for some moments, making no move to get up. There is something both fragile and intimate in the tableau.

Alina, shaking, suddenly pushes Troy away. 'Don't touch me,' she says hoarsely.

Troy is shocked.

Alina says, 'I'm sorry. It's just that I thought . . .' But she can't say it. She can't tell him that for a fleeting moment she had been transported to hospital again, thought Troy was her husband David clutching at her in a suffocating embrace meant for the photographer.

'My wife is alive, she will be able to walk, that is all that matters,' David is saying to the interviewer from

43

the English newspaper. 'She has me, she has our daughter Kate.'

It is not enough, Alina is thinking, but she cannot say it, for David is overwhelming her with his own strength and power, posing for the camera, putting words in her mouth. She wants to push him away, but her hands do not respond to what her brain tells them to do. Nerve damage, the consultants say. They are silent when she asks whether it is permanent; they shrug, as if it were of no account. Alina lies flat on her back in the hospital bed as she has already been lying for months. She cannot hold a book to read, cannot turn her head, cannot move. Every few hours she is turned on the bed slightly to one side, later the other. To occupy the endless days and nights Alina hums scores to herself. She sometimes thinks she is going mad.

She stares unseeingly at Troy, who is looking at her with a hurt expression. Alina pulls herself together, shakes her hands in an unconscious gesture, as if to reassure herself that those days are over; that she has recovered. She remembers that Troy is not David, and apologizes again. 'I've become very clumsy since the accident,' she says to Steffie. 'Always dropping things.'

'It's only because you haven't got your strength back fully,' Troy tells her. 'You know it takes time. Anyway, you're not any clumsier than I am, than the rest of us, I promise you.'

Alina says nothing. She can be powerfully contradictory in her silences, Steffie reflects.

Troy slices the fresh bread that Steffie retrieved from the terrace and passes around butter. Eggs are boiling on the cooker and the rusty stove in the corner is lit, warming the kitchen, taking away the damp.

'About this baby . . .' Troy begins, then tails off to take a bite of bread and butter.

Steffie understands that her brother is ready to talk about it now. She knows him, knows how he mulls things over silently before he is ready to discuss them.

'This isn't a whim, you know,' Steffie says. 'I've always wanted children. It never happened; I never met a man I wanted to have children with, and I'm not into getting myself impregnated by just anyone when there are so many unwanted babies in the world.'

Alina gets up to get the eggs. Steffie can see that Troy is aching to do it for her, but for once lets her be. She takes them out of the boiling water and puts them in the eggcups without any problems. Troy looks proudly at her, as if she has accomplished some mammoth task.

Alina turns to Steffie. 'Is it hard for a single woman to adopt?'

'Not in the States, that's primarily why I settled there. Oh, it's not easy, and it's quite costly, but it's not impossible, if you're willing to take on a Third World child.'

'Why Peru?'

'It's open for adoption now; I know several women who have had babies from there. I've already been to Lima. I've got a lawyer there who deals with this sort of thing. I'm at the top of the waiting list now; the next infant girl that is brought in for adoption will be mine, I hope.'

'You won't take a boy?' Alina asks.

'I think I'd do better at raising a girl, without a permanent man in my life.'

Troy thinks of Al, the American journalist who was the most recent man in Steffie's life, and is relieved he is no longer considered permanent. Troy met Al in Florida two years ago, having gone over to escape London when his marriage was in the throes of disintegration. He thought Al noisy and disorganized, unsettling.

Steffie knows Troy is thinking about Al, but will not ask, so she says, 'Al doesn't like kids, tried to dissuade me from adopting. Either a baby or him, were his words. Needless to say, I haven't seen him for months.' Troy notices she says this with no seeming regrets. She seems sure of herself, of her decision to adopt. Though he is happy for her, he is uneasy. He knows, from the terrible job their parents did, just how difficult it is to raise a child. If two parents were unable to give stability, confidence, security, how would one? He marvels that Steffie is willing to give it a go. He himself has never wanted children. This was another source of discord between him and his ex-wife.

He doesn't want to think about Steffie, and is appalled by his own selfishness. But for the past two months he has lived in a mythic utopia in this Irish paradise with his Celtic princess, surrounded by nothing but platonic love and music, by harmony. The intrusion of the real world jars him, like a beautiful sonata played by a bad musician.

Steffie is talking about adoptions, single parenthood, extended families, education, and his uneasiness vanishes with the ordered plans she lays before them. He decides she must know what she is doing. When she is finished he is relieved to be able to say honestly, 'I'm pleased for you, Stef.'

Steffie, satisfied, lets go of the subject. She knows that in their different ways, both Troy and Ivo will be supportive of her.

'Tell me about your concerts,' she now asks Troy.

Troy is relieved to be talking about something he understands. 'They've grown enormously. We now have between fifty and seventy people for each one, usually. We get a lot of English and Germans and

Dutch who have settled here, and the locals have begun to take an interest too.'

'When is the next one?'

'Next week. Marcel LeLeannic, the French recorder player.'

Steffie knows from his tone of voice that this is indeed a *coup*, but she has never heard of this Marcel LeLeannic, and when she thinks of the recorder, she remembers the dreadful noises she and Ivo produced when forced to take up the instrument in primary school.

Alina, seeing the blank look on Steffie's face, says, 'Marcel is brilliant, the most talented recorder player I've heard. You would not think it is the same instrument when he plays it; he makes it do things you wouldn't believe possible.'

'Alina knows him, you see,' Troy explains. 'They've met frequently on the concert circuit. After her accident, he was constantly in touch from Brittany, where he lives. He'd like to see her, so she bribed him by promising her presence in exchange for a concert.'

'Don't make up things,' Alina admonishes. 'I don't have that kind of influence on Marcel. He's actually arriving a few days sooner, to have a bit of a holiday. I've been extolling the virtues of Heron's Cove to him over the telephone.'

'He's coming earlier to see you, my dear,' Troy says with just a touch of asperity that he cannot quite hide. How possessive he is of her, Steffie thinks. How odd, if they are not lovers.

'So Heron's Cove is starting to fill up.' Steffie gets up and begins to clear away the breakfast things. 'First me, then this Marcel, then Ivo—'

'Marcel's accompanist, the pianist Claudia Dushnik, will be coming as well,' Alina says.

'Another excellent musician. I heard some of her solo concerts before she teamed up with Marcel. They work well together. I've never met Marcel, but I saw him perform once, in Paris. He's a wizard, a magician, had the audience spellbound.'

'None but the best for Heron's Cove, right?' Steffie teases, but Troy answers, quite seriously. 'I only want the best.' Music, to him, is too precious to be squandered on the second-rate.

Alina has begun helping Steffie with the washing-up. Troy rushes to take the tea towel from her hand, pushes her gently but firmly back to her seat at the kitchen table. 'I'll do that. You rest.'

'No!' Alina is trembling as she stands up, pulls the tea towel away from him and cries again, 'No, Troy!'

Her response is out of all proportion to the little incident, and both Troy and Steffie stare at her. Alina is shaking uncontrollably. 'Don't you see?' she whispers through quivering lips. She is talking to Troy, seemingly unaware of Steffie's presence. 'Don't you see I have to stand on my own two feet? Take control of my life again?'

Once again she is in hospital, and it is not Troy but David standing in front of her. The operations are over and she is walking, slowly; her hands have begun to move. David is watching her as she sits on the hospital bed, exercising her weak fingers as vigorously as she can. 'Don't torture yourself,' he is saying. 'You're lucky you can move them. You can write, comb your hair, do anything.'

'Except play the harpsichord,' Alina replies grimly, pressing her fingers onto a spongy ball, strengthening them little by little.

David sits at her side, puts a strong arm around her shoulders, glances to see if the nurses are watching. A tired young sister is studiously looking at the notes at the foot of Alina's bed. Her streaked blond hair has fallen appealingly from its severe clip and trickles down her neck.

David reluctantly turns his attention back to Alina. 'You can take on more students,' he says. 'You have two or three you give special lessons to, but you can become a proper teacher now. Pupils will come flocking from all over.'

'I don't want to teach!' she shouts at him. The sister, frowning slightly, looks at him. David smiles winsomely and sadly at her, a complicit smile indicating that they both know how nervy Alina is, how unwell still.

'Is everything all right?' The sister asks this of Alina, but looks covertly at David, acceding his to be the most commanding presence.

Alina closes her eyes, momentarily defeated. She is weak and exhausted, and sometimes feels it would be such a relief to let David take over, tell her what she must and must not do.

But it is her life. As David and the sister flirt amicably above her drowsing body, Alina squeezes the spongy ball again and again, again and again . . .

She forces herself back into the present and finds Troy and Steffie both staring at her, surprised at her outburst. Alina, distraught, says, 'Oh, Troy, I'm sorry, you've been so good, *too* good, it's made me lean on you.'

Troy says stiffly, 'I didn't realize it was upsetting you.'

'It wasn't, it isn't. Or rather it is because of my own inadequacies, my own fears. My accident has made me afraid of things. First physical things, like tripping or moving too quickly, hurting myself again. Then the

49

fears grow, become demons. Like being afraid of everything, doing anything. Playing music. Facing life again.' She looks at him with anguished eyes. 'Don't you see? It would be so easy to lean on you. That's why I must stop.'

She cannot explain it any better than that, and hopes Troy understands. He does and he doesn't. All he knows at this moment is that he is unbearably moved. 'Whatever you need,' he says softly, eyes on her face, 'whatever I can do, or not do, to help you completely recover, is fine with me.'

Steffie, watching this little scene from the kitchen sink, wonders when Troy will realize that he is quite in love with Alina.

The moment ends awkwardly. 'Well, it's good I'm here,' Steffie says pragmatically, trying to bring them all back to some kind of normality, something she often finds lacking in the world of professional music. 'With all these visitors coming, I mean. I can help you get the bedrooms ready, and the kitchen too. We'll have to get organized.'

Alina and Troy look genuinely perplexed. 'But the piano and harpsichord are both in tune,' Troy says. 'The programmes are printed and have been sent to our regular guests, and the music room is in perfect shape.'

'Did you notice the chandelier?' Alina adds. 'It came from Venice, Troy ordered it months ago. We were afraid it wouldn't arrive in time for this concert.'

Bloody musicians, Steffie thinks without rancour. What priorities! No food in the house, everything but the music room a shambles, Alina in some kind of crisis and a concert for fifty plus people in a few days' time. Yet there is something sweet, something naive, about their faith, their wholehearted belief that music

50

is God, is omnipotent, benevolent. It drives her barmy sometimes, yet she has to admit that it is a rather welcome antidote to the cynicism of Al and her other journalist colleagues.

'Well, I look forward to meeting this wizard, this Marcel the magician who has obviously cast his spell on both of you,' she says flippantly as she dries her hands on her towelling robe, unable to find anything else as Troy has managed to saturate the tea towel with soapy water. 'I hope he doesn't start roaming the hills bewitching the locals. I'm sure it wouldn't do.' She thinks of Jack, of the parents he described, the farm at the foot of the mountains.

Alina, calm now after her outburst, smiles. There is something archaic about that smile, something singular yet reminiscent of ancient drawings, legends; old as the mountains. She belongs here, Steffie thinks suddenly. She is exactly right in this strange isolated place surrounded by nothing but misty hills and the fathomless sea and the mythological past of Ireland.

As if reading her thoughts Alina looks up at Steffie and nods slightly. 'You'll like Marcel,' she says. 'He's not like the rest of us.'

Steffie doesn't know what Alina means by the rest of us: other people, musicians, Europeans, Celts, wizards, gods? She's being fanciful, but Alina's smile is so enigmatic and other-worldly that she feels slightly on edge, as if the world has tilted a fraction.

'I'm getting dressed now, going for a walk,' she says, feeling the need to get outside into the real world. 'Explore the area a bit, get some much-needed exercise.'

When she leaves the house, Troy and Alina are already at the harpsichord, playing Bach. Steffie listens a moment, then goes outside onto the terrace facing the cove. The rain has stopped and a powerful sun has emerged from behind the dispersing clouds. The house looks less ramshackle in the late morning light, the sea at the back, the mountains in front.

Steffie feels her equilibrium returning. It was getting altogether too heady in Heron's Cove with all that perfect music, perfect harmony broken only by Alina's sudden discordant outburst. A healthy tramp up the mountain is just what she needs after her long journey and the emotional toll of telling her family about the baby.

Taking a deep breath, Steffie heads off towards the mountains. The tinkling notes of the harpsichord follow her for a short distance, then blend into the crisp clear air but don't quite disappear. For a long time they follow Steffie around in her head, the harmony repeating itself, the music floating up into the clouds, haunting her as she walks steadfastly uphill.

Chapter Three

Thunder rolls discordantly down Le Val-sans-Retour and settles like a wrong chord over the yellow lake. Marcel, oblivious to the approaching storm, sits on a granite slab playing his recorder. It is a very old Dolmetsch, battered, scarred, and though he has more than twenty recorders now, he still, in his more contemplative moments – of which Marcel has many – goes back to his firm favourites.

Marcel is playing a selection from Purcell's incidental music to 'King Arthur', which he finds fitting in this woodland permeated with the legends of the Camelot king. As he plays he thinks of the concert he will be giving in Ireland, at the secluded haven where his darling Alina has been holed up for months. Already he is torn between a reluctance to leave his beloved forest, and a burning need to see her again. To Marcel, Alina is an angel, a princess he is dedicated to serve, through his music and the magic he creates with that music. He adores her, has done for years; unruly and pagan himself, he sees Alina as a Holy Grail, untouchable, inviolable.

The Valley of No Return is growing dark with the thunderstorm now rapidly approaching. Lightning rips the sky in the distance, but Marcel doesn't notice. He's used to this valley, used to the summer storms that sometimes tear it apart. He welcomes the storms in the summer now, for they disperse the many tourists who have discovered this part of Brittany. Le Val-sans-Retour is at the edge of the ancient forest of Brociliande, a deep mysterious place of silent oaks and beech trees where it is said the court of the great King Arthur once disported itself. Marcel was born here, grew up here, in the tiny village where he lives, in the heart of the forest. He knows that this valley was where Morgan Le Fay lured unfaithful knights to their death; knows that Merlin once roamed these woods and indeed is said to be here still, trapped by the sorceress Vivienne. Marcel knows the bridge where Lancelot proclaimed his love for Guinevere, knows the dense part of the forest where Tristan and Isolde hid to indulge themselves in illicit love. The legends are as much a part of him as his skin and blood and the recorder he is rarely without.

He learned to play here, in these woods, in this valley. A recorder was given to him for his sixth birthday, and it was like being given a first set of clothes to cover the nakedness he had felt since he took his first steps. Marcel's family was large and noisy, the cottage, though sturdy and in good order, was small and crowded. Marcel, the youngest, knew no privacy, felt, before he could even talk, exposed, vulnerable to the clamouring world around him. He was a slight child, with bones like a bird, covered with nearly translucent flesh which seemed inadequate protection from the overwrought vitality of his larger and more boisterous brothers and sisters, who, though adoring of this tiny fledgeling in their midst, often intimidated him with their physical prowess and terrifying good humour.

The recorder permitted him to escape. Bernadette, his mother, told him as he unwrapped it, 'My family always made music. Your *grand-père* played the accordion at weddings and on feast days, and as a child I sang. You are like my side of the family. You will make music too.'

First Marcel played it in the garden, the only spot where he could find some peace and quiet. 'Where's Marcel?' his older siblings would shriek, amusing themselves with a game of hide-and-seek.

'Hush,' they would say to each other. 'If we stay quiet, we'll find him.' And sure enough, if they waited long enough Marcel would give himself away, unable to resist taking out his recorder and piping out a melody.

When his obstreperous brothers and sisters became too much, Marcel wandered further afield, around the village. 'It's the Merlin,' the villagers would say good-humouredly.

'I'm not a magician,' Marcel would reply.

'Ah, but don't you know the story? The Merlin was a fine musician as well as a magician.'

The villagers in fact adored Marcel. Though not without a streak of mischief, he was benign, lovable. It seemed entirely natural to see him, as he grew older, roaming the myth-laden forest playing his haunting music, and it seems natural to them now, catching glimpses of him as he stalks the forest with his recorder.

It begins to rain, reluctantly at first and then harder. Marcel is finally forced to notice. He stops playing, tucks his recorder under his brown suede waistcoat and scuttles around the lake. While he walks lithely up the dirt and stone track, across granite rocks, past bleak trees, the lightning comes perilously close, but he hardly notices. When he reaches the top of the hill he takes a long look back down the valley. The wind has come up, dishevelling the trees around the murky lake, and there is a moaning through the valley that the villagers would call the sighing of Morgan Le Fay. Marcel takes it all in, knowing that he is leaving for Ireland this evening. Although he is already saturated to the skin, his frizzy fair hair clinging wetly to his neck and his clothes sticking uncomfortably to his body, Marcel is not in a hurry. He takes several deep breaths, storing it in his lungs and blood and heart where he can call on it later, when he is far away from this place he loves with a passion he has never felt for a woman or man.

Finally, he turns from the valley and begins the long walk home.

Claudia is playing the piano when Marcel appears, like a sodden satyr, at the French doors.

'You are so pathetic,' she says disdainfully, not missing a note of the Liszt *Hungarian Rhapsody* she is playing.

Despite the music, she is being Western European today, Marcel thinks with amusement; predominantly English: cool, disdainful. Her true reaction would have been more fiery, accusing him with many words and gestures of abandoning her when they should have been practising for the coming concert. Claudia is Ukrainian, but she has lived in England and France for several years, since the dissolution of the old Soviet state.

Marcel goes into his bedroom, once his parents' room, the room in which he was born. It has been altered, of course, but the essential things have remained: the blackened beam in the ceiling, the wide windows overlooking the forest of Brociliande. What was once a rough wooden floor has been sanded and polished and peppered with thick creamy rugs, and the walls have been papered richly but tastefully.

When Marcel's father died, his mother, who for years had been wanting to move to a pleasant modern bungalow in the heart of the village, put the house on the market. Marcel promptly bought it for much more than it was worth and renovated it sumptuously, adding bedrooms and balconies, without changing its central character. Bernadette, happy in her new bungalow, enjoys visiting her son in her old home, but is delighted to return to what she considers her far superior dwelling place. She cannot understand this modern trend of making do with the old, no matter how tarted up, when one can afford the new.

Marcel showers, towel dries his pale-yellow hair which fluffs around his head like goose down. He dresses in suede dark-tan jeans, a white collarless silk shirt and a loose black linen waistcoat. He tries to comb his fuzzy hair but gives up, and goes back downstairs to the living room where Claudia is still at the piano.

He listens to her finish the piece with a flourish, pleased at her playing. She has been his accompanist for four years now; they work well together, now that they have got over that messy emotional business of being lovers.

Claudia, finishing, stands up and faces Marcel. 'I'm going to pack,' she says distantly.

Marcel grins wickedly, looking like a cross between an angel and an elf. Though he has not lost the slight frame of his childhood, there is a lithesome grace to his body, a confident juxtaposition of muscle and bone, not unlike that of a cat. He is surprisingly strong, and has the large brown eyes of a watchful but calm animal. There is a naivety there also, however, that often worries Claudia. She fears that, for all the power of his music and fame, an unscrupulous woman is

57

bound to hook on to that naivety and entrap him. She herself tried, to no avail. Marcel lusted after her, coveted her, even needed her, but would not be committed to her. She finally gave up on him as a man and embraced him wholeheartedly as a musician, and since then their relationship has been satisfactory to both.

'I don't know if you even remember,' Claudia goes on with quiet sarcasm, 'but we are leaving for Ireland tonight.'

Marcel looks up at her, mock-pleadingly. She is six feet tall, five inches taller than him, and several stones heavier. Claudia is a big woman, in every sense. She has big black hair, thick and shimmering with a vitality all of its own. Her cheeks are high and broad, her nose defiantly snub, her eyebrows bold and dark. Usually she paints her full lips in a deep purple-black colour, not unlike overripe blackberries, but today they are as pale as lilies, contrasting sharply with her olive skin that turns golden in the sun. Marcel still lusts for her on the odd occasion, but keeps this under control. He needs her more as an accompanist than as a lover, for the latter are plentiful, the former scarce.

'Let's be friends, Claudia, *mon petit bijou*,' Marcel pleads winsomely.

Claudia whirls around on the piano stool and says, 'Don't try your goddamn French bullshit with me, honey,' lapsing into an appalling parody of an American accent.

'I'm not sure your extended visits to the major cities of the West have helped either your accent or your vocabulary, Claudia,' Marcel says mildly, 'though I can appreciate it was necessary to your career.'

Claudia becomes wholly Ukrainian. '*Te durni hlop.*

You stupid man.' She swears thoroughly at him in her native language, emphasizes her points with sweeping gestures, then says in English, 'Are you out of your head, wandering around in the rain when you have a concert this week? Are you crazy? And what about our rehearsals? I come all the way from Paris to have some practice time with you and you do your usual disappearing act.'

Marcel makes all the right noises, in both English and French. Claudia is proficient in both languages, and Marcel's English is superb, so they often combine the two in heated discussions, much to the confusion of anyone overhearing.

Soon Claudia comes around, as she always does. They have been together for so long that they each know and play their allotted roles perfectly.

Marcel says, 'Come, let's rehearse for an hour or so. I had to get away alone, away from everything; you should know how I work by now.'

Claudia shakes her head. 'I know you are too bloody dependent on that forest of yours. You use it as a crutch, Marcel. It's time you learned to stand alone.'

Marcel doesn't agree, but he doesn't argue. The woods are where he finds his inspiration, his creativity, his very soul as a musician.

They rehearse for an hour, forgetting everything in their absorption, the familiar alchemy changing their base and solid selves into the music itself, so that both become one. When they finish they sit in silence for a few moments, unwilling to go back into that other world, the world they are forced to live in when they are not making music. 'It should go well,' Claudia says at last.

'Yes.' This is an understatement for both of them. They know that the magic is there, will entrance the audience in Ireland as it has countless audiences all over the world.

Coming back to earth, Marcel sneezes. Immediately Claudia takes umbrage.

'There, you see? You're getting a cold, I knew your drenching would do you no good. I'll brew up some herbs for you. Now what have I brought with me? Elderflower, I think, that's good for colds. And peppermint. And I have myrrh oil to rub into your chest, and ginger to put in your bath . . .'

'I don't want a bath,' Marcel says petulantly. 'I've only just had a shower.'

Claudia ignores this and rushes from the room to collect her herbs and oils. She knows Marcel will follow her instructions on this, as does everyone who has benefited from her knowledge of healing. Marcel has been a recipient many times, rising from debilitating sickbeds and performing brilliantly, after being ministered to by Claudia. Sometimes he thinks she is a witch, Morgan Le Fay herself with her strange knowledge of bitter and ancient medicines. He is glad she is a friend and not an enemy, though to be fair he has never known her to use her herbs for reasons other than benevolence.

So meekly Marcel goes up the stairs, to run his bath and have his chest rubbed with the myrrh oil. Claudia is in the guest room rummaging through her bags and cases, and holds up vials and bottles, inspecting their colour, sniffing their contents.

'You'll be fine in no time,' she promises.

Marcel knows this to be true. Thankfully, he lets himself go in her powerful hands.

Steffie is on the telephone to Lima when Troy comes into the house with Marcel and Claudia. She acknowledges them with a distracted nod and takes the phone upstairs to her bedroom, for they are unpacking their various cases and equipment from Troy's van and are exclaiming over the house.

From Peru, her lawyer Luis is telling her with excitement that a woman has come to the orphanage, to give her unborn baby up for adoption. It is due to be born in a month's time, Luis says.

'The mother,' Steffie whispers breathlessly. 'Is she certain? Why does she want to give up her baby?'

'The mother is distraught. She is twenty-seven years old and has six other children. Her husband has just disappeared, no-one knows why or how.'

'He'll come back,' Steffie says, not wanting to indulge in false hopes. 'She'll change her mind.'

'I think not. She came to the orphanage when her last child was born, wanting to give up the infant, but was convinced to keep the child. The father was around then. Nothing will change her mind this time; she's tired, at the end of her patience.'

Steffie allows herself to rejoice. 'I'll come over as soon as the baby is born.'

'And if it's a boy?'

'It will be a girl, Luis. I have a feeling this is it.'

Luis curses in Spanish. He deals in concretes, not feelings. But he promises to phone her the minute the baby is born. Steffie hangs up, sits on her bed and stares unseeingly out the window, towards the sea. She holds on to her stomach tenderly, as if the infant were there and not in the belly of a strange Peruvian woman thousands of miles away. Her stomach feels rounded, swollen, pregnant; she knows she is being fanciful, but she swears she can feel movement.

She has known all along that her baby was about to be born. She has felt it in her bones, in her belly, in her soul.

61

All she has to do now is wait.

Steffie does not leave her bedroom until dinnertime, though she is called by Troy to come downstairs and meet the new arrivals. She apologizes, says she has a headache and would like to rest for a few hours.

In truth, she wants to be alone to savour the overwhelming fact that she will soon be holding her baby. Her body is weak and trembly with excitement, her skin prickly with thorny happiness. This, then, is what it is like to be on the brink of a fulfilment of a dream, she thinks with awe. But there is fear scratching at her joy: will she be up to such an epiphany, she wonders? Having been blessed by the gods, will she be unworthy?

Her joy turns to terror. She has wanted a baby for too long; she feels suddenly unable to cope with the approaching reality. In childhood, she had realized with a pang how unsuited for parenthood her own mother and father were, and longed to do it herself, to do it better. Steffie knows that this in itself is not a good reason for having a child, but there are worse, she tells herself. Besides, she has loved babies and children all her life. If her own education had not been so wayward and disrupted, she might have become a teacher. If her own relationships with men had not been so disjointed and unsatisfactory, perhaps she would have had a brood of little ones of her own. As it was, none of these things happened, but for Steffie it is not too late. She is having a baby, and as she vacillates between panic and euphoria, she feels her hour of reckoning has come at last.

Dinner at Heron's Cove is usually a haphazard thing. When there are no guests, Troy and Alina, and now

Steffie, eat home-made seafood chowder in the local pub, or munch on apples and cheese, or grab some chops from the butcher in Ballycaveen and grill them unceremoniously in the gas cooker. Now, however, more ritual is called for, and Troy has announced that they are going out to dinner in Dingle.

Steffie comes downstairs dressed for this occasion in a navy linen suit with a white T-shirt. She slips quietly into the music room, where Claudia and Marcel are rehearsing. Troy's grand piano has been moved to the centre of the music room for Claudia, and Marcel stands in front with his recorder. Troy and Alina sit listening, drinking Campari and soda. 'I'll get you a drink,' Troy whispers.

'No, thank you. I don't drink much since I've been expecting the baby.'

Troy and Alina look at her oddly. 'I know I'm adopting, not having it myself,' she stumbles on, 'but I *feel* as if she is living inside me. I feel she's already part of me.'

'I suppose that makes sense,' Alina says kindly.

Steffie is not sure that it does. She knows she is being whimsical, knows Alina and Troy think so too.

They turn back to the two musicians who are playing a rousing gypsy number that Steffie does not recognize. The pianist is a large woman in voluminous, colourful layers of silk and velvet. She plays intensely, and plays well, but not theatrically, which is surprising since her physical presence is so bold.

The recorder player, on the surface, looks ordinary except for the downy pale hair that frizzes around his head like a halo. But as Steffie watches him play, he seems to change in front of her eyes. His face, reddened with the exertion of the intricate piece he is playing, is animated with a passion that his eyes as

63

well as his body communicate to the audience. His slight frame is rippling with the harmony; his body moves and yearns and quivers with each nuance of the music. Even his clothes – ordinary enough except for a loose long satin waistcoat in a deep rich blue, like Yeats's embroidered cloth of heaven – seem transformed as the piece continues, becoming part of an entire symphony composed only of the recorder, the piano, the flesh and blood and spirit of the man playing it, and the strangely reticent figure of the pianist. The whole performance is both dramatic and moving.

'You haven't lost your touch,' Alina says composedly, after a moment or so of silent, almost stunned admiration. 'The magic is still there, Marcel.' She turns to Claudia and adds, 'A wonderful performance, Claudia. Marcel is lucky to have you as his accompanist.'

Marcel, triumphant, goes to Alina, and without a word, kisses her hand in the most courtly and romantic of gestures. Overwhelmed at how lovely she looks – he has only seen her twice since the accident, and then she was flat on her back in hospital, deathly ill, skeletal – he overcomes his confusion by suddenly beginning to play again, a composition by a seventeenth-century Dutch composer, Jacob van Eyck, titled 'Engels Nachtegaeltje', or 'The English Nightingale'. This piece is just right for the recorder, an instrument sometimes compared with birdsong, and Marcel himself is like a bird at this moment, a sprightly peacock, or an animated tropical mating male, strutting for a female admirer. For it is obvious that this virtuoso performance is for Alina, and Alina alone, and Marcel pours all his musicality, all his creativity, into the song.

When it is finished, everyone spontaneously bursts

into applause. Marcel accepts Alina's smile triumphantly. Though he can live perfectly happily without her, when he sees her he is flushed again with his courtly love, his unrequited passion. Marcel secretly rather cherishes this tragic doomed love of his; it enhances his playing, keeps Claudia at a manageable distance, and doesn't prevent him from having other, less intense love affairs with available females if the opportunity arises.

At last Steffie is noticed, and introductions are made. Marcel sees how excited she is, how her green eyes glitter when she welcomes him to Heron's Cove. He understands that he has made another conquest.

Marcel is not a vain man, but he is used to the adulation of women, who note the sexual nature of his performances, and make the fatal mistake of thinking that this ardour can be diverted to them. Marcel has never encouraged this, but there is something about him that makes women feel they know him better than he knows himself. Because he likes women and adores going to bed with them, Marcel is not as distant to his pursuers as perhaps he ought to be. And so it is always a surprise to them, to find that his intensity, his passion, is not for them but purely for his music, and for the forest from which he derives his inspiration.

'I enjoyed the concert,' Steffie says to both Claudia and Marcel.

'It was just a rehearsal,' Claudia says, adding mischievously, 'though to Marcel, of course, it was perhaps even more important than the concert.' She looks at Alina meaningfully.

Marcel glares at her, wishing she would be more subtle, more sophisticated; more *French*, he thinks crossly. Claudia glares back defiantly. Though she has, like Marcel, no desire to become lovers with him again, sometimes odd moments of possessiveness rack her with uncontrollable emotion.

'Well, I look forward to hearing the complete concert,' Steffie is saying politely.

'No doubt you will be sick of it by then, after you have heard Claudia and myself practising all week,' Marcel says breezily, not meaning it.

Troy interrupts, trying to get everyone together and out of the house. 'We're going to a new Italian restaurant which has just opened. I hope that's all right. Alina loves Italian food, and needs to be coaxed to eat these days. She still hasn't put back on all the weight she lost in hospital.' He shepherds them out of the music room, oblivious to the annoyance in Marcel's face on hearing the affection in Troy's voice for his beloved Alina. This is Marcel's role, and he looks at the usurper suspiciously.

During dinner Marcel gets both indigestion and several unpleasant jolts. Though the food is good, he unfortunately chooses squid, forgetting it never agrees with him. The Italian owners, now settled in Dingle, are gregarious to the point of hysteria, and Marcel finds them tiresome.

As the pains in his gut begin to mount steadily during the coffee and dessert, Marcel realizes with a shock that Alina is not oblivious to the attention Troy showers on her. Though she occasionally chides him when he is too solicitous, she looks at him with something that seems suspiciously more than affection as she does so. He notices, to his alarm, that she is smiling at Troy far more than she smiles at *him*, Marcel, though he has not seen her for months and is lavishing all his charm on her.

Alina is looking regal tonight, with her blond hair pulled straight back into the thick plait, which she has coiled like a sleeping serpent around her head. Tiny pearls twinkle on her earlobes like the tears of an ice maiden. Marcel wishes fancifully that he could kiss, dry and chastely, the snowy tears on those delicate lobes. But then she says something softly to Troy, who reaches across the table to touch her hand, and Alina responds to the touch like the opening of some rare night-blooming plant, her bosom expanding in a deep breath, her lips curling in the sweetest smile Marcel has ever seen. He is so distressed by this exchange that he says to Claudia, seated next to him, 'I'm not well, Claudia, we must go home.'

Claudia hisses softly in her native tongue, '*Te variyat*, Marcel. Crazy idiot, fool! We can't just walk out, and anyway I'm enjoying myself.' Indeed she is; she has had a sumptuous meal, and is now allowing herself to be entertained by Alina and Troy, who seem, despite their polite banter with the others in the party, to be in some private world of their own. She is also amused by Marcel's discomfiture.

Marcel realizes he is being childish and tries to pull himself together, but he feels betrayed. He does not want to be Alina's lover, but he wants her to be faithful to him anyway, at least in spirit.

'Where is David?' Marcel blurts out. 'I would have thought a loving husband such as he would never leave your side, Alina, after your near brush with death.'

He says it lightly, but it produces the reaction he wanted. There is an uncomfortable hush, fortunately filled by the arrival of more coffee and another flurry of maniacal attention from the Italians.

Steffie, sitting opposite Marcel, frowns slightly as he mentions Alina's husband, registering that this is a naughty thing to do. But she does not reflect on this for long, reverting to her own inner world of nourishing puréed food, the clean smell of a freshly bathed infant, the sleeping face of a baby in the middle of the night. She has still to learn the more unpleasant realities of motherhood.

Marcel is definitely sulking. He has come to Ireland at Alina's call, prepared to spend hours at her side, coaxing her into health with his music, sending Claudia out on the hills to gather medicinal, healing herbs to restore the invalid to her previous vitality. How upsetting it all is, to find another man horning in on this vision! Not just another man but a musician to boot, and not nearly so talented as Marcel himself.

Troy says something to Alina that Marcel cannot hear, and Alina turns to Troy with a look Marcel has never before seen on her face. The knowledge, dreadful but irrevocable, comes to him that they are in love.

'Lighten up,' Claudia mutters, blowing foul smoke from one of her herbal cigarettes in his direction. She knows perfectly well what is wrong with Marcel, but wishes he would stop being so blatant about it.

Marcel pulls himself together, remembering that he is a professional, that he is here officially to perform. He wants nothing more now than that this concert be finished, so that he can return at once to his beloved Brittany and nurse his broken heart, not to mention wounded pride, in the forest of his birth.

In the meantime, there is this infernal evening to get through, and his digestion feels totally destroyed. 'Meadowsweet,' Claudia mutters, knowing about his indigestion as she knows most other things about him. 'I will give you a good dose when we get back to the house. I picked and dried the flowers and leaves myself when I was last in England.'

Steffie, sitting opposite, wrenches herself away from

68

thoughts of her baby to say sympathetically, 'Not feeling well? What a shame.'

Marcel looks at her properly, something he has not done since they met. She is shining; healthy, effervescent. There is an agitaiton, an excitement in her, that is most attractive. Her neat though plain features are made beautiful by this reckless beaming glow, rather like a lighthouse gone slightly berserk.

Marcel recognizes these symptoms; he has witnessed them often enough, usually after an especially highly charged performance. They occur always in women, and in women who are available, even though they had not realized their availability until then. Steffie's restlessness, her unconcealed joy, her heightened colour, are all the signs of, if not love, then infatuation, an intense physical attraction.

Marcel's spirits lift as his bruised pride begins to be soothed. Alina has disoriented him, cast him from his role as chivalrous knight, as courtly lover. He will revert, then, to his other role, his old self, that of magician, wizard; he will bewitch the delightful Steffie, who is already under the spell of his music and magic, and have a tumultuous affair with her. Alina will notice him then, and perhaps regret what she has lost. Perhaps, after all, he will not rush from Heron's Cove when the concert is over.

Marcel turns his attention to Steffie. He visibly changes as he does so, like a sorcerer able to change shapes at will. He becomes Marcel the brilliant musician, the charismatic performer, the medieval Merlin. His body becomes alert, vibrant; energy courses through him like lightning.

He begins innocuously enough. 'I played a concert in Miami once. An interesting city, don't you think? Though I can't imagine what it's like to live there.'

'It has its good and bad points, like most other cities. The sun and warmth is a big plus.' She goes on to describe the other merits. Marcel listens to the words, but is not unaware of her over-bright eyes, the high she seems to be on.

'How long are you staying at Heron's Cove?' he asks.

Steffie is vague. He takes this to mean that she is available, and will stay on if *he* does, or move on with him if necessary. Marcel must be forgiven for this rather vain assumption; it has happened exactly like this so often – women following him all over the world at a moment's notice – that he no longer thinks it unusual.

Steffie, spurred on by Marcel's interest, begins to talk about herself. She had watched his charismatic performance during the rehearsal at Heron's Cove and fantasized about her child being given her first recorder, then imagining her daughter an accomplished musician. As she watched him playing his heart out she saw her own child there, grown into young adulthood, enriching people's lives with her music.

'At what age do you think my daughter should be given her first recorder?' She blurts the question to him during a brief pause in their conversation.

Marcel is thrown by this reference to a child. He asks politely, trying to hide his chagrin, 'You have children?'

This opens floodgates. 'I will have shortly. I'm adopting a Peruvian baby. I only found out today that there will be one available, all being well, in a month's time. I'm so thrilled, so overwhelmed! I haven't even had a chance to tell Troy and Alina yet. But when I watched you play, listened to your music, I could see my child there; I couldn't stop dreaming of what she will be. I'd like to expose her to music at an early age;

after all, we have musicians in the family, look at Troy. I keep saying *she*, even though Luis, he's my lawyer, warned me it could turn out to be a boy. But I have a gut feeling, you know?'

Marcel doesn't know, but lets her carry on. Once again he is stunned into silence. The love blazing from this woman's eyes is not for him, but for an unborn baby. The pain in his gut intensifies.

He doesn't know how to deal with this. First Alina, now this woman – English, American, whatever she is – untouched by his magic, unbewitched by his spells. Steffie's green eyes are staring intently into his, but he knows now that the intensity is not for him. Before he can take this all in, Troy is paying the bill and the party starts to scrape back chairs and shuffle towards the door.

Marcel walks behind Steffie, notes her small neat body, her prim navy suit, the clean hair like a scoop of orange sherbet resting on her long neck. A pleasant scent emanates from her, like the roses in his garden back home. He remembers that flush on her face, the lusting brightness of her eyes, and wants that desire to be aimed at him, not at some mewling infant who sounds like a figment of the woman's imagination.

The night air is pleasantly cool, the evening only now beginning to get dark. A slither of moon hangs torn in the sky, and a few bright stars have ventured out. The mountains are raised bruises on the darkening landscape, their origins ancient and unknowable.

Marcel decides he likes rural Ireland. There is a challenge here, a mystery. The sea not very far away sprays a faint scent of salt and kelp into the air, the lush grass of the hills and fields whisper in a soft breeze. The homesickness he felt this evening, compounded first with Alina's treachery, then the brutal realization that Steffie is not at all interested in him, has abated slightly. (The fact that his indigestion seems gone is another factor.) Alina's defection is too great to contemplate just yet, but Steffie's now seems a challenge. He licks his slashed vanity and prepares to go back into the fray.

'I'm thinking of staying on for a bit after the concert,' he says to Steffie as they get into Troy's car. Claudia, overhearing, looks at him disdainfully.

'Well, you *did* order me to take a break after this, didn't you?' he says playfully to her. 'We have no bookings for a bit, and you said I needed a holiday. And our host very kindly suggested I stay as long as I wanted.'

'You're both more than welcome,' Troy says. He means it too, at least on one level. His house will be full of music and talk of music.

But on another level, a deeper one, partially hidden even to Troy, there is disappointment. His and Alina's retreat from the world is coming to an end. Though, of course, he knew it would, and looked forward to it, for it meant that Alina would be wholly well again, the prospect has unsettled him.

Alina, in her role as gracious hostess of her temporary home, says, 'It will be good to have you with us, Marcel. And you too, Claudia, if you decide to stay.' She looks in Troy's rear-view mirror, catches Marcel's eyes and holds them for a moment. Marcel, shot through with hope by this, decides that perhaps he should not abandon her too soon; perhaps she has suffered some great mental trauma after the accident which has caused her to act so outrageously out of character with this man, Troy. Marcel may be needed still, to break this bewitchment with magic of his own making.

Steffie's face, near his in the back seat of the car, is silver in the starry evening. Marcel puts his arm lightly over the back of the seat, grazing her shoulder. Claudia, on the other side of Steffie, notices, but her face is as enigmatic as stone. Turning to look out of the window, she decides to walk the hills tomorrow searching for plants, for wild flowers she can dry and use for her medicines. She has a feeling they will be needed. Alina, whom she has met only once or twice before, is still obviously not in complete health, and Marcel, indigestion aside, needs something potent to pull himself together. And this Steffie . . . Claudia ponders on Steffie for a few moments. On the surface she is so vibrantly healthy, but there is a longing there, something that could sicken her if she is not careful.

Claudia mixes, in her head, her dried leaves and flowers, her herbs and oils. The others, silent for once, each in a world of his or her own, gaze at the dark landscape going past the car windows, oblivious to the potions that Claudia, like a sorceress, is planning for them.

Chapter Four

'What a magnificent morning!'

'Perfect spring weather.'

'Just think, and it's only the beginning.'

'We should be outside. What about a picnic?'

The sun is burning through the kitchen windows at Heron's Cove, where Troy and his visitors are lingering over breakfast. 'What beautiful bread,' Claudia says, helping herself to a third slice.

'One of the locals dropped it off this morning,' Troy says. 'Appeared at the door saying it was for Steffie.' He smiles avuncularly at his sister and says, 'Typical Steffie, always picking up friends, hobnobbing with the natives wherever she goes.'

Steffie cringes, wondering why Troy on occasion embarrasses her, why he sometimes seems a generation older than she, even though he is two years younger. Perhaps because he has led such an insular life despite his sojourns in major cities all over Europe and America. Wherever he goes, he inhabits the same world, that rarefied world of the professional musician that can drive those who live with them into headbanging frustration. Steffie has often thought that her brother hasn't a clue about life, or life as most people know it.

She eats the bread Jack has brought, remembering their conversation this morning. He appeared quite early, jaunty and confident, with two loaves of his mother's bread. 'She's becoming deeply suspicious,' he grinned. 'My confiscating all her bread for some hitch-hiker I picked up.'

'I believe it was me who picked you up,' Steffie bantered.

'Why don't we finish this argument at dinner one night. I'll take you to my favourite restaurant in Dingle. Name a night.'

But Steffie, unsure of Troy's plans for his guests in the next few days, put him off. She could not help feeling slightly flattered as she sensed his disappointment. Steffie thinks Jack is exceedingly sweet, and possibly a bit of a lad. She has not forgotten the girlfriend in Tralee, the regretful way she looked at him when she asked him to come back soon. But Steffie is in the fortunate position of being able to enjoy the overtures of lusty carefree young men without any worries about falling into temptation. Her overwhelming love for her unborn baby leaves no room for other commitments, other desires. She can watch Jack's attraction to her with detachment, enjoy it for what it is. This is a unique feeling for Steffie, who ordinarily becomes totally involved, and committed, to people she is fond of. Motherhood has changed her already, and she's not even had her baby.

Now, Jack having reluctantly gone back to work, the others are dithering around, wondering which country joy to sample first. The concert is not until tomorrow night, and Claudia and Marcel feel the need for some relaxation today. They are enjoying this holiday; they have had an arduous year, performing all over Europe and twice in America; they are both exhausted.

They decide, finally, on a walk from Heron's Cove along the coast to a nearby sandy beach, where they will lounge about on the shore and eat their picnic – bread and various cheeses and white wine which they have some notion of chilling in the sea.

Troy, sitting next to Alina, puts his hand solicitously on hers and says, 'I hope it won't be too far for you. You mustn't overdo it, you know. Remember, the doctors said it would take years for you to entirely gain your strength back.'

'If you ever do,' the physiotherapist had said, when Alina was home and convalescing. 'Not to worry, though,' he had told her cheerfully. 'It's mostly your hands now. And they will be ninety-nine per cent perfect by the time I finish with you.'

He had not understood why Alina had turned away from him, said in a muffled voice that she wasn't feeling well and could he please go now.

Her daughter Kate had been there and heard the conversation. Alina, when she could pull herself together, said, 'It is not enough, ninety-nine per cent.'

Kate said, 'Mum, I think it's brilliant news. Dad can't believe how well you're doing. You'll still be able to play, to teach . . .'

'I don't want to teach. Or play for myself.'

David had come in on this last sentence. 'Don't you think that's being rather selfish? You could have been permanently paralysed. Or dead. Can't you be grateful for what you have?'

Kate, shocked by his bluntness, left the room. Alina, defeated, said, 'Why can't you understand? You're a musician too.'

David's face took on the soothing look he used to placate temperamental first violinists. 'And so are you. So will you always be. Even if you never perform in concert again. Which you won't, Alina. It's better for you to accept it now.'

He said this so firmly that for a time she began to believe him.

*   *   *

In the kitchen at Heron's Cove Alina pulls her hand away from Troy, and he remembers, too late, her need to be less dependent on him. It pains him that he has become a burden to her by his caring and concern. Alina says, 'Of course it's not too far for me to walk to the beach. But I think I shall stay behind. There are things I'd like to do, letters to write. I must phone Kate; I haven't spoken to her this week.'

'Perhaps it's just as well; the path is rather treacherous in places.' Troy continues to the others, 'You won't mind that we don't go with you? I'll direct you to the coastal path and the rest is straightforward.'

Claudia, Marcel and Steffie politely murmur that it will be no problem. 'That's settled then,' Troy says, feeling he has got around the problem rather well. They would both stay home, he and Alina, and there will be no argument whether Alina is fit enough or not for the walk. He beams benevolently at her, and Steffie thinks how besotted he is. She has never seen her brother like this before, not even with his ex-wife in those heady early days.

Alina stands up and fills the coffee pot again. 'There's no need for you to stay behind, Troy,' she says.

'But I want to. Actually, I have things to do too, before the concert.'

'No you haven't; you know perfectly well that everything is done,' Alina retorts. 'You must go with your guests; you mustn't leave them to wander on their own.'

Claudia and Marcel protest, but Steffie understands that there is something more going on here. 'Troy, please,' Alina says softly so that the others cannot hear, 'remember what I said the other day? I don't need to be coddled any longer.'

'I'm sorry that my concern is becoming a burden,' he says stiffly.

'Oh, Troy, it's not, believe me. It's been too easy to lean on you. That's why I must stop now. Please, go with the others; let me be alone for a time.'

She says this so sweetly that Troy cannot take offence, but he is bewildered, unsettled. He can't help saying, 'We'll be several hours, you know.' The implication is that terrible things can happen to Alina in those few hours.

'Troy, stop it. Please, stop.'

Troy, helpless, begins to fuss around gathering a picnic, some blankets. They finally leave, laden down with baskets and rucksacks. Marcel has his old recorder and Claudia her various herb containers, hoping to find some interesting samples of kelp. Steffie packs fresh fruit, apples and grapes that she finds in the fridge.

Finally, Alina is on her own. She has hardly been alone since her accident, she realizes. First there were the months in hospital, then a long period of convalescence at home in Dublin. She had had a nurse to help her as she relearned how to dress and feed herself, how to cope with living again. Her husband David was there for some of the time, and so was Kate, but both had commitments outside of Dublin which she urged them to fulfil. Their undisguised pity distressed her, convinced her that she would never be quite normal again.

Her convalescence was slow and frustrating, even though the spacious flat was never empty, even when David and Kate left. Musician colleagues from all over the world made detours to come and see her, for her accident – a totally senseless one involving only herself, a skid on a slippery road, and a parked lorry – had shocked them all.

Alina tries to scrub all details of the accident and its aftermath from her mind, but her mind betrays her. Walking back to the house from the terrace, where she waved the others off, she remembers her first step, after months of lying immobile. Her neck and spine had been wired and fused after a series of operations; her legs, no longer paralysed, had regained their mobility. Propped up on both sides by a nurse and a physiotherapist, Alina put her feet on the floor and walked.

It wasn't a walk, more a shuffle. 'You're doing fine,' the nurse said as Alina faltered, her legs so weak they couldn't hold her emaciated frame.

'I can't,' she said, tears of frustration building up behind her eyelids.

'Just to the end of the ward,' the physiotherapist said.

It was visiting hours, and the ward was full. As Alina began her walk, everyone fell silent. The medical staff stopped what they were doing to watch; the patients, eager to believe in miracles, crossed their fingers or prayed.

Twice she almost fell, but was propped up by a strong firm arm. When she got to the end of the ward everyone cheered. She looked up from her trembling feet, face wet with tears and perspiration, to see Troy watching her.

'Well done,' he said. It was inadequate to the point of ludicrousness, but he was too moved to say more.

'It's only the beginning,' she said softly.

'I know.'

'My hands next.'

'Yes.'

'I can do it, whatever they say.'

'Yes.'

Alina closed her eyes, let herself be placed in a

wheelchair and taken back to bed. The look on Troy's face was not of pity, as it was on Kate's, or of contradiction, as David's had been when she spoke of her determination to perform again. It was of hope. The scent of it was sweeter than any of the flowers she had surrounding her bedside.

Alina walks into the house at Heron's Cove and phones Kate, knowing that David will be out at a rehearsal. She has of course spoken to him since she has been here, but to do so needs energy; she hasn't that much of it now, and what she has she must conserve.

Kate is glad to talk. 'So much to tell you, Mum; so many wonderful things happening. But I'll save them until I see you.'

'Will you be coming down again soon?'

But Kate is suddenly cagey. 'Uh, do you need me? Do you want me to come?'

Alina is moved by this obvious willingness of her daughter's to put aside her own concerns and visit her mother. She says, 'No, I'm fine, I really am. Troy's looking after me almost too well, and the house is filled with musicians and family. And I'm practising. Hard.'

Alina can hear the worry travel along the telephone wires from Dublin to the Dingle peninsula. 'Oh, Mum, I'm glad for you, but are you sure you won't be too heartbroken if—?' She breaks off her sentence.

'If I fail?' Alina asks gently.

'Look, I'm sorry, I didn't mean – it's just that we worry, Dad and me.'

'I know you do, and I appreciate it. But I'm all right, love. I truly am.' And for a moment she is, because her daughter needs her to be.

When they hang up Alina goes into the music room. She looks at her hands. She has the habit of staring at them these days, as if they are strange animals lying pale and curved in her lap. She knows they are still not right. They are ninety-nine per cent right as the therapist promised, but she needs that extra one per cent if she is to perform again.

She goes to the harpsichord and begins to play. It is not one of the pieces she usually practises with Troy, but a Scarlatti sonata. It is one she often played at concerts before the accident, for it is technically demanding, full of arpeggios, scales, leaps, single and double trills, octaves, all requiring a virtuoso performance. She begins the piece and before she has gone very far she falters. She tries again and fumbles again. This happens five, six times.

Alina stands up, goes to the window of the music room, the one facing the mountain. It is clear and well defined today, the usual mist hovering over it evaporated into the clear air. She stares at it for some time, emptying her mind, meditating only on the earthy brown/green colour of the range of hills, the hot blue of the sky. She remembers learning to walk again, how her feet took ages to begin to obey her. Then she returns to the harpsichord.

This goes on for a couple of hours: the attempt at the same piece, the breaking off at various parts, until at last Alina relents, stops being so hard on herself and plays it through to the end. When she has finished, she bows her head and sits without moving for a long time.

It is not good enough, not nearly good enough, but it is there. There is still some tingling in her fingers, some numbness that comes and goes, but despite that she has got through the piece of music. Perhaps, after all, she *will* perform again. This is the first time she has allowed herself that thought.

*   *   *

Claudia drinks tepid white wine (the sea-chilling idea somehow never worked) and watches Steffie and Marcel frolicking in the sand at the edge of the small secluded cove where they have had their picnic. They are like daft elves, splashing water, burying their feet in wet sand, teasing each other. Marcel is wearing cut-off jeans, a black T-shirt and his loose black waistcoat, and Steffie a miniskirt and striped blouse. She looks plump and girlish, her roundness somehow giving the impression of baby fat, innocent and ephemeral.

Claudia watches these frolics with a jaundiced eye. She has seen it before, Marcel impish and light-hearted as he approaches a conquest. Ignoring their splashes and merrymaking, Claudia hikes up her kaftan, which is golden and shiny and drapes around her voluptuous body like robes of sunbeams. Holding it up from the water, she wades into the sea, picking up odd bits of seaweed, scrutinizing them closely, throwing back some bits and holding on to others.

Troy approaches, his cord trousers rolled up to his knees. 'Cold,' he winces, yet does not move. He has been wandering morosely up and down the beach, wondering if Alina is all right at home alone. What if she has fallen, or become ill? 'Um, I wonder if we should be making a move,' he mutters to Claudia.

'Oh, no hurry,' Claudia replies breezily. 'Such a fine day.'

'Yes. Of course.' His disappointment is obvious.

Claudia takes pity on him. 'She'll be all right, you know. I'm sure it'll do her good, some time on her own.'

'Oh. Of course. Yes.' Troy is nonplussed at this stranger digging into his secret thoughts.

'Geranium, that's what she needs.'

'Pardon?'

'For her hands. She needs to rub geranium oil into them twice a day. Better yet, you can do it. Much more relaxing to have someone do it for you. I have some back at the house, I'll give it to you.' She scrutinizes him carefully. Troy, uncomfortable, mumbles something about going back to the beach blanket.

'I'll come with you,' Claudia says. She waddles out of the sea trailing seaweed and flops down onto the blanket, indicating to Troy that he should sit also. 'Here, have a sip of wine. No, not that, it's not very nice, too warm.' She reaches into her capacious straw basket and pulls out an unlabelled bottle that looks like wine. 'This is special, I brought it all the way over from France. It's my own brew. Or rather my *babcha*'s, my grandmother.'

Troy takes the proffered glass and sips. It is a sweet wine, normally something he dislikes, but this has a slightly bitter taste mingling with the sweet which is not unpleasant. He has another sip, then takes notice of Claudia for the first time. She is looking at him frankly and inscrutably, but this time, instead of this making him uncomfortable, he finds he wants to confide in her. This is so unusual for Troy that he wonders what was in the wine he has just drunk.

'You've heard her play,' Troy blurts. 'Last night, before we all went to bed. She and I did the Rameau together. Then she did that Couperin prelude. I think she's still bloody brilliant.'

'Of course she is.'

'But she won't have it. I want her to do a concert at Heron's Cove; it is a perfect place for her to begin again. No critics, no-one to judge.'

'Only herself,' Claudia says.

Troy gazes mournfully at two seagulls come to

scavenge the remains of their picnic. 'That's right. She is judging herself too harshly.'

Claudia rolls over onto her side to face Troy more squarely. Her kaftan billows around her like a tent. He notices the bare chubby brown feet, the scarlet polish on her toenails. She says, 'Give her time. That's all she needs.'

Troy shakes his head. 'I thought so too, but now I'm not so sure. She's already put off two tentative dates for a concert.'

Claudia waits. She rolls over again, this time onto her back, and closes her eyes to the sun. She looks like a golden mountain, a magic mountain, Troy thinks irrelevantly.

She pours more wine for Troy. He drinks, then surprises himself by beginning to talk. 'I went to visit her in hospital. I've known her for years, but not very well. We were actually students together at music school, when David was teaching, but we were in different years. Then she married him, had her baby, dropped out for a while. I got to know David; we were friends for a time. Off and on, of course, as these things have to be when you live in different countries.'

'I don't know him,' Claudia says, her eyes still shut, 'but, of course, one hears things. That he is volatile, temperamental, passionate. But an exceptional conductor.'

Troy is silent. He doesn't like the word *passionate* applied to Alina's husband. She is so fragile, so cerebral somehow.

'Go on,' Claudia orders.

Troy looks at her, shocked. He doesn't want to go on, doesn't want to spill out his most private thoughts to this virtual stranger. To cover his confusion he drinks more wine. The taste grows on him; it really is quite special. It smells of honey and musk and cloves. It doesn't seem like wine at all somehow.

He goes on. 'It was a shock, seeing her in hospital the first time, unable to move. She was so determined to survive, though.' Troy looks out over the sea, which is deep green and still. 'I didn't realize until later that survival to her was playing the harpsichord, nothing else.'

Claudia is silent, but opens her eyes and turns her head to stare at him like some Eastern European oracle. Troy cannot now stop talking. 'I kept coming back. I was doing a music festival in Belfast, but I kept coming back to Dublin to that hospital. I saw that her hands were not getting better; they were still paralysed. David, Kate, her friends, listened to the doctors and tried to warn her that she might not be able to play again. They talked hopefully of teaching, even composing. They didn't know her at all, you see.'

The golden mountain beside him stirs. 'But you did.'

Troy nods. 'Call it instinct, whatever, but I did. I knew that Alina wanted life, but life was performing. And so I lied to her. I told her that I saw movement in her fingers, more each time I came to visit. I helped her exercise them, showed her what to do to strengthen her hands, even in her weakened, semi-paralysed state. I consulted other neurosurgeons, physiotherapists.'

'And if it hadn't worked . . . ?'

'She'd have hated me, but that's not important. She'd have given up, died, whatever. I'm sure of it. Despite David.'

Claudia notes the bitterness in his voice and remains silent. Troy drains off the wine in his glass and says, a cold anger underlining each word, 'Her husband fought me every step of the way. Said I was raising her hopes falsely. Said she was finished as a concert harpsichordist. He even ordered me out of their house one day, in one of his fits of . . . passion.' He spits the word out distastefully.

There is a long silence. Claudia has closed her eyes again, seems asleep, but, of course, she is not. Troy's eyes are burning from staring at the sunlight reflecting on the bright sea, but he hardly notices. He remembers the scene in Dublin in every detail.

'I don't understand,' he had said to Alina. 'Since you've been home, you seem to have lost all your determination. You're nearly over your convalescence, you've improved more than anyone thought possible, yet still you won't attempt to play music again.' He was worried about her. She had become resigned, but in doing so, had lost her will to carry on with a life that would always be incomplete.

'David says I'm only fooling myself. He tells me I need to face the truth.'

'How can you face the truth when you haven't tried to find out what the truth is? At least try. Try playing again, take that first step. How do you know you'll never perform again if you don't try?'

David had walked in then. 'How dare you. How dare you raise my wife's hopes. Do you know what it will do to her if she fails?'

'I know what it will do if she never gives herself a chance.'

David, furious, said, 'Get out. Get out of my house.'

'David, stop this,' Alina cried. 'Troy is only trying to help.'

'By telling you you will perform again? By creating illusions? He's not the one who will have to live with you when you fail. Get out, Troy. Stop interfering in our lives.'

Troy, white-faced, left, too angry to even say goodbye to Alina. He never set foot in their house in Dublin again.

She came to Heron's Cove a month later. Though her doctors had pronounced her fully recovered, she looked wan and listless. 'Help me,' she had said simply.

By then the music room was complete and Troy had already had a few concerts. During the weeks between, Troy worked with Alina in the mornings, while in the afternoons he went to his workshop and she practised on his harpsichord. Troy was never far away. His workshop, the converted stables near the house, was close enough for him to return on any pretext, listen to her practising, delight in her progress. His own work suffered, is still suffering, from his preoccupation with Alina, but he has worked hard this past year and does not feel pressured. He feels confident enough now as a craftsman of fine harpsichords to know his customers will wait, if necessary, for the completed product.

Besides, this is important. All music is important to Troy, but the harpsichord is his cherished instrument, and he refuses to let one of its greatest players be lost.

Shouts and laughter from Marcel and Steffie, cavorting on some nearby rocks, cause Claudia to open her eyes and sit up. Steffie seems to have momentarily forgotten to carry herself with the dignity she thinks belongs to a future mother and is lying on her stomach trying to catch tiny fish in a rock pool. Marcel is perched above her, squatting on his haunches. Claudia hopes he doesn't fall off the rocks and graze his hands before the concert. She is glad she has brought along her special marigold ointment, which she made herself from freshly picked marigold flowers last summer. The ointment is excellent for cuts and sores and minor burns.

Troy is gazing broodingly out to sea. Claudia says, 'David must resent Alina being here, then,' as if there has not been a long silence since Troy last spoke.

'Yes. He's in a rage. But then he so often is. This passion you attribute to him is, I suspect, mere bad temper.'

'They say', Claudia goes on, 'that he was very supportive of his wife after the accident.'

Troy shakes his head bitterly. 'Oh, they do, do they? He indulged in selfish histrionics, caused numerous unpleasant scenes at the hospital and tried to cash in on the drama of the whole dreadful thing to publicize his own career.'

Claudia is surprised at his vehemence. She herself had heard something along these lines, from the more vituperative musicians of her acquaintance, who maintained that David's constant presence at his wife's bedside was instrumental in keeping him in a limelight he was beginning to lose to young, up-and-coming conductors.

'Have some more of my wine,' Claudia says. 'It is made from elderflowers I collected in the forest of Brociliande when I stayed with Marcel.'

'It doesn't taste like elderflower wine.'

'It has other things,' she replies vaguely.

Troy lets himself relax. It is the first time he has done so since Alina has arrived. He has some notion that his constant alertness, awareness, is necessary to prevent her from relapsing into the somnolent state she was in during her convalescence. When Alina is around he feels constantly on guard. Though this is a role he has chosen for himself, has accepted unconditionally, it is sometimes stressful.

Claudia waits, playing with the sand, covering her sturdy feet with the dry grains. Troy begins to speak again, as she knew he would. 'I don't like Alina going back to him,' he murmurs, as if to himself. 'I am afraid he will undo all the progress she has made at Heron's Cove. I don't think she wants to go back either, but of course she will. She obviously loves him, he's her husband.'

Claudia shakes her head at the obtuseness of men; she has only been here a short time and it is obvious to her that Alina is in love not with her husband, but with Troy. And now Steffie and Marcel are approaching; she eyes Marcel: another example of men's obtuseness. Any fool can see Steffie is not ripe for sexual love; she is stuffed with nest-making hormones like any prospective mother and neither needs nor wants a potential lover hovering around at this moment.

'Perhaps we should head back,' Steffie says, drying her feet on a towel. 'I want to phone Luis, see if there are any new developments.'

'Have some of this wine,' Claudia offers. 'It's my own home-brew. Find the glasses we used with our picnic.'

They taste the wine, exclaim at its strange but compelling flavour, its richness. Marcel takes his recorder from the brown leather rucksack he has been carrying on his shoulders and begins to play. It is a merry tune, a dance melody, and as always when he performs, his body joins in: eyes, forehead, torso, feet all wrestling eloquently with the music. The beach in the small secluded cove is empty except for themselves, and Steffie, exuberant, begins to dance, a sprightly waltz with twirls and whirls and her own nimble steps. She is dancing for her child, her dear daughter, whom she will soon be cradling in her own arms. She is dancing because the excitement and joy she feels can no longer be contained.

Marcel thinks she is dancing for him and plays most eloquently. When the music finishes, he almost fancies himself in love with this ginger-haired sprite. Claudia notices this and sighs. Marcel always fancies himself in love at the beginning of a new affair. It never lasts more than one or two couplings.

'We'd better go,' Troy says, firmly now. 'The day is no longer so promising.' He waves vaguely towards the sky, where dark clouds are beginning to gather over the sea. As they begin to trudge home, thunder rumbles in the distance.

'Ivo would like this,' Steffie says. 'It looks like there's going to be a storm at sea.'

'I wonder if he'll make it over here,' Troy says. 'You never know with Ivo. He's never seen Heron's Cove, you know.'

'I don't even know where he is right now. Off chasing lightning somewhere, I suppose. We're so restless, our family, always running off chasing clouds, wild dreams. Except for you, Troy. You have your music, you don't need to keep looking.'

They walk in silence, thinking of Ivo as the storm draws nearer. He would be a good uncle, she decides, despite his rather strange preoccupation. He is the most effusive of all of the Ginger Nuts, especially when a storm is brewing. Steffie thinks he should have married, had bundles of children, but his many relationships with women have been brief and sporadic. Ivo leaves them without warning to chase a tornado in Kansas or an electrical storm in Arizona.

Once a woman called Dulcy moved into his Miami Beach apartment and Steffie thought that this might last. But after two months she came to Steffie in tears. 'He's gone. Left in the middle of the night. He heard a forecast about a low-pressure area moving into the Midwest and is staying there indefinitely.'

'He'll be back.'

'Sure, for a day, a week, if I'm lucky. He's never in his goddamn place long. I think he prefers living in slightly seedy hotels, or on friends' sofas, or in his van, chasing goddamn rainbows.'

'Not rainbows. Storms.'

'Whatever. They give him a high I never can.' Dulcy looked defeated.

Steffie had to admit this was true. Mentally she said goodbye to Dulcy, hoping that Ivo's storms would make him happy, because a woman never could.

She says now to Troy, 'I worry about his health. He's smoking again now and drinks more than is good for him. He's getting podgy too. He was always chunky, but he's more so now.'

'How is he fixed for money?' Troy worries about money. Their parents had thrown it around like confetti at a wedding, which even as a child had made him nervous, though they had plenty of it to throw.

'All right, I think. He doesn't spend money on anything except his equipment and travelling to where the storms are. He's become quite acclaimed, you know, as a photographer of storms. Picture spreads in glossy news magazines, that sort of thing. He never stops working.'

Troy is relieved. He finds Steffie's and Ivo's lifestyle erratic and is constantly concerned about them. It never occurs to him that his is too. At least he hasn't any money worries now. Not only are his harpsichords in demand and fetching outrageous prices, but also the aunt that owned Heron's Cove was found to have a substantial amount tucked away in an obscure safe deposit box. Troy had offered this too, to Steffie and Ivo, but both had refused, telling him to use it to do up the house. They are as unconcerned about money as their parents were, though they do not flagrantly toss it about. Having had to work hard in their chosen professions to obtain it, they know its worth.

Troy and Steffie are both silent for a few moments, thinking fondly of Ivo. 'I hope he gets here soon,' Steffie says finally. 'We can keep an eye on him.'

They turn a bend and Heron's Cove comes into view. From this distance the house looks grand, impressive. It is only when one comes closer that the effect is one of shabbiness rather than grandeur.

Both Troy and Steffie forget their brother at once. Troy is seized with anxiety, wondering if Alina is all right. Steffie wants to get quickly to the telephone, to phone Lima.

Marcel and Claudia are lagging behind, oblivious to the approaching storm and speaking belligerently in French. 'You're being a complete fool over Steffie,' Claudia says, jumping right in. 'You are misreading all the signs.'

Marcel says coolly, 'Remember, Claudia, you are merely my accompanist, not my keeper.'

This incenses Claudia. She tells him in no uncertain terms that without her, he would be nothing. The old argument is so familiar to them that they can conduct it in either English or French, and Claudia has been known to shout it in Ukrainian. Marcel understands, even then, exactly what she is saying, though he doesn't understand the words.

Troy and Steffie increase their pace, leaving the others behind, rushing towards Heron's Cove, not noticing the drama of the coming storm, the way the sea darkens and swells, the way the mountains grow purple in the dimming light. Indeed, most of the day was wasted for them. As Steffie larked about with

Marcel, and Troy paddled distractedly in the shallows with Claudia, the beauty of the day and of their surroundings was barely registered by either of them. Steffie's thoughts were in Peru, with her embryonic child; Troy's at Heron's Cove, with a woman he does not know he loves.

That night, after a dinner of cold meats, various cheeses and a large salad, Steffie says, 'Why don't we all go out tonight?' She has not been able to get hold of Luis and feels restless, in need of distraction. 'We can go into Dingle, show Claudia and Marcel a bit of Irish pubbing.'

The five of them set off in festive spirits. Alina seems particularly happy. Her day alone at the harpsichord has lifted her spirits. Troy's consistent hope is becoming contagious; she can feel it beginning to surge through her own bloodstream, though she has not yet let on to anyone about her solitary and intense hours of practice. She looks good, dressed in a long summer skirt festooned with tiny red flowers and a red blouse with a scooped neckline. The scar on her throat seems to reflect the colour of her clothes; it seems more vivid, scarlet. Alina has made no attempt to hide it; her plait is intricately wound around her head and her neck and throat are bare.

In Dingle, they are spoiled for choice. There are countless pubs, many with tempting music coming from within. Troy, though he has lived in the area for some time, hardly knows the town, which is not large but busy and compact, the main street crammed with colourful pubs, numerous restaurants and perky shops. The smaller streets snake sideways and look interesting enough to wander down; the one they are on has a second-hand bookshop, a grand brick house that seems to be a doctor's surgery, and a pub that looks like an old-fashioned ironmongers. Unfortunately the evening, chilly and damp, is not conducive to aimless strolling, but there are too many pubs, too many choices, and no-one will make a decision.

Steffie, becoming impatient by all this dithering, spots a pub near the harbour called Patrick's, which she remembers Jack mentioning. 'Let's try this one,' she says and goes inside, not caring by this time whether the others follow her or not.

Patrick's is a square pub which resembles a small barn inside, but is festooned on every available wall and beam with old newspaper clippings, advertisements from years ago for Irish stout, ancient posters and postcards. Numerous photographs of all sizes, mostly of the past history of the fishing community in Dingle, hang in heavy wooden frames, some with other yellowing photos taped around the edges. The pub is crowded tonight, noisy. In the summer it will be packed with visitors, but now the customers are mostly Irish, both local trade and weekenders from Cork and Limerick. Many people are standing, but there are tables and benches pushed against the sides. Troy, standing at the long bar going down one length of the pub, orders drinks while the others squeeze into a rickety corner table which has just been vacated. He hustles his way through the gregarious crowd to deposit his drinks, then returns for Steffie's Guinness which is settling on the bar.

When he finally gets back with her drink, she barely thanks him, so intent is she on watching some musicians playing at the table next to them in front of a lit fire. The spring day, which promised this morning to be so fine, has disintegrated into a cold drizzle, and the warmth of the turf fire is comforting. It smells like

Ireland, Steffie thinks, like I remember it, turf smoke, wet grass and earth, thick stout. She is suddenly very glad to be here.

Troy follows her gaze to the musicians and recognizes Jack, the young farmer who brought them his mother's home-made bread this morning. Troy thought this both quaint and rustic; he loves these little things that reinforce his decision to leave the city and settle somewhere so spectacularly rural.

He thinks the music quaint and rustic also, and is delighted that he can appreciate it as such. He recognizes that the musicians are good, even excellent, for what they are. There is a man with a beard playing the accordion, a black-haired woman on an acoustic guitar and Jack playing a rather battle-scarred fiddle. The music is fast, lively, fun. Three young men from West Cork, who are talking in Irish to each other, break off their conversation to do an improvised jig in the middle of the pub. When the music and dancing stop, the crowd cheers, applauds. The men grin, shy now, and push their way boisterously to the bar to order more drinks.

'It's a wonder anyone comes to your concerts at all, with free music in every pub in Ireland,' Steffie says to Troy, delighted with what she has just heard.

'Oh come now, Stef,' Troy says, 'you can't compare someone like Marcel here, and Claudia and Alina, to people who just wander off the streets into pubs and play a few folk tunes.'

'You are a terrible snob about music,' Steffie says with some asperity. 'Just because it's not your kind, it doesn't make it less important, or enjoyable, or enriching. Anyway, I thought Irish instrumental music evolved from the same roots as your beloved baroque music. The origins of both were the dance.'

'The roots of early recorders were in dance too,' Marcel says.

Alina nods. 'And there are other elements in Irish music as well. The harp, of course. The music was highly complex and developed. There was an Irish harpist in the seventeenth century, Carolan he was called, who was influenced by Vivaldi and Corelli.'

'I only meant—' Troy tries to speak but Alina has not finished.

'And what about the "Sean Nos" tradition of music? Sung without instruments, handed down orally for centuries. It's sophisticated stuff, Troy, with elements taken from medieval bardic poetry, which was as scholarly and élite as even you could wish for.'

Though Alina speaks gently, Steffie can see that Troy is nonplussed. But he says, with a rather embarrassed little smile, 'I take your point. Perhaps I do become a trifle insular about music.'

Alina puts her hand lightly on his, and looks at him so warmly that he actually flushes in her gaze. Steffie thinks, This woman is good for him. Anchors him to the solid earth when he's floating too dangerously far in his clouds of music.

This conversation has triggered off a lively discussion of traditional music. Marcel begins by praising the folk music of his beloved Brittany, and Claudia then tells of her grandfather in Ukraine who played a melancholy instrument called a bandura. 'He was magnificent when he played,' she recalls. 'I would never consider myself a better musician than he, though I was trained in the classical tradition.'

Troy, having given in gracefully, buys them all another round of drinks. The musicians in the pub are playing a ballad now, and Jack, having abandoned his fiddle, is singing in a good strong voice:

Remember me, when the candles shine in the evening;
Remember me, when you close your eyes to dream.

It's a catchy refrain, and Jack grins at Steffie, flirting with her as he repeats the chorus. When the song is over, the man and woman with him also put down their instruments. The people in the pub understand that Jack is going to sing unaccompanied, and a hush occurs in the crowded pub. A low murmur – 'shush, ssh,' – goes around to those in the back who have not realized what is going on.

When the pub is entirely quiet, Jack begins to sing a slow haunting song in Irish. Though Steffie cannot understand the words, she finds it both powerful and moving, and Jack sings with great strength and clarity. Applause nearly rips out the walls when he is finished, and cries of 'More, Jack, give us another,' ring out from around the bar. Jack obliges, but with his fiddle this time, giving them a rousing number with a difficult instrumental passage that he sails blithely through.

The pub audience is appreciative. Jack beckons the other two musicians to join him and they play for another half-hour, taking requests, bantering now with the crowd. Jack is a born showman, Steffie notices, not unlike Marcel and his recorder, though Jack's performance is earthy and grounded, while Marcel's is somewhere in the clouds. Steffie thinks how refreshing it is to be here in this down-to-earth pub, drinking Guinness instead of fine wines, mingling with real people. She's fond of all of them at Heron's Cove, loves their company, but she does need a dose of the outside world sometimes to purge herself after gorging on exquisite music, brilliant musicians, a house heady with passionate creativity.

When the musicians finally take a break, Jack gets

up and pulls up a stool next to Steffie. He sits quite close to her, flushed, triumphant. It irritates the hell out of Marcel.

Claudia, huge and resplendent tonight in leggings and a long salmon-coloured shirt topped with jumbo strands of ebony beads and a profusion of multi-coloured scarves, is losing her tolerance somewhat, all these men preening themselves with their music in front of Steffie. The thought fleetingly crosses her mind that perhaps Steffie could do with a dose of senna pods: the laxative effect would keep her confined to the house and give the besotted Irishman and the pursuing Frenchman time to cool off.

Claudia banishes these thoughts immediately; she would never use her knowledge of medicinal herbs in any other way than benign. Her grandmother never did, though Claudia does sometimes wonder if the tonics she gave to her husband, after too many late-night sessions on the bandura, might not be suspect. Her grandfather was a homebody for days after one of her doses, too lethargic to go down to the village with his pals and imbibe vast quantities of vodka as was his inclination.

Jack stays at their table for quite some time, though the other two musicians have begun to play again. Troy, feeling guilty over the dismissive way he reacted to the man's music at first, engages Jack in conversation and is surprised to find himself warming to him, drawn to his humour, his easy charm. When he finally gets up to join the others, Troy invites him to the concert the next evening.

'You'll be there, Steffie?' Jack asks boldly.

'Of course,' she grins.

'Then so will I, so.'

Marcel glowers.

'Chill out,' Claudia says to him kindly, trying to tease him out of the foul mood Jack's presence has induced.

'I don't know where you pick up that foul English slang,' he says belligerently.

She thinks again about senna pods. Perhaps she should give them to Marcel, leaving out the cardamom or fennel she usually mixes it with to soften the effect and prevent griping.

Actually, Claudia finds Marcel's frustration, the bruising of his artist's ego, rather bracing. She is very fond of Marcel, but has never quite forgiven him for ending their carnal relationship all those years ago. Claudia, back in Ukraine, was used to being the one to decide when something should end; there was a small fleet of pallid music students in Lvov who adored her. She discarded them one by one as each proved too inept to cope with either her prodigious talent or her voracious sexual appetite, inherited no doubt from her grandmother, who was reputed to have seduced much younger men with her herbal wines and spirits whenever her husband strayed too far.

So a little bit of pain won't do Marcel any harm, she decides. Besides, it won't affect his performance tomorrow night. And that, after all, is the only thing that matters.

Back at Heron's Cove another storm is gathering over the sea. Clouds have obscured the starry night and the house sits black and sullen at the water's edge.

Ivo, squatting on the terrace, watches the approaching storm with wild satisfaction. He believes that it is an omen, this gift from the gods at the moment of his arrival.

Unpacking his camera bag, he finds a vantage point underneath the French windows and squats down again. He does not even notice that the house is dark and empty, has not knocked or tried the door or looked inside a window.

A streak of lightning lashes over the sea.

'Yes!' shouts Ivo. 'Yes, yes, yes, yes!'

He stands up and spreads his arms out to the sea and to the storm.

Chapter Five

Alina spots Ivo first. They have returned from the pub and are fumbling about in the dark while Troy tries to find his keys. 'I keep meaning to get some outside lights,' he mutters as he empties out his pockets.

The storm that has raged over the cove for the past half-hour has abated. The rain has stopped and the thunder is now merely a low rumble somewhere over the hills. Lightning beams weakly and harmlessly in the distance.

'Good God,' Alina cries. 'Someone's there, beyond the terrace, half in the water. Quick, he's not moving, there's something wrong.'

Troy gets to the man first. 'Christ, it's Ivo. Steffie, it's Ivo, he seems to have passed out or something.'

'God, is he breathing? Troy, *do* something. Marcel, don't just stand there, help him.'

They haul Ivo out of the shallow water and into the house. He is saturated, unconscious. Steffie hysterically tries to revive him while Troy flutters helplessly around her.

'Stop hovering,' Claudia says. 'Give him room to breathe.' She pushes the others out of the way and feels for the pulse in his neck, but already he is coming around, moaning softly.

Everyone talks at once. 'Ivo, what happened?'

'I didn't know you were arriving tonight.'

'He's shivering, get him out of those clothes.'

'Quiet. Let him have some quiet, some peace.'

'Shall I call a doctor?'

Claudia is briskly rubbing his chest and shoulders, as Alina rushes in with clean dry towels. Troy disappears and returns with a warm woollen dressing gown for Ivo. Steffie is trying to strip him off, but he is powerful and bulky and seems to be making no move to help himself.

Finally Ivo is dry and wrapped and drinking brandy in front of the elegant fireplace in the music room. He is reclining on the pale cream sofa newly arrived from Cork, having insisted he does not need a doctor. The others hover nearby, on armchairs or the floor.

'My camera,' Ivo gasps between sips of brandy. 'Oh hell, my camera!'

'It's here, I brought it in, I've got everything: camera bag, tripod.' Troy says.

'Jesus. Oh, Jesus hell. I thought it was lost in the sea.'

Ivo himself looks like something out of the sea, Neptune perhaps, or Caliban, with his wayward red beard flicked with white, his corpulent belly, his massive arms, his short legs. He takes no notice of Alina and Marcel, who are gaping, nor of Claudia, now rubbing a strong-smelling unguent she has fetched from her bedroom into his powerful shoulders. 'Made from Chinese herbs,' she explains to whoever is listening. 'Very soothing, calming. He's had a nasty shock to his system.'

'What happened?' Steffie asks, now that Ivo seems revived and undamaged. 'I take it you were photographing that storm.'

'Fantastic, it was. Hovering right over me. All I can remember is the lightning crashed around me, then I lost consciousness. Do you think I was hit?' He says it almost eagerly, and there is a strange, almost fanatical gleam in his eyes which have deepened to the colour of burnt sienna.

'No, of course not,' Steffie says sharply. 'If you had been hit you'd be dead, or burned to toast, or scarred in some manner.'

'It must have struck very nearby, though, probably just missed you,' Marcel says thoughtfully. He's used to lightning storms; he's witnessed many in his forest.

'That would explain it,' Troy says. 'The force would have knocked you senseless. For Christ's sake, man, you're lucky to be alive. I don't know why the hell you do it; you must have a death wish.' His anger is brief but lashing, like a relieved parent's when the child is found safe.

Ivo, in fact, always feels like a recalcitrant child when he is with Steffie and Troy, but this doesn't bother him. It makes him feel young, like his storms do. Ivo, far from having a death wish, wants to stay young for ever, having ancient memories of how pleasant it was to be fussed over by his older brother and sister, in those innocent days before he realized that they were the only ones in the family who cared.

Sometimes, when he is photographing his storms, he knows that he will be forever young. At these moments he knows he is not mortal, not merely flesh and blood and bones, but something golden and eternal.

He felt it first when he photographed a storm in England. He had paid a duty visit to his mother in London and then rented a car and drove down to the West Country, shooting a series of landscapes in Thomas Hardy country: a commission from an American magazine after a spate of Hardy movies had made the author fashionable.

He wasn't much excited about the prospect. Photography up until then had been a job; he had not the passion for it that Troy had for his music. 'I envy

Troy,' he had once said to Steffie. 'He is so in love with what he does.'

'Aren't you?' Steffie had asked, surprised.

'I like it. I have this desire to be the best in my field. I suppose that's the same?'

It wasn't, of course. Troy also wanted to be the best in his field, but was enamoured of the work itself.

'I know what you mean,' Steffie said. 'I feel like you; I like what I do fine, but I feel I want more. I'm not quite sure what it is yet.'

'Why do we need more?' Ivo had asked. 'Why do we have this need to be possessed by something, like Troy is?'

Steffie had shrugged. 'The parents, perhaps. They were blown about like petals on the wind by their whims, never feeling intense about anything much. Not even us.'

Ivo was thinking about this conversation as he drove down the A303 into Wiltshire. He was on his way to Stonehenge, to do another tedious shot of the standing stones, obligatory for a piece on *Tess of the D'Urbervilles*.

He arrived late, too late for the photographs he wanted. Going past the monument, he found a bed and breakfast several miles down the road and set his alarm for an early start.

He had intended to photograph the sun coming up behind the stones: banal and overdone, but his imagination had become stale. Unfortunately, the morning was stormy, the sky bruised with yellow and purple. There was no way the sun would be even remotely visible.

Ivo never made it to Stonehenge. The storm broke over the plain beyond the stones, the lightning lashing the air like knives through that wounded sky. The air seemed to turn green, then pale orange, then deep blue. Lightning cut through it again and again, altering the colour with each flash.

Ivo took photo after photo. Oblivious to the lightning striking around him, the rain soaking him, he took photographs until the storm petered out. Then he lay on the sodden earth in the now drizzling rain and understood for the first time how Troy felt about his music. Suddenly, Ivo's existence made sense; suddenly, there was passion in it. He lay on the ground for a long time, shaken and exhilarated.

Steffie is shaking him gently. 'Ivo, what's wrong, you're still not right.'

Ivo takes a couple of deep breaths and tries to control his excitement. 'Don't you feel it, Stef?' He reaches out his hand to her, and indeed she does seem to feel a slight shock, almost imperceptible, as their fingers touch. She is sure it is her imagination.

'You're crazy,' she says crossly. 'You sound like you *want* to be struck.'

'I think I've become immune to lightning, Stef. Like you do with germs if you're constantly exposed to them.' He looks boyish and eager.

'That's a dangerous idea,' Steffie tells him, beginning to tremble herself as she thinks how close her brother was to death.

Ivo knows enough not to push it, so he keeps quiet.

'I think he should be put to bed,' Claudia says. 'I will make a drink of valerian and other herbs, to restore him to some kind of equilibrium. Then, he must soak in a bath of vervain oil, and finally, a massage of lemon grass and lavender oils. Keep watch over him while I go and prepare my potions.' She stands up and majestically sweeps out of the room, her numerous scarves floating along behind her like wispy coloured clouds.

Ivo doesn't find this at all strange, this stately, mountainous woman pronouncing his cure. He is spent, now, as he always is after photographing a storm. Nothing matters but the photos he has taken, which he will develop tomorrow.

He lets himself be led by Steffie and Troy into a small cell-like bedroom looking out over an impressive mountain, with other lesser hills behind it now drenched in moon and starlight. There is no sign of the thunderstorm, or even rain clouds, confirming Ivo's belief that the awesome spectacle had been arranged exclusively for him.

The bath is hot, steamy, scented. Ivo has been travelling for almost twenty-four hours, what with airport delays and missed connections. He feels out of this world and strangely euphoric, unlike his usual post-storm depression. Perhaps the lightning really did strike him, he thinks. He rather likes this idea, of being struck and surviving. It happens, he knows. Perhaps if he was truly hit by lightning he is now filled with its power, and storms will be drawn to him like iron to a magnet. What photos he could take then!

'I am going to give you a healing massage,' Claudia says. 'Take off all your clothes and drape this towel around you.'

Ivo allows her to massage and oil him, soothe him with herbal drinks and then, finally, with her bitter-sweet wine. As she strokes and kneads his naked body, he imagines she is making love to him; in his odd exhausted state, he dozes, dreaming it is true. This strange, big, alien woman is, in his present state of mind, a goddess, another gift from the lightning which has already given him so much.

106

Claudia, her hands glistening with oil, watches the sleeping Ivo speculatively. Something about his wildness intrigues her, reflects longings of her own. She is tired of ordinary men, with ordinary concerns, ordinary ambitions. This is why she remains with Marcel, as his accompanist and closest friend, because he never bores her; because something in him, some magic, some charm, touches on her own sorcery.

But she and Marcel are no longer lovers, and she needs a lover. Perhaps Ivo is a man who will be her match, who will wean her away from the hold Marcel has on her, the hold she only admits to in contemplative moments.

She looks at Ivo again. His sleep is disappointingly ordinary; he is even beginning to snore. Perhaps he is not the man she is looking for after all.

Claudia, like a technicolour ghost with her scarves wafting behind her, floats out of Ivo's bedroom and down the corridor to her own. From downstairs she can hear the sounds of a harpsichord and a piano and a recorder; Troy and Alina and Marcel are amusing themselves in the best possible way they can.

Claudia runs another bath, this time for herself. The tub is ancient, with iron claws, a deep womb in which to rest. She puts a selection of scented oils into it, and sprinkles in a handful of ginseng.

As she soaks, she is not unhappy. Ivo might prove to be somewhat less than adequate, but she is willing to give him the benefit of the doubt. Perhaps, with the help of her herbs and unguents, he will shape up and become the powerful partner she needs.

Claudia sinks deep into the spicy bath, her ebony nest of hair rising from the steam like a flock of ravens, her golden face thoughtful and serene.

*   *   *

Downstairs, Steffie listens placidly to the music, sitting in an armchair by the remaining embers of the fire. Troy is playing the piano, Alina the harpsichord, and Marcel the recorder. Steffie wishes that she could knit, but she has tried, she is useless at it. She somehow feels it would hasten the arrival of her baby, were she able to knit little pink bootees and soft woollen caps. She aches with longing to have her baby here right now, in her arms, cradled and soothed by the music. She thinks she will go mad if she has to wait much longer.

Steffie is finally aware that the music has stopped. Troy, yawning, says, 'Tomorrow will be a busy day. I'm off to bed. You must go too, Alina. You look tired.'

'I'm off too,' Steffie says. 'I'll look in on Ivo first, make sure he is all right. Good night, everyone.' Alina says good night, but Marcel, looking out of the French windows at the starlit night, scarcely acknowledges Steffie. If she hadn't been so preoccupied with thoughts of her baby, she'd have wondered why he is ignoring her after his fulsome attentiveness of the past twenty-four hours. As it is, she doesn't even notice.

Alina does. She is used to Marcel's mercurial changes of mood and knows there are things that must be said. She tells Troy, 'I'm not tired yet. I'll sit here for a bit with Marcel. Good night, and see you in the morning.'

For the second time that day, Troy is dismissed. He is too shocked to protest. He had been so used to being the only person in Alina's life that he does not know how to cope with other claims on her attention.

She smiles reassuringly at his troubled face and watches as he reluctantly leaves the room.

Marcel and Alina are now alone in the music room. Marcel perversely keeps his back to her, looking out of the small window facing the sea and pretending to be engrossed in the stars. His dark-gold embroidered waistcoat, loose and flowing and medieval, glows dully in the dim light of the chandelier.

Alina waits. It is something she learned in hospital, to wait. Her skin is pale in the light, her hair flaxen.

It is Marcel who speaks first. Without turning, he says softly, 'How could you, Alina?'

Alina still waits, her face implacable. She is not going to carry on a conversation with somebody who will not look her in the face.

Her silence forces Marcel to turn at last. He looks distraught. The sight of Alina, breathtakingly fragile and still, drives him frantic. 'Why did you do it?' he moans. 'I thought you were untouchable, unlike the others. I thought nothing could tempt you. I didn't *want* to tempt you, I wanted to protect you, shield you; I wanted you to be pure and incorruptible. What made you succumb? This . . . this bloody place, this music room? Did he create it just for you, Alina, this fucking temple? Or did you go to bed with him because he makes harpsiochords – has he promised you the most perfect instrument ever made? You *are* sleeping with him, aren't you? *Mon dieu*, explain, Alina, or I shall go mad.' He is so overcome he repeats the whole tirade in French.

Alina looks at him with pity. 'I never asked you to worship me, Marcel.'

But Marcel will not be placated. 'You are the only woman I've ever loved, Alina. You must know that, though I never burdened you with the responsibility.' He is pacing around the room now, still holding his recorder, swinging it from side to side as he makes sweeping gestures to go with his words. Finally he comes to her, sits by her side at the harpsichord. 'Put me out of my misery, Alina. Admit you are unfaithful to me – to David, I mean. Was it the accident, Alina? Oh God, was it that? If I had been there at your side, would you have turned to me? Would you have made love to *me*, instead of to Troy?'

Alina, who has been listening to all this calmly, suddenly slams her fingers on the keyboard in an ominous chord and then walks away to the dying fire. 'What do you know about my accident, Marcel?' she whispers, so that he has to strain to hear. 'What do you know about any of it?'

Now Marcel slams his hands on the keyboard, causing such discordance that both pause for a moment and listen, wondering if the entire household is eavesdropping. But there is no sound anywhere, only uneasy echoes from the harsh chords.

Marcel goes to her, throws himself eloquently, if somewhat theatrically, on some cushions at her feet. 'Is that what happened, *ma chérie*?' he says brokenly. 'This is a punishment for me, because I was not there?'

Alina shakes her head, trying to hide a small smile. 'Sure, but you're a trial to me, Marcel LeLeannic,' she says broadly. Then, more seriously, 'Oh, Marcel, you poor fool, jumping so to conclusions. Of course I'm not sleeping with Troy. I love him dearly; he is a wonderful friend; he saved my life when I wanted to die because I could not play any longer.'

'You're not having an affair with him?' Marcel says eagerly, hopefully. Then his face drops. 'But you do love him; you're in love with him, it's so obvious.' His body droops in dejection. 'You want him, Alina. I can tell.' He flops down again tragically.

Alina sits down on the sofa and beckons Marcel to join her. 'Do get off those cushions, you look like you're in a swoon or something. Oh, don't look so offended. I'm starting to lose patience with you. What I want, and indeed what Troy wants, is immaterial. We don't even discuss it.'

'He's in love with you too, Alina. Any idiot can see that.'

'Perhaps.' Alina is quiet for so long that Marcel groans and puts his head in his hands.

'You have destroyed me, Alina,' he whispers hoarsely.

'Don't be so bloody silly, Marcel. I've been necessary for you, a fantasy, some nebulous madonna figure which you seem to need, for some reason. Maybe it's all these women throwing themselves at you after your performances; I've always thought that it did you more harm than good.'

'*Merde*, Alina, you talk bullshit.' Marcel perks up, sits up straighter, indignant now.

'Not at all. In fact I'm absolutely delighted that that nice Steffie is too besotted with her coming baby to take any notice of you.'

This wounds Marcel. He sighs, picks up his recorder and begins to play, as he always needs to do when he cannot cope with life. Soon he is standing up and the music, a Corelli violin sonata transposed for the recorder, begins to invade Alina, lift her. Marcel may be an imp, a goblin, a naughty elf at times, but when he plays he is a magician. His charms work on her, and when he finishes the melody she is ready to make her peace with him. She has great affection for Marcel, is sorry she has hurt him, however unintentionally.

'Don't worry, Marcel. My relationship with Troy is as platonic as yours and mine. I'll be leaving Heron's Cove soon anyway, going back to Dublin, to David and Kate.' She says it rather forlornly, but Marcel chooses to ignore this.

111

'Perhaps that is for the best,' he says, somewhat pompously. 'David must be frantic, wondering what you are up to.'

'Do you think he cares? What worries him is what people will think, what he cares about is his own reputation, his adoring wife going off to salvage her career with another musician. It wounds his professional pride.'

Her bitter vehemence surprises Marcel; he has never heard her speak a word against David before.

'You've changed,' he says rather inadequately, not quite knowing what he means by this. 'Your accident has changed you.'

'I was never what you fantasized me to be, Marcel.' She gets up, kisses him tenderly on both cheeks and smiles. 'Good night, dear. You are playing more brilliantly than ever, by the way.'

This appeases Marcel. He decides that after all nothing has changed; he can still love her from afar, as obviously Troy seems to be doing. Still, he'll be happier when she leaves Heron's Cove and goes back to Dublin.

Restless, he plays the Corelli sonata again, the music following Alina upstairs. On the landing she meets Troy. 'Oh . . . hello,' he says somewhat awkwardly. 'I couldn't sleep, thought I'd go downstairs, have some cocoa perhaps.'

'You need one of Claudia's brews.'

'Her wine is something else.'

There is a moment's silence. Troy says, 'You wouldn't . . . uh, care to join me?' The question hangs oddly in the air. 'For a hot drink, I mean.'

Alina would like to. More than anything else she would like to, and if they were alone she would. But Marcel is still downstairs; he would be hurt if, after saying good night to him, she came down with Troy.

'I won't, thank you. I'm a bit tired.' But she makes no move to go into her bedroom.

Troy is ridiculously disappointed. He makes no move either. The sound of the recorder drifts to where they are standing, making them both smile. The music seems to enchant them, hold them spellbound. When it comes to an end they seem surprised, somewhat dazed.

'Marcel is still up, obviously,' Troy says, pulling himself together. 'Perhaps he'll join me for a drink in the kitchen.' He kisses her lightly on the cheek. 'Good night, Alina.'

Alina watches him go downstairs just as Marcel watched her leave the music room. She is not tired; on the contrary, she feels restless, unsettled. She wonders what it is about her that makes men content to love her chastely from a distance. She supposes this is a good thing, given her married status. Alina, depite her stormy marriage, believes in it. She and David were wed in church, and though neither of them practise their religion now, she believes in the sacredness of the vows they made. Besides, she has invested a great deal in her marriage, worked hard at it. To dissolve it now would be to admit failure.

She married David because she was pregnant and wanted a decent family life for her child. By the time of the actual wedding, she knew she did not love him, that what she felt when she let herself be seduced by him was a mixture of admiration and infatuation, laced with an edge of vanity, that this talented and respected man fancied *her*.

Love would grow, Alina told herself, but somehow it never did. But by then she had Kate, whom she adored, and a blossoming career carefully nurtured by her husband. Love, she believed, didn't matter.

A few tentative notes on the harpsichord tinkle up from the music room, followed by a trill on the recorder. Troy and Marcel begin to play together: Handel, excerpts from his opera *Rinaldo*. Drawn by the music, she creeps downstairs again and sits in the kitchen where she can listen through the open door and not be seen.

She empties her mind of everything except the music. This is her life; now that Kate has grown, it is all she has.

Her hands, resting on her knees, begin to twitch, as they do now and again since the accident. It is something that will pass with time, she has been assured. Nonetheless it bothers her. It is as if her hands are separate from the rest of her, reminding her that all is far from well.

The thought frightens her. Unable now to enjoy the music, she creeps from the kitchen and hurries upstairs to her room.

Troy breaks off his playing and says to Marcel, 'Sorry, but I thought I saw someone rush through the kitchen.' He gets up, looks, but it is empty.

'Ghosts,' Marcel says breezily. 'We have many in Brittany; I am sure Ireland does too. Shall we begin again? Music soothes the spirits, as they say.' He chuckles over his little joke.

But the occupants of Heron's Cove are far from soothed. Upstairs Steffie tosses and turns, dreaming bad dreams of out-of-reach children, while Ivo, awake, imagines bolts of lightning emanating from every nerve ending in his body.

Claudia is also awake. She feels an unsettled energy coursing through the house and is wary. Vague forebodings, apprehensions, seem to thicken the air;

fears of unknown origins. Getting out of bed she rummages through her infusions and finds the special extract of the aspen flower that she is looking for. Mixing it with water from the jug by her bed, she dips her fingers in the distillation and begins to sprinkle it around the room, like a priest with holy water.

'That's better,' she says aloud, climbing into bed again.

She feels the house and its spirits settling around her, and promptly drops like a stone into a deep well of clear healthy sleep.

'Brilliant, darling!'

'An amazing performance, both of you.'

Accolades flurry over Marcel and Claudia, snowflakes of praise which settle gently on their shoulders. The concert has, of course, been a success. The music room is full, the audience comprising professional colleagues, in Ireland for work or a holiday, as well as neighbours, visitors, music lovers from all over.

'Almost as good as the music in Patrick's on a Saturday night,' Jack says, 'and sure you can take that as a compliment.'

'You're as vain as Marcel,' Steffie laughs.

'Not vain,' Marcel bristles. 'We know what we are worth.' He smiles at Jack complicitly. In the triumph of the moment he has forgotten that the Irishman is a rival.

He is reminded by Jack himself, who has turned to Steffie to say, 'Now that the concert is over, will you come out for that meal?'

'I'd like that.'

Marcel stiffens. Claudia notices, and sighs. 'But Steffie cannot,' Marcel says. 'She is coming to Brittany with us.'

'I didn't say that,' Steffie protests.

'You're going back soon?' Jack asks Claudia.

She nods. 'We had hoped to stay longer, take a well-deserved holiday. But our agent phoned this morning. He's arranged for us to do a recording, so we must return for intensive rehearsals.'

They are interrupted by other people, congratulating Marcel and Claudia on the concert. Jack takes Steffie aside. 'And you're going too?'

'Marcel's trying to persuade me. I need to keep working, you see, and he keeps telling me what a great story I could get from his forest.'

'But I thought you came to Ireland to see Troy.'

'Jack, you seem worried,' Steffie teases. 'Can it be you'll miss me if I go? And you hardly know me! Well don't worry, I'm not. I have no intention of leaving Heron's Cove, not for a while.'

He's relieved. Troy comes up to them, tells Steffie there's a phone call for her. Steffie takes it upstairs to her bedroom, the only place where there seem to be no people milling about.

It is Luis on the phone. 'My baby,' Steffie gasps. 'What's wrong? It's too soon.'

'The baby I had hoped for you is gone. The mother had it prematurely, far too early, and the infant was born dead.'

'Oh, no. That poor woman.'

'The mother was greatly relieved,' Luis says curtly. 'Sometimes a dead birth can be more welcome than a live one. But listen. Another child, a girl, has been taken in by the orphanage. She had been abandoned, but the mother has been found and is totally unable to keep the baby. The woman is ill, destitute, terrified that she will have to have the child back.'

Steffie cannot speak, though Luis is waiting.

'She is three months old,' he continues. 'Can you come immediately to Peru, sign the necessary papers and begin adoption procedures?'

Steffie nods, forgetting she is on the phone.

When they finally hang up, she sits on the bed for a long time. It is Alina who finds her. 'Was it bad news?'

'There is a baby. I must go to Lima at once.'

Alina squeezes Steffie's hand. 'I am so happy for you.'

'I can't believe it, I really can't. I'm over the moon, I'm flying, I feel dizzy and sick and numb with shock.'

'Come downstairs, tell the others. All the audience has gone, except Jack. He's waiting for you.'

Steffie can scarcely remember who Jack is. 'Oh, God, I'd better explain. He doesn't even know I'm adopting. But then we've hardly been alone together, except in the car the day we met. There hasn't been time to talk to him properly since then.'

'You'd better come down and tell him. He's worried that the phone call was bad news.'

'Tell him I'll be down in a minute, OK?'

Alina leaves. Steffie whirls around the room in a fit of joy, then suddenly crashes on the bed. The enormity of what she is about to do overwhelms her, obscuring everything else. She is filled with terror.

Immediately her mood vacillates again; a fistful of joy knocks the fear right out of her. 'Oh God,' she exclaims. 'I'm having a baby.'

The others are waiting for her when she returns to the music room. Jack stands and says, 'Are you all right?'

Her smile is radiant. 'Didn't the others tell you?'

'They said you'd probably like to explain.'

Steffie does. Jack, stunned, can hardly take it in. This is just not on, he thinks. It is not on. The first woman

117

that has really attracted him, both emotionally and physically, in years, is about to get herself a baby? He sits back down, his thoughts scrambled. Whatever he had expected from Steffie's call, it was not this. It most certainly was not this.

The others are also reacting to Steffie's news. Troy is filled with trepidation at the very thought of parenthood, while Ivo feels a fleeting jealousy which, to his credit, he immediately banishes and hugs Steffie soundly. 'Congratulations,' he says, and the others chime in.

'Not yet,' Steffie warns. 'Wait until I bring my baby home.' But her eyes are round with awe, with joy.

Claudia feels an odd stirring inside herself, a strange empathy with this woman she hardly knows, who is about to have a child. Something trembles inside her as a flood of hormones threatens to drown all logic and rational thought processes. She finds herself gripping the arm of her chair to steady herself.

Marcel is shattered. He had been envisaging Steffie in Brittany, soothing him from the shock of seeing Alina and Troy together. He feels his world has tilted, destabilized. He needs some healthy adoration from a besotted female to revitalize him.

Their thoughts are all on Steffie. Except Ivo, who has heard a rumble of thunder and is away with the gods.

Chapter Six

Two English tourists are tramping around the forest of Brociliande, wearing shorts and unsuitable sandals and laden down with maps, rucksacks, flasks and guide books.

'Bloody hell, this is the third time we've passed that fallen tree. We're going in circles,' the young man says.

His female companion snorts, 'What happened to your impeccable sense of direction?'

'According to this map of the forest, Merlin's tomb is supposed to be on this path.'

'Maybe the French don't want us to find it,' the woman says dreamily, taking off her backpack and collapsing on the trunk of the fallen oak tree. She is also young, with a pert face, a tiny gold ring in her nose and half a dozen dangling things hanging from her earlobes. 'Maybe the site is too sacred.'

'Wouldn't surprise me.' The man joins her on the tree trunk. 'Don't blame them, I suppose. Don't want every bugger tramping around here, spoiling the vibes.'

The day is hot, and the young man pulls back his long curly hair into a ponytail, with a rubber band he manages to find in his backpack. The forest is still, eerie in its silence. The trees are old, gnarled, mostly oak; the ground is spongy, pungent with spring. The woman says, 'You can feel it, can't you. The humming, the vibes, the magic. It's just like Glastonbury.'

The man closes his eyes. 'It's all around us, isn't it;

it's cosmic. Merlin's tomb must be around here, I can feel it.' He opens his eyes. 'Come on, let's get moving.'

They pick up their bags, trudge for five minutes through the dense woods, then stop at the edge of a small clearing. There, in front of them, is the tomb, a huge granite slab sheltered by a craggy oak tree. Though unmarked, they know this is what they have been looking for, for on the giant stone are scattered several crowns made of leaves, twigs, flowers, most of them dead now.

The couple stop, awed and reverent. There is still no sound in the forest, no birdsong, no rustling of little animals foraging in the undergrowth – nothing. It is uncanny and gives them the creeps, as they tell everyone later.

She hears it first. A thin piping sound, which she mistakes for birdsong. Then he hears it, and looks at her, perplexed. They stand motionless as the sound becomes louder, and they recognize it as music, but not anything they know. It seems ancient, medieval.

'Shit,' the young woman mutters.

Her companion licks his dry lips and forgets to breathe. Both stand paralysed, transfixed, as the music comes closer.

'Oh fuck,' the man moans as a figure moves slightly behind the trees at the edge of the tomb. It seems to be a man and he is the source of the music. He has what the couple will describe later to their friends as a primitive instrument, some kind of a pipe or early flute. The man himself looks medieval, wearing rustic suede trousers and a loose flowing waistcoat of the same material.

For several seconds the couple watch, mouths open, hearts beating wildly, as the man, seated on a rock,

120

partially obscured by the undergrowth, continues his strange haunting tune.

'Oh shit, oh fuck, it's Merlin,' the woman whispers. She turns and runs like hell, back the way they came, the man right behind her.

It is not until they have reached the safety of the gravelled path which leads out of the forest that they stop and collapse in a heap on the mossy ground. 'I knew this place had a spell on it,' she says, panting, breathless. 'Oh God, do you realize what we've just seen? Merlin *lives*. Oh, wait until we tell the others. They'll never believe us.'

But of course many of them do. The story fills out, grows with each telling, adds to the myths and legends of Brociliande.

Back at Merlin's tomb Marcel plays on, oblivious.

At Marcel's house Claudia is sitting in the courtyard sunning herself. She is sleek and well-oiled, like a seal. It is still and quiet here too; not even the bees are buzzing around the wild roses and unkempt rhododenrons.

Ivo, sitting on a wooden bench under a crab-apple tree, wonders idly if the deckchair will hold all that solid ample flesh. Claudia is topless – she is being French today – and her breasts tremble and heave like Vesuvius as she breathes deeply in and out. Ivo would like to make love to her, but he's already tried that and was rebuffed. This annoys him, for he still thinks of Claudia as his, part of the storm at Heron's Cove, part of the electricity that he still feels coursing through him. And at Heron's Cove it seemed as if this were true, for she ministered to him tenderly, giving him bitter herbal drinks to sip, pouring sweet-smelling liquids into his baths.

Here, in this godforsaken village in the middle of the forest, power seems to have shifted. Ivo finds himself massaging *her* with camomile or may chang oils, or wandering around the fields and forest gathering plants and petals. When this makes him irritable and intractable, Claudia brews him a murky tea and commands him to drink, saying it will soothe his nerves, or pours him another glass of her rich aromatic white wine.

Ivo has been bad-tempered a great deal since coming to France. Claudia had told him of the spectacular thunderstorms in the forest, and Ivo became intrigued. He has photographed lightning in the most dramatic of places – in the middle of rain forests; in Tucson, Arizona, where the atmosphere is electric and lightning is rampant; on Baldy Mountain in New Mexico; in Florida's own Lightning Alley which averages ninety days a year of lightning and has been the location of some of Ivo's best photographs. But he has never filmed in an enchanted forest still haunted by the Court of King Arthur. He'd like to plug into this magic. Who knows what photographs it will produce.

But since arriving, there have been no storms. The air is sultry and promising, but nothing materializes. Ivo wishes he hadn't left Heron's Cove, then remembers why he left. Steffie has gone, and Troy is preoccupied with the Irish princess, or so she seems to Ivo with her old-fashioned music, her pale face, that heavy plait wound around her head like a tiara.

Ivo is not used to both Steffie and Troy being preoccupied with someone else, to the exclusion of their younger brother. Troy seemed distracted, falling into odd silences when Alina was out of the room, and following her around with his eyes when she was.

And Steffie. They were supposed to be having some

kind of a reunion, the three of them, and here she was rushing off to South America. He was pleased for her, that she was getting her baby, but felt slightly bereft by her lack of attention.

He needs a storm, that's all. To fill the temporary gaps left by Steffie and Troy, and the deeper, more damaging ones left by his parents. He is waiting, and the waiting is preying on him. He needs a storm in this forest which is old, ancient, pagan, despite the stories of the Holy Grail and other such Christian additions. Ivo feels that the spirit of the place must permeate the very skies, enhance their energy. He senses that a storm here must be unlike any other, for its source would not be just the ground and air temperature, the friction of warm moist air and icy crystals, but something mystical. He longs to photograph it.

Claudia watches him, as she is watching now, obliquely from her half-closed lids. She notes that he is restless. He has a book in his hand, some American novel, but he's not reading it. He picks it up, puts it down almost immediately, gazes off past the cornfields and towards the forest. He looks blotchy from the sun, though he tries to stay out of it, and his tangled hair and beard are wet with sweat. Impatiently, he brushes away a couple of flies buzzing maliciously near his head, then stands up and looks around him irresolutely.

Claudia sits up, alert. She wraps a red kimono around her near-naked body and says, 'You need a cold drink, something soothing, cooling. I have just the right herbs, I think.' She reaches for his hand and takes him languidly into the house.

When Marcel returns home from the forest, Ivo, relaxed now after several glasses of Claudia's chilled

123

brew, is in the spare bathroom he has turned into a makeshift darkroom. He is enlarging the photographs of the lightning at Heron's Cove, ones he took before he was knocked unconscious. They are spectacular and will sell well. Ivo's earlier foul mood vanishes completely as he looks at his work. He's photographed lightning from every angle; he's committed to paper some of the most tremendous storms in recent memory. He has become part of each storm, he feels them living in him, as they do in his photographs. It is a breathtaking thought.

Marcel finds Claudia still in the courtyard, dressed now and drying basil and bay leaves, and other strange herbs that Marcel can't identify, in the sun. 'You're restless too, Marcel,' Claudia says. 'You need a tonic. I have just given Ivo one.'

'Not now.' Marcel is wary sometimes of Claudia's potions. She has healed and strengthened him enough times to make him uneasy over the power of her herbs and oils.

Marcel sits on the bench vacated by Ivo and puts down his recorder lovingly. It is a treble recorder, one of his favourites, made for him by a craftsman in Amsterdam. He often wonders how pianists and harpsichordists cope, not being able to have their instruments with them at all times. Marcel is rarely without one of his, usually his smaller descant recorder either tucked in a large pocket, or carried in a rucksack. He would feel skinned, vulnerable, without it; he would feel stripped of his powers.

Claudia is watching him as she watched Ivo. 'You're spending more and more time in that forest of yours. Every afternoon, after we have finished rehearsing, you wander off.'

'It's not unusual. I've been doing this for years.'

'Perhaps, but not so often, not for such long periods of time.'

Marcel shrugs eloquently, indicating Gallicly that such is life and there is no point in discussing this further.

Claudia is not dissuaded. 'This is the first time I've known a woman to throw you, Marcel.'

'Oh, that pallid redhead,' Marcel says dismissively. 'She was just a diversion. I haven't thought about her since we were in Ireland.' He realizes, with the merest touch of remorse, that this is true. 'Besides,' he continues, 'what is it to you? You are more than preoccupied with that mad photographer. Why you asked him here I'll never know.'

'It was *you* that did the inviting, to lure his sister.' This time Marcel looks slightly shamefaced, for indeed he had done just this, had invited Ivo to stay at his home in Brittany for as long as he liked. This was, of course, before Steffie had received her summons to Peru.

'Are you jealous, Marcel?' Claudia purrs. She rather likes the idea.

'*Tu es folle*, Claudia. Crazy, mad, out of your head. I have never been jealous of another man.' He turns his back dismissively on her, sniffing a red rose blooming exuberantly in the centre of the courtyard.

Claudia does not like to be dismissed. 'Oh no?' she says loudly. 'Not even Troy? Get real, Marcel, you're jealous as hell of him.'

Marcel frowns, but carries on smelling the roses insouciantly. 'There is nothing to be jealous about,' he says, not looking at her. 'Alina has confided in me. She and Troy are only friends, not lovers.'

Claudia roars with laughter. She becomes wholly Ukrainian, chortling '*O yoi yoi*,' slapping her thighs, making extravagant gestures, while asking God how he could have made such an idiot in his own image. Marcel forces himself to keep smelling the roses, though his nostrils are so dilated with repressed irritation that he sneezes.

'For how long, Marcel?' Claudia is finally able to speak. 'You are so dense, you cannot see the signs? They are aching to fall into bed with each other; they love each other. It is only a matter of time.'

This time Marcel loses his cool, becomes seriously angry. He shouts, hollers, berates Claudia in French and English, even a few Breton words he has picked up from his mother. She in turn does the same, except instead of the Breton language she uses her own native tongue.

In the midst of this harangue, a woman enters the courtyard through a wooden gate and says, calmly in French, 'Are you two at it again? Such carrying on. It is good this house is at the very edge of the village and not too near the next neighbour.' She goes straight to the roses and begins plucking away the dead ones. '*Mon dieu*, you have let the garden go, Marcel.'

'Maman,' Marcel cries, embracing the woman.

'Bernadette!' Claudia shouts, pushing Marcel out of the way so that she can kiss the woman soundly on both cheeks, several times.

There is a little tussle as Marcel and Claudia fight to escort Bernadette to the most comfortable garden chair. Claudia, being larger, wins.

'I have brought you presents from Paris,' Bernadette announces proudly, taking items from her large stiff basket. She gives them each a beautifully wrapped gift which they open at once. Marcel's is a garish print of Notre-Dame, framed in cheap gilt. He will hang it proudly in his house, along with his fine collection of paintings. Marcel loves his mother and would not hurt her for the world.

'*Merci beaucoup, Maman, c'est très belle,*' he says, kissing her again.

Claudia's present is an ornate rosary, with flashy red glass beads. Claudia also thanks her profusely, meaning it, for she too adores Marcel's mother.

'It may come in handy one day,' Bernadette says cryptically. She knows Claudia does not go to church, but knows too that she comes from a devout Ukrainian Catholic family. She has great hopes that one day Claudia will lead Marcel back to his own abandoned religion. She feels that this lapse, for both of them, is a temporary aberration, which time and common sense will remedy.

'How was Paris?' Marcel asks. He enquires about his brothers and sisters, the nieces and nephews. Bernadette visits them every summer for a month, staying a week with each of her married children. She recounts all the family exploits, then asks the other two about Ireland. They chat amicably for almost an hour, Claudia and Marcel forgetting their quarrel, much to Bernadette's quiet satisfaction. She likes Claudia, thinks she is a steadying influence on Marcel, despite the fact that she too is a musician. Bernadette distrusts most musicians. She, like Steffie sometimes does, finds them ungrounded, floating in some puffy world of their own, unanchored to real life, which to her takes place mostly in this small village and occasionally in Paris where all of her children have gone. It saddens her, the loss of her chicks to the big city, though she understands it was necessary; there is no work for them here. She is relying on Marcel to bring the family back to Brittany, starting with his own children, living in the house where Marcel himself was born.

That fact that Marcel has told her he doesn't want children, not now, not ever, does not stop her from making plans. She needs grandchildren *here*; one day she will be too old to keep trudging to Paris, and though they visit her in Brittany, it is not enough. She longs for the daily contact, longs to spoil them all year round, wants to teach them the old songs, the old language, before everything is forgotten.

Claudia brings out aperitifs and some savoury snacks. Bernadette allows herself a Kir, white wine and cassis, the sweet blackcurrant cordial she so loves. A small neat woman in her early seventies, she feels quite modern in her new Parisian skirt, a gift from one of her daughters-in-law. With it she wears a tidy grey polyester blouse she bought in the town of Josselin when she went with the church group to see the chateau. Her grey hair is permed stiffly and her feet are shod in wedged silver sandals. Bernadette prides herself on not letting herself go, though she is a widow and lives alone. She organizes dances every month in the village hall for the over sixties, goes on every coach trip the numerous church associations organize, and reads the West France newspaper avidly. Though not a day goes by that she doesn't say a rosary for her dead husband's soul, she is not unhappy. Life fascinates her; she is avid for it.

Just as she is about to go Ivo rushes out of the house. 'It's coming!' he shouts. 'I've just heard it on the radio. Massive thunderstorms are coming in tonight, all over Brittany.'

'Ivo, why didn't you come out when I called you?' Claudia cries. 'Come meet Marcel's mother.'

'I'm happy to,' Ivo says. Marcel make the introductions. Ivo says all the right things, but it is obvious he is miles away. Bernadette thinks scornfully, Another musician, flitting about on some other plane.

Marcel explains what Ivo does. Bernadette is clearly perplexed. Who would want photographs of storms, when the real thing is available for anyone who looks out the window? Why not photograph something sensible like weddings, which only take place once, which *need* to be captured for posterity.

Bernadette leaves and Ivo races back inside to get his gear. Though the storms aren't due until tonight, he will go to the forest now, find some possible spots with good vantage points. He will wait all night if he has to. It won't be the first time.

The thunder begins, ominously in the distance, at two in the morning. Ivo, still alert despite his long wait, stands up from behind the rock where he was half sitting, half reclining. Though he was cushioned by a blanket from the damp ground, he feels stiff, aching. Rather than following this storm as he usually does, driving through fierce rain to get to the core of it, the place where the lightning is – rather than this, Ivo has this time decided to wait at the spot he wants to photograph. He has not decided lightly; he has consulted weather charts and forecasts, studied the skies, knows that his chances are good. The fact that it is night helps enormously: shooting in daylight is much more difficult, with the risk of overexposure.

And now as the storm rolls inexorably over the top of the trees and into Le Val-sans-Retour, where it settles above the lake like a crow settling into its nest, Ivo is satisfied. He is perched above the valley, on the flat exposed bit on the top of the barren hill. Here, he can capture the view not only of the valley, but of the surrounding plateau and the forest on the opposite hill.

At first the lightning is innocuous, distant. The thunder rumbles and complains but doesn't amount to more than a few threats. Ivo waits, expectant, and soon he is rewarded. As if gathering force, rallying its strength for one final display, lightning fills the air, one flash after another, one crash of thunder topping another in a splendid cacophony of noise and chaos.

Ivo laughs, takes photos, laughs again. He shouts at the thunder to deafen him, mocks at the lightning to try and strike him. 'Try, go on, try!' he bellows. 'I'm not afraid. You can't hurt me. Come on, here I am!'

A blaze of lightning hits a tree halfway down the valley, a tall pine standing alone on the bleak hillside. Ivo has captured the moment with his camera and howls with victory. 'See?' he shouts. 'You can't touch me. I've captured you, tamed you in my photos.'

The lightning is everywhere, lighting up the entire sky, the lake, the Valley of No Return, the barren plateau. Ivo takes photo after photo, exultant, victorious.

Gradually the storm abates. The thunder rolls ignominiously down the hill and away from the valley, and the lightning that slashed the sky is now no more threatening than a picture postcard. Even the wind has gone. The rain that held off while the lightning came closest begins now in earnest, chilly and relentless.

Ivo lays face down on the rock with exhaustion. The aftermath of the storm is almost too much for him this time; he cannot bear the return to reality, the loss of his exhilaration. Once again there is that emptiness, the one that is always there, the black hollow space that only a storm can fill.

A deep chill going through his body returns him slightly to normal, enough to make him reach for the hip flask in his back pocket which Claudia had put there before he left. He drinks the alcoholic herbal brew greedily. It is strong, potent. He lets it course through his bloodstream, heat his skin. When it is all gone, he gathers his equipment and staggers home in an unremitting downpour.

Claudia is waiting up for him, as he expected. But there is no hot steamy bath, no heated oil to rub into his aching limbs. Wordlessly, she strips off his clothes and pulls him into bed with her. The realization that at last he is to have Claudia, his gift from the gods, staggers him, and he fumbles for her. But the storm has taken its toll, enervated him. 'I can't,' he whispers after a time. 'I'm knackered, spent.'

And indeed he is. The energy which consumed him as he was photographing is gone, leaving him weak and flaccid. Within moments he is sound asleep and snoring in the big brass bed.

Claudia leaves him, not only physically but emotionally. She had had hopes for him; she had engaged his interest, had first pampered him with her lotions and potions, then seen that he did the same for her. She had thought that at last he was ready, had become a match for her.

Lying in her own bed, Claudia listens to the birds singing in the dawn outside. She has already forgotten Ivo, realizing that he is one of her mistakes, that she can no more love him than any of the other men she has tried to relate to since she left Ukraine, before she met Marcel.

She cannot sleep. There is an unfamiliar ache inside her, as if something is missing. She gets up, drinks a bit of the wine that is not really a wine but medicinal, magical too she often suspects. It does no good. She opens a vial, pours oil into an aromatherapy burner and inhales the scent. Still she feels no better.

Lying back on her bed, Claudia stays awake until long after the roosters in the village have stopped their raucous crowing.

Steffie also sleeps uneasily this long night. She has been in Lima for four days and has not yet seen her baby.

Luis met her at the airport. A dusty wind gritted her eyes, dried her hair and her skin, and Steffie can still hear it moaning outside her hotel. The room she has is small, neat but cheapened by plastic tables, a lumpy bed and thin postage-stamp towels. The pale-pink wallpaper manages to be both grotesque and faded. It is not inexpensive, this hotel, and Steffie had hoped for better. From her window she can see mountains outside the city, but she isn't interested in views.

She needs comfort, because she has been in her room most of the time she has been here. Luis told her vaguely that there was some legal work to be sorted out before she could see the baby. Then the director of the orphanage had to go away for a day or so, on some mysterious business. 'What does that matter?' Steffie wailed. 'Can't I just see the child?'

Luis placated her, told her not to be so impatient. 'How can I be patient? I've waited so long,' she cried.

'And now you must wait a bit longer,' he had replied maddeningly.

And so she must wait. She is in his hands, at his mercy. She dares not cross him because he is her lifeline, the person who will find her a baby.

Finally the long night is over. Today Luis is taking her to see the baby. They go in his car, something black and shiny like a funeral car, and drive out of the city for what to Steffie seems like hours, but is less than thirty minutes. The road goes along the coast and Steffie is aware of miles of sand dunes on one side, and on the other, mountains of sand and rock. She registers small bleak white houses, ramshackle filling stations which seem to double as seedy restaurants, rest stops for coaches.

The orphanage is a long low concrete building standing on its own in the middle of a seared dry lawn. Inside the building are closed brown doors, with only the occasional sound of a baby's cry, a child's voice.

The director leads them into a small room, newly painted green but already beginning to flake. Inside there are two seedy armchairs and a squat wooden table.

'Wait here,' the director says.

Steffie and Luis and the interpreter, Anita, wait. Steffie had questioned why she needed an interpreter – the fees are exorbitant – since Luis speaks perfect English and could do any necessary translation. She had been told only that it was necessary. Anita is immaculately dressed in a smart black skirt and white blouse. Her heels are very high. She is smart, bright. She will certainly not be in Lima for long; she has her heart set on America, on New York City where her boyfriend has gone.

Luis and Anita speak in Spanish, laugh at private jokes. Luis is not Peruvian, but Steffie has not yet figured out where he comes from. His native language is Spanish, but he has blue eyes and fair skin, which contrasts oddly with his thick dark hair which is sleek like the fur of a cat.

The director returns. Behind him is some kind of uniformed nurse or assistant, carrying an infant which she places in Steffie's arms.

Steffie is shaking and has to sit down. 'There, what a fine baby,' Luis enthuses. Anita looks at her finger-nails, notices one of them is chipped and frowns.

Steffie holds the baby to her breast, moved beyond words, beyond thought. The infant is wrapped in a worn but clean blanket and smells of soap. Steffie holds her like this for some time, while Luis and the director talk heatedly in Spanish. They seem to be arguing, though Steffie does not know why this should be so.

'They are saying that the mother, she is strong and healthy. This baby will be so, as well,' Anita says, chewing on her broken nail.

'I thought the mother was ill, that that was why she can't keep her child,' Steffie says.

The director does not understand English, but Luis dismisses Steffie's remark without waiting for Anita to translate. 'She's tired, exhausted, that's all. But her baby is robust.' He takes out a cigar and lights up, offering one to the director who accepts greedily. Obviously neither of them has heard that passive smoking is not good for babies.

Finally Steffie dares to look at her child, her daughter. The baby is asleep, deeply so, in fact she looks almost drugged. Steffie feels the first stirring of unease. 'Leave me please,' she says. 'Leave me with the baby.'

Anita looks relieved, no doubt anxious to go and repair her fingernail, but Luis does not like it. Steffie insists that she needs time alone with her baby.

When they have all gone, she tries to wake the sleeping infant. This takes some time to accomplish, but at last she does so. The baby stares mindlessly at her. She can see, but her eyes are vacant, her face expressionless. Steffie has been around enough babies to know that at three months old there should be some reaction somewhere. She places a finger in the baby's hand but there is no instinctive tightening of the infant fingers around it. She coos and sings and smiles to the baby, but nothing. No reaction. Nothing at all.

Luis comes back, but she sends him away again. She walks around with the baby, desperately. She talks to her. Nothing. The baby is in some world of her own and Steffie cannot get through.

When Luis comes back Steffie says, 'Where is the director? I want to talk to him. I want Anita here too.'

When they are all assembled, Steffie says to the director, 'Has the baby been checked by the doctor?'

Luis starts to protest, to say with great annoyance that of course she has. But Steffie interrupts with a warning look. Anita translates and the director answers in Spanish. He seems troubled, and Steffie curses herself that she doesn't know the language, that in their travels, her parents never lived, when she was growing up, in Spanish-speaking countries. The director seems distraught, and Steffie senses there is something important here which Anita and Luis are keeping from her.

Anita says, somewhat sulkily, that the director says all babies are automatically checked by a doctor when admitted, and what kind of a primitive place do North Americans think this is anyway. Steffie says, 'Tell the director, Anita, that I would like to see the doctor.'

There is a good deal of consternation over this. The director looks perplexed, and Luis says with annoyance that the doctor is a busy man, but Steffie, rigid and angry with dread and foreboding, says she wants to see him at once.

Luckily, the doctor is in the building, visiting a sick child. He is old and frail and harrassed. Steffie asks about the health of the baby, and he gives a long harangue in Spanish. Anita translates unwillingly, 'He says there are too many babies, too little money. He is doing all he can, but the problem is growing. He is on call all hours of the day but still it is not enough.'

'For God's sake I know all that!' Steffie cries. 'What does he say about the baby? Is she all right? She doesn't seem right to me.'

Anita looks quickly at Luis, who nods almost imperceptibly. 'The baby is healthy,' she says. 'The doctor says the baby is just fine.' She glances slyly at the doctor, who of course does not understand a word she is saying.

Steffie despairs. The director left when the doctor came in, and the nurse is nowhere in sight. Luis says, 'Come, you are overwrought, becoming a mother at last. We will go for lunch, and then we will go and sign the adoption papers.'

Steffie looks at the sleeping baby still in her arms. 'No,' she says. 'I will go to lunch by myself, and you will find me another doctor, an English-speaking one. I want a second opinion about this baby.'

Luis is angry, but he tries to hide it. He pats Steffie's shoulder with his thin fingers and promises to find a doctor. 'Though it will have to be paid for, the consultation.' Steffie knows this. She knows everything in connection with this adoption has to be dearly paid for.

The doctor cannot come until the next morning. Steffie drinks two bitter black coffees for lunch in a pleasant square near the heart of the city, but she is totally unaware of her surroundings and paces around the square restlessly before impulsively finding a taxi and directing the driver back to the orphanage.

The same nurse is there, and seems to understand

Steffie's need to see the baby again. The nurse stays with her while she holds the child. She is a brisk young woman who clucks kindly at both Steffie and the baby. Steffie again desperately wishes she could speak Spanish; she feels she would get some straight answers from this sympathetic woman, or even the director who, though bristly and clearly stressed, seems an honest man, as did the doctor who is nowhere to be seen this afternoon.

The baby is as listless as before, even when the nurse coos and chuckles at her. This makes Steffie despair even more, for obviously the nurse knows the infant, and if anyone could get a reaction, she would be the one. But the baby merely lies in Steffie's arms and continues to stare vacantly into space.

Steffie returns to the hotel, drinks a half bottle of bitter red wine, and goes to sleep on an empty acid stomach. She is too numb and in shock to eat or sleep, and lies staring at the shadows on the ceiling all night, listening to the hot wind, her eyes as vacant as the baby's.

The second doctor is tall, handsome, elegant. He has several gold rings on his fingers and a Rolex watch. He treats Steffie with charming superiority, telling her in his excellent English that he is sure she is just suffering from post-natal nerves. He says this with a condescending laugh and takes Steffie's elbow as he leads her into the little room. Anita is not there, but Luis of course is. He and the doctor exchange glances, and smile slightly at each other, and Steffie knows without a doubt what will come next. She scarcely watches as the doctor makes a great show of examining the baby, placing her on the table on a blanket, and when he is finished, says, 'The baby is one hundred per cent fine, nothing to worry about. All children develop at different ages, you mustn't have expectations for your own infant because all are not the same.' He watches as the nurse dresses the baby, wraps her in a white shawl, then takes the child and hands her to Steffie. 'Congratulations, *señorita*, you have become a mother. I salute and honour you.' He nods his head gravely.

Steffie wonders wearily what favour Luis once did for this man, who may or may not be a doctor. It doesn't matter. Suddenly nothing matters, nothing in the world. She has lost her baby. It is like losing her life.

Once again she irritates Luis by asking to be left alone with the infant girl, but this time he is convinced she is taking the child, so he finally leaves in good grace, promising to wait in the director's office.

Steffie sits down on the misshapen armchair and clings to the baby, who is awake and silent. For the first time, she lets the tears fall, powerless now to stop them. They roll down her cheeks and onto the baby's face, but the infant remains oblivious. Steffie rocks the baby and slowly, brokenly, begins to talk to her. 'I'm sorry, baby. I'm so, so sorry. I just can't do it, I can't take you home, can't take you on. Oh God, baby, I feel such a shit, leaving you behind like this. But you're not right, there's something wrong with you. I don't know what, nobody will tell me. Maybe they're really not sure themselves exactly what it is. I don't know what it is either, sweetie, but whatever it is, I can't handle it.'

Steffie breaks off, unable to go on. The baby, oblivious, stares into space. 'I'm sorry,' Steffie whispers. 'I feel like such a coward. But I'm on my own, you know? If I had a partner, maybe I'd think about it. I don't know. I'm just not brave enough, baby. It's hard enough going through the emotional and physical stress of having a normal kid when you're single, but you, baby, would do me in. I can't do it. Forgive me, OK? Oh God, forgive me!'

Steffie goes on brokenly like this for some time, an hour maybe, until the nurse comes and literally prises the baby out of her arms. She hands Steffie a tissue, and holds her while she finishes crying; Steffie on one arm sobbing her eyes out, the baby in the other, unmoved. While Steffie cries the nurse murmurs soothing words in Spanish, which Steffie doesn't understand but finds comforting.

Luis is furious, of course. But he cannot say too much, for there will be other babies, other opportunities for Steffie – and for himself. He needs to hold on to her desperation, her need to have a child. He doesn't understand this, has never understood it in the dozens of women he has found babies for, but he has never tried to understand. They pay his huge fees and he delivers the goods, that is all he needs to understand. Sometimes there are setbacks, like today. But Steffie will have her baby eventually, a healthy normal one as she insists upon.

Steffie knows all this. She knows she has to rely on Luis, knows that in the end he will find her the right baby. She hates him for what he has done today, what he has tried to do to her, but she understands it is all part of the game.

They part at the airport in mutual hidden antipathy and outward politeness. Steffie flies to Miami, remains home for almost a week, but feels she will go mad with grief and guilt and frustrated longing. She phones Troy and Alina answers. Troy has gone to Cork to pick up another visiting musician, so Steffie cries over long distance to Alina. She hangs up the phone feeling

139

comforted. Alina had urged her to return to Heron's Cove, but Steffie is aware that the couple have so little time left together. There is no doubt that when Alina feels ready to play professionally again, she will return to her husband. Steffie loves her brother, wants Troy to have his small bit of seclusion with this woman who has so affected him. Ireland, Steffie feels, will have to wait.

Yet she feels an overwhelming need for family. Her mother and father are useless, but there is still Ivo. Steffie puts a phone call through to France.

Ivo answers the phone, for Marcel and Claudia have gone to Paris to make their recording. 'Steffie, how are you? How's the baby? Why haven't you been in touch?'

'There's no baby, Ivo. I don't want to talk about it now, OK? And I'm sorry I haven't phoned. I couldn't, you know?'

'Fine, it's all right, we'll talk when you want to. Look, I'm sorry.'

'It's OK. Oh, Ivo, it's so good to hear your voice! Tell me what you're up to.'

Ivo is glad to oblige. 'You won't believe the photographs I've taken here. In Marcel's forest. There really is something extraordinary about it.'

Steffie begins to cry.

'Stef, what's wrong?'

'Everything. The baby . . . I need family, Ivo. I feel I've just lost mine. My baby . . . I wish you were home, Ivo. Troy is so . . . distracted these days.'

'I know.' He doesn't add that she has been distracted as well. 'Look, come here, to Britanny. Marcel would love to have you. He begged you enough to visit him.'

'Maybe I will. I need to work anyway. Maybe I'll do a series of travel articles on Brittany.'

By the time she has hung up she is determined to go. The thought makes her feel slightly better. Perhaps tonight she will sleep and not be haunted by a lost baby staring at her with large, vacant, but somehow, to Steffie, accusing eyes.

Perhaps. But Steffie doubts it. She knows that it will be a long time before that baby will let her go.

Chapter Seven

Everyone at the house in Brociliande is delighted to see
Steffie, for separate reasons, not all of them altruistic.
The latest outbreaks of thunderstorms in Brittany have
put Ivo on a rather precarious high. He has taken
hundreds of photographs, and feels these are different
from any he has ever done before. He has not just
photographed lightning, he has captured the spirit of
the storm, the force of the cosmos. He feels like a bolt
of lightning himself, charged, crackling. He longs for
Steffie's arrival, so he can show her his photos, bask in
her admiration, be the younger brother she protected
and pampered as they were growing up.

Claudia also welcomes her arrival. She no longer
feels annoyed by Steffie, who is so distraught over her
experience in Lima that Claudia cannot help but feel
sorry for her. Indeed, Claudia hopes that Steffie and
Marcel will be a harmless diversion for each other.
Both need distracting: Steffie, from the baby she left
behind, and Marcel, from his ceaseless brooding about
Alina.

Claudia's prediction that Troy and Alina will soon
be lovers – if not already – has niggled Marcel. Claudia
is worried, for she is afraid this preoccupation will put
Marcel off his performances. Though his moods are
erratic and plummet in a matter of minutes from the
heights to the depths, this low is going on far too long,
is out of character. Claudia has invested a great deal in
Marcel, in their partnership. She gave up a modest, if

142

not spectacular, career as a soloist before taking up with him, and her own sparkling success now relies on his virtuoso performances. Life had not been easy for Claudia, before meeting Marcel. She took on any booking her agent could get for her, no matter how low the fee, how appalling the venue. She supplemented her meagre income from performances with music lessons, teaching many more hours than any of her colleagues. Marcel had changed all that. He sparked her, brought out her own creativity. In the concert hall they are a potent duo, each providing the other with the necessary harmony and friction to give a dynamic performance.

And so Claudia wants no other person, man or woman, to come between her and Marcel, between the spell they have created by their music. Alina was fine at an untouchable distance; Claudia knows quite well that she was, before Troy, a fantasy necessary to Marcel. The odd lover, Claudia accepts, especially for Marcel, who finds it hard to resist available females. She herself never takes a man into her bed unless he has something to offer her. Good sex, even love, is never enough on its own, for Claudia. She needs to be filled not just with sperm or endearments, but with vitality, with a creative bolt that will enhance her own energies.

This is why Ivo has proved so disappointing. He is not, she has realized, touched by the gods but is merely obsessed. She is sorry about this. She could have given him so much in return, had they clicked as a couple. Claudia is a generous woman: where she takes, she also gives copiously. It is the lack of either giving or taking these days that is making her life so frustrating.

*   *   *

143

Steffie is exhausted and depressed when she arrives in Brittany. She has been having nightmares since she left Peru, black dreams of an ill, damaged child lying shunned and abandoned amidst hundreds of healthy laughing children. She wakes moaning with fear as the rosy smiles of the robust girls and boys turn into malevolent poisonous snarls.

The daytime is no better. The baby she left behind haunts her; she sees the vacant eyes, the unnaturally still face, everywhere; when she closes her eyes, when she looks at strangers, when she sees her own face in the mirror.

She is grateful, then, to be welcomed warmly by Marcel on her first day in Brittany. Ivo is out somewhere with his cameras and Claudia is in the fields collecting herbs.

Marcel kisses her cheeks, offers her coffee, food, an aperitif. She accepts some cheese, olives, wine, and they take it out into the garden with its small sheltered courtyard framed with healthy blooming roses of crimson and deep pink which dazzle in the sunlight. 'How vibrant they look,' Steffie says.

'Yes, you can tell my mother is back home,' Marcel replies. 'You must meet her.'

Steffie eats some olives and looks around her. The garden has an insouciant, well-loved feel about it, with its blowzy roses, its scent of honeysuckle. It is early evening and the swallows are darting and flying purposefully through the sky above them. In the field bordering the garden there is corn growing, and beyond that is the forest.

'How peaceful Europe is, how prosperous, after South America,' Steffie sighs.

'Brittany, prosperous?' Marcel says incredulously. 'My parents would have roared with laughter, hearing you say that. I can't remember a time when there was enough money when I was growing up.'

'Still, compared to Peru . . .' Steffie trails off, is grimly silent for a few moments. She thinks of the brief journeys outside Lima on her way to the orphanage, of the poverty she had glimpsed through car windows.

'Of course. You have just been there. Ivo told us you have come home alone.'

Steffie wants to talk about it, indeed almost does, for Marcel is waiting expectantly for a reply. He would be reassuring, would assuage her guilt by saying that she had made the right decision in not bringing the ill child home. But what she feels is too deep for glib words of comfort.

So she only says, 'There turned out to be no baby, in the end.'

'*C'est dommage*. So it was a wasted trip? I am sorry, but surely these things, these hitches happen. You are still waiting, then?'

She nods, but somewhat doubtfully. Marcel notes the doubt and it secretly pleases him. Why anyone, particularly someone free, unattached, with a good career and a sophisticated lifestyle, would want to burden herself with a child is beyond Marcel's comprehension.

Steffie, tired, leans back in the garden chair and closes her eyes for a moment. France usually relaxes her; she has been here often, likes its easy harmony. But the air is sultry, oppressive; the evening sun shaded by a nebulous mist. There is a thickness in the sky, something opaque, hard to breathe in. Low rumbles of thunder echo in the distance.

Steffie opens her eyes and says, 'I feel that everything is waiting for something. The air, the trees, the forest over there. Like I've been waiting for this baby I

145

despair of ever getting. What are *you* waiting for, Marcel?'

Marcel thinks about this for a moment. 'Nothing at all, Steffie,' he says. 'When I am here, in this old house, in this forest where I grew up, I am waiting for nothing, for I have everything.' Except Alina, he thinks angrily. I should have had Alina, I have always been waiting for her, and she has betrayed me like this.

He surprises himself at the vehemence of his thoughts. To purge himself of these, he turns with predatory charm on Steffie, becoming the enchanter, the siren musician, the Merlin. He begins talking to her about the recording he has done with Claudia, and at one point, to illustrate what he means about a Bach sonata, he takes one of his recorders and begins to play.

Marcel throws heart and soul into even this little demonstration as he does with everything he plays, and slowly Steffie responds, becomes less desolate as the music charms and bewitches. She can't help but succumb, especially as this display of virtuosity is for her. She realizes that she is ready to be enchanted. She has come back from Lima shaken, uncertain. For the first time, she doubts her capabilities for motherhood. Where once she felt so sure of herself, so ready, so pregnant with anticipation, now she wonders if she is really cut out to be a parent after all, let alone a single parent. This shattering of her expectations has left her in a state of panicky confusion. If one setback has so knocked her down, does she really have the stamina needed to adopt a child? The longing is still there, but she feels it has become a hopeless addiction, laced with fear and uncertainty.

And so when Marcel plays, glancing at her with eyes that seem to thrust his wayward soul into her keeping,

Steffie succumbs. Perhaps he can take her where she no longer is shaken by cravings for babies and motherhood; where she is no longer haunted by the hopeless helpless future of the baby she has left behind.

She has had enough, she feels now. She is tired, she is confused; she has had enough.

When Marcel finishes playing, he goes to her and puts his hand lightly on her shoulder. 'It's good that you are here,' he says. 'I've missed you.' He is somewhat embarrassed by this lie, and surprised at himself for uttering it. He usually never lies to his women. He never has to. But Marcel too has obsessions to exorcize; he needs Steffie, at this moment, as she needs him.

Steffie nods and lets his hand rest on her shoulder. The hell with babies, she thinks passionately. The hell with longing and wanting and waiting. It's time to be light-hearted again, and carefree.

She turns to Marcel and smiles.

At that same moment a baby is born in a small village outside of Lima, a baby girl. Her sturdy little body is covered with blood and slime and as soon as her lungs fill with air, she lets out a gusty cry.

Steffie turns away from Marcel and raises her head. 'Did you hear that?' she asks. 'That cry?'

Marcel looks around, annoyed that his spell has been broken. 'It's the wind in the trees. *Rien,* nothing.'

'There's no wind at all. The air is oppressively still.'

'A bird, then. Of no significance. There is no-one here.'

Steffie is looking out towards the forest, straining to hear . . . what? She's not sure herself.

In the distance thunder mutters warningly. But it is too far away to intrude.

Steffie shakes her head, looks back at Marcel and

forces herself to concentrate on him again. 'It's good to be here.'

Marcel, satisfied, kisses her lightly four times, twice on each cheek, as is the old Breton way. 'It's good for me too,' he replies.

The thunder rolls in closer.

Ireland is spattered with storms as well; it is June now and bleak. Jack Murphy is deep in his dung-spreader trying to get out the string tangled in the chain, which must have been in the dung. He's done half a field, and needs to finish it before the rain starts again and it becomes impossible to get the tractor onto the wet soggy earth. As it is, the field he's working on is muddy enough, and it's the driest on their land. 'Spring,' he mutters as he jumps on the tractor. 'Jesus.'

The chain is still not working. Jumping off again Jack takes a packet of cigarettes and lights one. He had given it up, but after Steffie left, started again. It annoys him that this woman he barely knows has affected him so much. He's not even been back to Tralee to visit the woman there.

Jack looks up at the mountain, which is dense with black cloud. 'I know how you feel,' he mutters aloud to it.

It begins to rain. Hard. 'Oh feck, Jesus and Mary, not again.' On days like this he wonders why he ever left England. Throwing away his cigarette, he kicks the dung-spreader hard before tackling it again.

In Heron's Cove the rain hits the water like hard buds, pockmarking it. Inside, a turf fire in the music room burns all day, as does the wood-burning stove.

Alina and Troy don't mind the rain, the grizzly thunder, the startling streaks of lightning. It is intimate huddling together by the fire in the evenings, reading, talking, sometimes going over some music.

During the day, when there is no concert, Troy works on his harpsichords while Alina practises alone. Her fingers, no longer stiff, have nearly regained their old alacrity, but Alina despairs that they will never cross that nebulous line between competency and brilliancy. Sometimes Troy comes back from his workroom and finds her sitting on the terrace, in a drizzling mist, staring at her hands.

Troy is helpless in the face of such sadness. He tries to help her in the only way he can, which is through music. Wordlessly he takes her back into the music room and while she listens he plays Bach to her. He is playing as best he can; he knows the Bach well. But he wants her to realize that however well he plays it, she can, even now, after the accident, play it better.

Alina is not thinking of the Bach at all. She is thinking of Troy and how she will miss him when she finally leaves Heron's Cove. She has decided she will go when she has mastered the Scarlatti to her own high standards. Or perhaps, she vacillates, she will stay until the end of summer. Her reluctance to return to Dublin hovers over her like a discordant cloud.

She wonders how she will cope without Troy. His endless encouragement has woven something silky though strong around her, and she is becoming less fragile, tougher, every day. She will need to be tough, to go back to her performing. If she survives as a musician, it will be thanks to Troy.

She watches him play, looks avidly at his slender body, his floppy hair. She loves him aesthetically, emotionally, totally. She would love him physically if all passion had not died in her with the accident. David, who has wanted an excuse not to make love to her in years, has completely stopped now.

'You're too frail, it's too soon,' he had said when she had hesitantly broached the subject, before coming to Heron's Cove. She had done it not because she wanted to make love, but because she felt he might, and wanted to tell him it was all right with her.

'I think I should be the one to decide that,' she had said with some asperity. She had hoped that by the act of lovemaking, her body would begin to feel again.

'Your accident has left you weak, disoriented. Give yourself time. I'm willing to wait.'

She stopped herself before saying, and why didn't you say that before we were married, before Kate was conceived? 'Are you?' was the only comment she permitted herself.

'All I want to make love to these days is my music,' he had smoothly replied.

Once again she held her tongue and didn't say, You mean your whole orchestra, or rather the female members of it.

In truth, she doesn't care. She dislikes her body now; it seems out of control, trembles at odd moments, betrays her with sudden exhaustion, a chill on the warmest day. Her muscles, after the months in bed, the enforced convalescence, are puny, weak. She is skinny, her skin slack. Bones and scars stare at her from the mirror in ugly proximity. She is sure she will never want to make love again, and she does not mind. She has, in the past, sublimated much of her passion into her playing, as David claims to be doing; in some ways, the imposed celibacy of the accident was a relief to them both.

This is not to say she will not go back to Dublin and pick up the shell of her marriage. It is there like Ireland itself, binding.

Troy has finished the piece and is looking at her. '*You* play it for *me*, now.'

She obliges. He sees that her fingers have grown strong, nimble, since the months she has been here. Her playing is stronger too; she is not far from making a total comeback, if he can only get her to believe it.

He watches her face, sees how animated it becomes as she plays. Her hair is as pristine as always, drawn tightly away from her face in the usual plait, but her face is less ordered, more impassioned. It is fuller too, he notices; she has gained weight since being at Heron's Cove. Despite what she thinks, her confidence, so necessary in her line of work, is returning.

Despite his genuine pleasure at seeing her so restored, Troy has a foreboding, too. He shakes this off as the restlessness caused by the encroaching storm. The music room has got dark though it is only late afternoon and there are still hours of daylight left. His uneasiness troubles him; he hasn't yet realized that when Alina goes music will no longer be his god, his soul and salvation.

Alina is playing part of Bach's 'Partita' in B minor for harpsichord; it is one of his favourites, and he abandons himself to the enjoyment of it.

Yet something still troubles him. Listening to the music, watching Alina's face, her fingers, noting her flowered skirt spread around the bench like a libation, he knows that he will remember this moment. Instead of giving him quiet satisfaction, the thought strikes him with a despair he has never known before.

Later, Troy is unusually quiet as they take a late evening walk. Alina, noticing, knows not to ask questions. She becomes silent herself, knowing he will talk when he is ready.

151

They are walking around the small harbour of Ballycaveen. The storms of the day have cleared, leaving the air clean and crisp. The days are long now, and it is still quite light. A local fisherman is unloading his catch, and they nod and greet each other. Troy and Alina lapse back into silence as they walk to the end of the pier, then back. Finally Troy says, 'It seems too pleasant an evening to go inside just yet. Perhaps a drink . . .' He trails off indecisively.

There is a pub tucked between two cottages at the mouth of the harbour with one lone table outside against the low sea wall. Alina pulls out a chair, saying, 'I'd love an Irish coffee.'

Troy goes inside to get the drinks and Alina sits watching the sea, wondering why Troy is so uncommunicative tonight. The truth is, he is still blanketed in the deep gloom that smothered him when he realized Alina's days at Heron's Cove must soon be coming to an end. He hadn't anticipated missing her. Before she had come, he had relished his solitude, broken only by the monthly concerts, the visiting musicians. He had his work – and Troy puts in long hours at his craft, or did before Alina came to stay – his music, his fine old house to restore whenever he got around to it. It was enough, he thought.

Now, standing in the pub waiting to be served, he perceives a bleakness in this existence that was not there before. He still does not quite grasp what has happened to him. He is like someone suddenly hit on the head, fuzzy, dumb, bewildered.

Outside, Alina sees a man and a boy talking to the fisherman out on the pier. The boy is animatedly telling him about a fish he himself has caught; Alina can tell this by the way he stretches out his hands to indicate the size of the fish. Finally, the story over, the boy pulls his father up towards the pub. 'Will you be getting me a packet of crisps, Dad, sure now, will you, please?' he wheedles.

The man good-naturedly lets himself be pulled. As he passes Alina's table she recognizes him at the same time as he does her. 'From Heron's Cove,' Jack says.

'And you're Steffie's friend. I remember the pub, Patrick's, and your marvellous playing, the song too.'

'This is my son, Tom,' Jack says.

The boy, who is about eight, greets Alina politely and, sensing his father is about to talk, sits down at the table. Alina asks Jack to sit, too, which he does readily. 'I was just at Heron's Cove, would you believe,' he says. 'No-one was in, so we came here. The fisherman over there is a mate of mine; I wanted to see how he was doing.'

'How nice that we ran into you here.' She knows why Jack came to Heron's Cove, and feels sorry for him.

Tom says, 'Will I have my crisps now, Dad? Please? And a Coke? For a treat?'

'Och, the boy torments me,' Jack teases, tousling Tom's hair as Troy joins them with two Irish coffees.

Troy insists on buying Jack and Tom drinks, so he goes back into the pub with an eager Tom at his heels. Alina wonders about the boy; she knows from Steffie that Jack lives on the farm with his parents. Is there a wife there as well? She is sure Steffie does not know Jack has a son.

She is too polite to ask, and anyway it doesn't matter now; Steffie is far away.

'Have you heard from Steffie?' Jack says, trying to throw it in casually.

'Yes, she phoned from France. She's there now.'

'I thought she was in South America.'

'She was, but she's back in Europe.'

'Will she be coming back to Ireland, then, or no?' Jack asks bluntly. His interest is obvious. 'With the baby,' he adds, though he is clearly not as interested in that.

'There's no baby, Jack. It was all very sad. She came back alone. I don't know what her plans are.'

Jack looks out over the bay at another small fishing boat heading back to the harbour. The sun is streaking the sea with pinks and oranges as it begins to set. He thinks of Steffie, wishes there had been more time for them, time for her to talk about this adoption and for him to tell her about Tom. He had wanted to, but it was a painful subject, hard to speak of. He had thought they'd get around to it eventually, when they had more space to be alone together, but it never worked out that way.

So that's it, then, he thinks resignedly. Tom and Troy return now, laden with drinks and crisps. 'Don't you go telling your ma how I've been spoiling you,' Jack teases the boy. Alina thinks: so there *is* a mother.

Jack and Tom leave soon after. Troy and Alina linger, watch the daylight fade, the stars slowly appear and a full orange peach of a moon light up the harbour. There is a cool breeze coming from the sea but neither wants to move. Each feels an aching need to draw out the moment as long as possible.

In the forest of Brociliande the storms have also lifted. Marcel is sitting by a small stone well where bubbles of clear water break the surface, the result of some constant mineral activity. At this well it is reputed that Merlin fell in love with the sorceress Vivienne. Marcel learned the story in childhood; he never thinks of it now, though it is in his blood, bred in his bones. As usual he has his recorder; he begins, slowly, to play. It is late evening, the only time during this busy season that he can come here without encountering a tourist. As he plays, Marcel feels that he is becoming part of the woodland, part of the ancient spirits that he knows still hover here. His Brittany ancestors recognized and acknowledged these spirits, and later incorporated them into the primitive Catholicism, which even today retains the roots of pagan myth. But tonight Marcel's magic is greater than theirs. He plays and plays, not caring that there is no audience, only the ghosts of the forest. He plays for himself, and for them.

Back at the house Ivo is in despair. He's always low when he's not photographing a storm, but this one is worse than usual.

'Perk up,' Steffie says to him when they meet in Marcel's sunny kitchen, or the rose-covered courtyard. 'It'll storm again soon, feel how hot and humid the air is.'

'I can't bear the waiting,' Ivo moans.

'I know. I feel the same. Sometimes I wonder if I'm waiting for nothing. If there *is* only nothing. No baby. Nothing.' Steffie, forgetting she has just admonished Ivo to perk up, droops like dead roses, lost in her own thoughts. This makes Ivo even more downcast. Steffie could, even when he was a child, be relied upon to cherish and comfort him, bind wounds, bandage the bruised spirit. Ivo is hurt, but it never occurs to him to comfort *her*. Their roles have been defined, were set in childhood. He leaves Steffie in a melancholy slump and wonders if he should find Claudia. But she's no help now. She has not repeated her offer of coming to bed with him, and has once again rebuffed his half-hearted attempts to reinstate himself in her eyes. Ivo doesn't even care. He is as impotent as the summer sky, devoid of electricity, of energy. He wonders how he will survive this day, let alone the summer, if the storms do not return. Knowing he should stir himself, go out and *find* thunderstorms like he used to do instead of sitting about waiting for them, Ivo is incapable of moving from Brociliande. The forest has bewitched and captured him.

In the garden during this pale June evening, Claudia and Steffie are gathering roses, Claudia so that she can dry the petals; Steffie to make flower arrangements.

Steffie is listless, distracted. Claudia says, 'Don't worry about it. About the baby.'

Steffie is startled. She has told Claudia a bit about the ill child, but not a great deal. 'She haunts me, Claudia,' she says now. 'I keep thinking of what I've done to her by rejecting her, what a pitiful future she has.'

Claudia is moved, but she says briskly, 'I don't mean the baby you left behind. I mean the one you will have one day. Stop fretting about it. What happened is over, done with.' She snaps off a white rose, deftly avoiding the thorns.

Steffie puts her flowers on the table and sits on the bench beside it. It is beginning to get dark; a full moon is etched clearly in the pale violet sky. It is far too beautiful to go inside. 'I'm not sure I can do it,' she finds herself saying. 'Go on with the adoption. I no longer can trust that I'll be even an adequate mother, let alone a good one.'

'Do you want to be a mother, still?' Claudia carries on plucking roses.

'Yes, passionately. But not if I can't do it decently. I wouldn't sacrifice a child just to satisfy some need of my own.'

'I would think it a good sign', Claudia says carefully, 'that you have doubts.'

Steffie shakes her head. 'I never did before. Not seriously. It was only until I held that poor baby . . .' She breaks off.

Claudia pauses and turns away from her roses. Something in Steffie's voice endears her to Claudia; perhaps it is the anguished uncertainty. Positive and confident herself, Claudia finds Steffie's confusion oddly touching.

She goes to Steffie, sits on the bench next to her and lights up a herbal cigarette. Steffie is so forlorn that Claudia impulsively takes her in her arms. Steffie bursts into tears, which surprises both of them. Claudia once again feels a shivering inside her, as she has done before when Steffie talked about her longings for motherhood. Some dormant seeds of maternal instinct seem to be sprouting inside her, as if watered by Steffie's tears. Yet how can she be feeling maternal about Steffie, who is older than she is? Claudia feels unnaturally bewildered and blames the fullness of the moon.

Steffie's sobbing eases off, and in the silence Claudia says, loudly and determinedly, 'If there's a baby out there somewhere for you, Steffie, you'll know, and find it, I promise you. Or it will find you.'

Steffie looks at her in amazement. She looks so sure, so complacent, so like an oracle. Somewhere in the night a child cries, and Steffie almost, but not quite, hears her. Her senses are alerted, but she is too far away. The child cries again, louder.

'I hope so,' Steffie murmurs fervently. And then she is quiet, straining to hear the sound she thought she heard in the night.

But there is nothing, not this time. There is only, from a distance, the sound of Marcel's recorder as he makes his way home. It is not unlike the cry of a baby and Steffie is comforted.

The two women sit in silence and in harmony, until Marcel appears, like a ghost of the forest, and joins them. Steffie turns to him eagerly, ready to be distracted from her tears, her confusion, the strangeness of the lingering moonlit evening. In the few days that Steffie has been here, the flirtation she is enjoying with Marcel has escalated. Begun as a distraction, to take her thoughts off motherhood, Steffie is finding herself drawn more and more to this slight enigmatic creature who plays like a god and entices her every day deeper under his spell. Steffie can't cope much with reality these days; it's far too painful. So she's an easy prey to magic.

Claudia, watching the two together, knows that Steffie is on the brink of going to bed with Marcel, of embarking on an affair that she herself has encouraged, thinking that it would take Marcel's mind off Alina and Ireland. Now, she is uneasy. She too heard the child's cry in the night, saw Steffie turn her head, recognized the longing still there, despite Steffie's new doubts.

She doesn't need to be distracted, Claudia thinks, watching as Steffie playfully waves a crimson rose under Marcel's nose. She needs to concentrate all her energies on finding that baby, following the destiny she has chosen, or that has chosen her. Besides, Marcel is trying too hard. He is acting too interested. Claudia after all does have her limits of tolerance.

Marcel is holding the hand that is holding the rose, and manages to kiss it as he puts his lips to the flower. This is all a bit too much for Claudia. Suddenly, she doesn't want this affair to happen, doesn't want to see Steffie hurt, discarded by Marcel like all women eventually are, like she herself would have been had she not been important to him as more than just a lover. And so she says, her voice ringing loudly in the moonlit garden, 'Steffie, this baby we were talking about . . .' She tails off enigmatically and waits.

Steffie turns from Marcel and looks at Claudia, who is sitting on a stone bench by the roses, looking like a granite carving in the fading light. She is dressed in some kind of a scarlet kaftan and her plump feet are bare, their golden colour gleaming on the soft grass. Steffie stares at them, mesmerized, and waits.

When she has got Steffie's complete attention, Claudia says softly, 'I know about herbs, about strange medicines handed down from medieval times, that make women fertile.'

Steffie tries to laugh, but it comes out croaking and uncertain. Marcel swears softly in French. Steffie says, 'But I don't want to conceive a baby myself. I want to adopt.'

Claudia nods her head. 'Of course. I understand that. But these charms are potent, inexplicable. Who knows but that they won't work in helping you get the baby you want?'

Marcel hisses at Claudia in French, then says in English to Steffie, 'What nonsense she talks. I hope you are not going to be taken in by witchcraft.'

But Steffie seems to hear the cry again, the infant plaintively wailing, and although it could be the night wind accelerating through the trees, the cry pierces her, just as the thorn on the rose she is holding suddenly pierces her skin. She looks at Claudia, only barely making out the black eyes, the profusion of hair. The night is opaque, whimsical. The scent of honeysuckle thickens the air. Not far in the forest of Brociliande, Steffie feels the spirits wake, stir and go out into the night.

She looks at Claudia and smiles. 'Why not?' she says

lazily. 'Why not try magic, since nothing else seems to have worked.'

Claudia smiles too, and stands up slowly. 'It's a perfect night for casting spells,' she says, and Steffie can't tell if she's teasing or in earnest. 'A full moon.'

Marcel watches the two women leave the garden, go into the house to rummage through Claudia's vials of oils and herbs. At first he is furious, softly cursing them both, silently vowing his revenge on Claudia, but then his mood changes, lightens. He thinks of the way that she has outmanoeuvred him and laughs aloud. The moon, silver now, has cast an iridescent light all over the garden, trapping Marcel where he sits on the garden bench.

She is a fit match for me, he thinks proudly of Claudia. I never realized it before, but she is indeed a match.

He picks up his recorder, silver too in the moonlight, and plays to the night's spirits, while on the balcony of the house above him, Steffie drinks infusions of raspberry leaves tinged with unidentifiable herbs and plays at magic. Claudia, listening to Marcel's music, sighs with relief that Steffie is no longer trapped in it.

Inside, Ivo, oblivious, dreams of lightning illuminating a silver forest, and smiles as he snores.

Chapter Eight

For the next few days Steffie and Claudia are barely out
of each other's sight. They spend hours walking in the
fields, the forest, gathering herbs and flowers and
plants, drying them in the sun, crushing them, mixing
them with oils. Claudia has a small but crammed herb
garden in a patch of Marcel's land, and there she
grows lemon balm, basil, thyme, rosemary, sweet
cicely, lemon verbena. 'Do you actually live here with
Marcel?' Steffie asked once.

'Not really. I have a small flat in Paris, but I'm not
often in it. I rent it out to colleagues when I'm away.
Marcel and I have a lot on, and need to be together to
rehearse.'

Claudia is certainly settled in Brittany now, as are
the others, at least for a time. She teaches Steffie about
herbs, when to harvest the various plants, how to dry
them and store them. How to make aromatic oils with
crushed flowers and olive oil, and medicinal ointments
with vaseline and dried herbs. Steffie is fascinated by
all this and learns quickly. It will be useful when she
has a child, Claudia tells her.

Marcel watches this with some amusement. He
thinks idly of interfering, of attempting to seduce
Steffie away from the influence of the other woman,
but decides against it. Their female solidarity unnerves
him. With their herbs and oils and charms they are like
priestesses, or wise women from some ancient tribe.
He's not sure that he wants to interfere in these

womanly rites, these feminine rituals. He's not sure he even wants to know about it.

So he watches from afar, half intrigued, half exasperated. His projected affair with Steffie has turned into a non-starter, but this doesn't bother him unduly. He fancies her, but not that much. Right now he's more interested in Claudia, in the way she has manipulated the situation to suit herself. Marcel cannot help but admire her.

And so Marcel roams his forest alone, seeking shade from the hot sun in secluded parts unknown to the tourists and the hikers. There, in dense still woodlands, he plays his recorder, dreams, dozes on the spongy mossy ground of the forest. Sometimes, on the way home, he comes across Ivo, his camera slung around his shoulders, sitting on a rock or a fallen log, looking vacantly at the sky. Marcel always stops and tries to talk. Sometimes Ivo is chatty and good company, but at other times he is distracted, preoccupied. Marcel finds the other man disconcerting when he is like this, but in an odd way, fascinating. Marcel knows Ivo's head and heart are in the clouds, and he can understand this, for his own are wrapped in clouds of music. And there is something splendid about Ivo, something almost regal, like a fallen god, a deposed monarch: Samson without his hair; a young demented Lear; Sisyphus doomed to endless toil, struggling to find that impossibly perfect bolt of lightning.

On one such day Marcel meets Ivo at Le Val-sans-Retour as he trudges up the hill out of the valley towards home. It is late afternoon, and the valley is quiet, empty, still. Marcel rounds a bend on the top plateau and sees Ivo standing motionless on the dry grass, looking out over the valley. His camera bag, unpacked, lies heedless on the ground a few yards away from him.

'No storms this evening, Ivo,' Marcel says gently. 'Let's go home.'

Ivo nods, pliant as a child, and picks up his bag. His hair and beard have grown longer and untidier, the white sprayed through the copper more pronounced. His thick eyebrows are the same colour, Marcel notices, and just as unruly. Under them the eyes are feral, manic.

The two men walk along silently, until Marcel says curiously, 'Why don't you try some other photography, since the storms seem to have stopped. Steffie tells me you do amazing landscapes.'

Ivo stops walking and grabs Marcel's shoulders with both his hands, which are large and strong and fleshy. 'The landscape is nothing without lightning, do you hear? Nothing! Lightning is the ancient god, the only god we've got these days. It transposes the earth from the mundane to the sublime. I need it, Marcel, I crave it, for it makes *me* sublime too.'

Marcel, startled, disengages himself from Ivo's grip and steers him down the path. The man's a lunatic, he thinks.

They walk on in silence for a good ten minutes. Finally Marcel, trying to break Ivo's preoccupation, says, 'Your sister and Claudia seem to be trying to conjure up a baby with charms and incantations. I think the forest and the moonlight have unhinged them both.' He says this with a short laugh, to show Ivo he is not serious.

Ivo says, fervently, 'Don't mock the power of magic.'

Marcel stares back at Ivo, wondering what is going on behind those feline eyes. 'Oh, I don't,' he replies sombrely. 'Believe me, I don't. Remember I was born here.'

163

Ivo nods, satisfied. Marcel decides the forest has unhinged all of them, and wonders uneasily whether it was a good idea to entice them all here.

Claudia and Steffie are in the garden when they arrive. Steffie is lying flat on her back in shorts and a sun halter, her eyes partially closed, her loose green shorts pulled down below her navel. Claudia, dressed in a sarong the colour of heather, her Amazonian legs emerging like trophies from the slit in the side of the garment, is massaging some kind of a scented oil into the skin on Steffie's stomach. The air around the blanket is pungent with heat, with the smell of sandalwood and roses. From the house the stereo is playing 'Love and Death' from Wagner's *Tristan and Isolde*.

Marcel and Ivo are both aroused by this sight, and by the mingled scents, the music. Marcel is aroused physically as he stares in fascination at Claudia's tanned firm hands knead Steffie's firm pale belly. The motion is both hypnotic and erotic. He wants those hands on his own belly, his own skin, rubbing, kneading, slowly, then faster and faster, until the magic takes and he is transported.

Ivo stares too, but his arousal is of a different kind. He sees the strength in Claudia's hands, the muscles in her calves, the inscrutable look on her face as she ministers to Steffie, and believes that she can save him, bring back the thunderstorms, the lightning, the energy. He needs her power and vitality. He needs her potions and magic, her heady wines and soothing oils. He needs her sorcery.

Ivo needs magic in his life. He had it in childhood, thought his mother and father were enchanted creatures, always racing through the night to some mysterious place or another, shimmering in their fine clothes,

164

smelling like exotic gardens as they hurriedly kissed him goodnight. When they were gone he would find solace with Steffie, who smelled comforting, like porridge and honey, and who dried his tears and assured him everything would be all right; she was there, he was safe.

Until the day she wasn't. Ivo was ten, Steffie sixteen; the family were living in Manhattan for a brief time. Ivo was ill, some childhood illness he has long since forgotten, and he was alone with the nanny. It was not unusual for the parents to be out, but normally either Troy or Steffie were around. But Troy at fourteen had gone off for a week to a music camp, and Steffie had, unfortunately for Ivo, fallen in love for the first time and was staying the night at the home of her boyfriend's family.

Ivo, feverish, had woken up in the middle of the night shrieking with a febrile nightmare that left him shaking with terror, drenched in sweat. The nanny tried to comfort him, but she was new and he hardly knew her. 'Steffie,' he moaned. 'I want my sister.' It was the first time he had needed her so desperately, and the first time she wasn't there.

That night was the longest of Ivo's life. He vacillated between desolation, fear and anger: Steffie, the one person he had trusted, had abandoned him. The nanny went back to bed, but Ivo stayed up most of the night watching a tumultuous thunderstorm roaring over the city. The fury of the wind and rain, the brilliance of the lightning, awed and strangely calmed him. It was as if the storm had become his own anger, his own rage, lashing out at the world, punishing it. The lightning slashed the city as Ivo himself would have liked to; it embodied all the power he had not.

He forgot the incident, as children do. But it came

165

back to him almost as an epiphany that morning near Stonehenge when he photographed lightning for the first time. It was as if at last he was in control; he had the power that had eluded him as a child, and he would never feel helpless again.

But he has, of course. The old feeling of vulnerability, of impotence, has seeped into his soul, despite the tranquillity of this rose-scented garden in Brittany. Only another storm will return his vigour.

Steffie, on the blanket, stirs, moves and greets Marcel and Ivo dreamily. Her slick belly glistens in the late afternoon sun. Claudia's hands are glossy with oil, golden, plump. Marcel longs for those hands on his hot skin, his burning flesh, but Ivo fantasizes that they are on his temples, gently massaging them, conducting energy from the centre of her being into the core of himself.

'Here, I've pulled over the other blanket, sit down,' Steffie says. 'You both looked dazed. Have you been out in the sun too long?'

Marcel and Ivo topple onto the blanket, watching Steffie pull up her shorts and roll back over contentedly. 'It's a fertility oil,' she explains, though no-one has asked. 'Claudia says that even though I'm not having the baby myself, this will bring me closer to her spiritually, so that when at last she comes, I'll be ready.' She smiles happily at Marcel, having forgotten that only a few days ago, she had intended to go to bed with him. All her concentration is centred once again on one thing only: a child of her own.

As if she were hugely pregnant, Marcel loses the last vestiges of lust for Steffie. Besides, next to Claudia she seems too pallid, too thin, too bland. Marcel rolls over onto his stomach so that his face is touching Claudia's bare calf, which smells of some aroma he cannot identify. Surreptitiously, he bites it gently. Claudia, feeling it, neither flinches nor pulls away. She sits inscrutably between the men, smelling of heat and scented oils.

The garden gate opens and Bernadette bustles over to them. Her coarse grey hair has been recently set and styled by the local hairdresser and sits primly around her ears; she is dressed in a summery polyester skirt reaching just below her knees, and a short-sleeved white blouse. She has put on a smidge of coral lipstick and wears her best gold earrings, as well as the tiniest splash of perfume, brought to her by Claudia from Paris, behind her ears. She is ready to go visiting.

'Good, you are resting, all of you,' she cries merrily. 'Every time I come, you are scurrying around like insects: Marcel off in the forest playing the recorder, Ivo looking for a storm, Claudia making her potions, Steffie working on her little computer on her lap.'

Steffie, who speaks French, says with a smile, 'I've done so little work really, Bernadette; only my basic weekly article, and I meant to do a whole series. This forest of yours encourages laziness.'

'Oh la la, it is summer, the vacation time. Even busy journalists and musicians and photographers need holidays sometimes.' She says this with tongue in cheek. Like Jack Murphy back in Ireland, she cannot believe these people really work, not real work, like her husband, God rest his soul, who owned the only garage in the village and worked day and night, seven days a week mending other people's clapped-out vehicles for whatever they could afford to give him. And not like she herself worked, raising all those children, helping her husband mind the garage, and still find time to go to Mass and novenas and do the flowers for the church and have poor old Père St

167

Yves, the priest, to dinner every Sunday.

'I've brought you *galettes*, freshly made,' she says, diving into her ubiquitous basket and passing around the sweet buttery Breton biscuits. Bernadette has been a frequent visitor at the house, getting to know all the inhabitants, treating everyone with the same insouciant affection she treats her own children. Even Ivo, who doesn't know a word of French, gets on with her in his distracted way, communicating with manic grins and gestures.

'And for you, Claudia,' she goes on, 'some peppermint from my garden. And dill.'

Bernadette wholly approves of Claudia's medicinal herbs, having an instinctive mistrust of doctors. She has followed Claudia's ministrations to Steffie with interest, knowing all about Steffie's desire to adopt a child. Though she can't quite understand why Steffie won't find herself a good man and bear his children (she had initially had some hopes for Marcel in this role), she nonetheless wholeheartedly approves of Steffie's strong maternal instinct. It is sadly lacking in her own son, Bernadette feels, this need to have children. She is hoping some of Steffie's craving will rub off on him.

'Delphine in the village has just had her baby,' Bernadette enthuses. 'Such a dear boy, so handsome already. I shall send her up with him for you to admire.'

The women coo approval. Marcel groans.

'And the Olivier twins, the butcher's children, you remember, Marcel, surely? They are so robust now. A joy to their parents, they tell me. And to their grandparents.' She looks pointedly at Marcel.

'Just as yours are to you, Maman,' Marcel says sweetly.

'In Paris? They bring me sorrow, so far away. I miss them no end, worry about them constantly. And they are not Breton, they are Parisian.'

'They are still your grandchildren.'

'Ah, what do you know, Marcel?' Bernadette sighs. 'What do you know of a lonely old woman like myself?'

This prompts a chorus of protestations, much to Bernadette's satisfaction. The talk then flits and swoops from topic to topic like starlings from tree to tree, until Claudia says, 'Will you have a drink with us, Bernadette? An aperitif? I'm ready for one.'

'That would be most pleasant,' Bernadette says. 'A Kir, if you please.'

Marcel goes inside for the drinks. An evening breeze has come up, dissipating the sultry heat of the day. Bernadette thinks how modern she is, sitting here with her sophisticated son and his cosmopolitan friends from all over the world. She thinks of her own mother, in her heavy wooden clogs and long black skirts, of the lace coif, stiff and starched white, she always wore on her head on Sundays and for every occasion. Bernadette's father was the village basket-maker, well respected in the community.

How old-fashioned they were, she muses. And yet . . . her mother had four children, and all stayed in the village, or at least went no further than the nearest town ten kilometres away. Bernadette's sister and two brothers, all older than her now, still live in the village or town. They and Bernadette all gave her mother grandchildren; there were hordes of them, in and out her parents' house all day long. Her mother spoiled them, scolded them, adored them; she spent every day at the stove making them savoury crepes, *galettes*. And what do I have? Bernadette sighs to herself in an uncharacteristic moment of self-pity. Grandchildren far away whom I hardly know; my house empty, my life without the laughter and tears of little ones to ease me into my old age.

'Are you all right, Maman?' Marcel asks gently. 'You are far away.'

Bernadette pulls herself together. She has a good life: a modern new house; her health; her many friends; and Marcel, her youngest son, nearby when he is not on tour, or in Paris making recordings. 'I am perfectly all right, Marcel,' she says determinedly.

She won't give up hoping. Marcel is still young, there is still time. Perhaps Claudia could use some of her potions on him, like she is doing for Steffie? Bernadette knows this is witchcraft, and that the Church wouldn't approve, but the Church in Brittany is somehow different, more earthy, more grounded in real life. Sometimes Bernadette sees no difference between the Church and magic, and wholly approves of both.

She looks up and sees that Claudia is looking at her. Their eyes meet and hold for a few seconds. A spark of something very like the electricity that Ivo is forever seeking crackles suddenly between them. It is as if Claudia has read her thoughts, as if some charge has passed between them.

This does not surprise Bernadette. Claudia, though not French, thinks like a Breton woman, has the same kind of blood. After all, she is from Ukraine which, like Brittany, was crushed by another larger neighbouring power, the language forbidden, the religion, the culture, persecuted. They are of the same background, Bernadette feels. They come from generations of survivors.

*   *   *

170

After Bernadette has gone, Steffie retires early to her bed, but Claudia and Ivo and Marcel stay outside. Each man wishes the other would leave, but neither does. Finally Claudia is the one who says good night to them both, and goes inside. Shortly afterwards the two men follow her.

Claudia bathes in patchouli oil, and walks out on the balcony, wrapped in a black satin robe. She looks out at the dark shape of the forest beyond and waits, her bare feet planted firmly on the stone floor.

Ivo comes first. He slips up behind her, pressing his body against hers, feeling the strength coming back to him again. But she walks away from him quickly. 'No, Ivo.'

'We don't have to make love, we needn't be lovers, not if you don't want to,' Ivo pleads, 'but let me stay with you tonight. I need you, Claudia.'

Claudia shakes her head, then takes his unkempt hair in two fists and draws him slowly towards her. Then she kisses him maternally, on the forehead. Ivo struggles to reach her lips, saying again, 'Please. I need you.'

Claudia pulls away from him. 'You don't, you know. Not tonight. Look, over there.' She points to the sky above the forest, which is black and starless. As they watch, a faraway flash of lightning illuminates the darkness for a second or two, then vanishes.

'You've done it,' Ivo breathes heavily. 'You've conjured this up, you witch.'

Claudia shrugs, but whether it is in agreement or dismissal, Ivo cannot tell. 'Thank you,' he whispers, then is gone. A few minutes later, he appears under the balcony, laden down with his camera bag. He waves to her, then bows awkwardly, like an encumbered medieval knight paying homage to a queen.

When he is gone, Marcel appears on the balcony. 'So you sent your fool away?' he teases, kissing the back of her neck, running his hands down the soft satin of the robe over her breasts and belly.

'He's not a fool,' Claudia murmurs. 'Mad perhaps, but not a fool.' She is not surprised at Marcel's appearance, though he has not made love to her in years.

His hands slip inside the soft material onto her bare skin, which is silky with the oils from her bath. She lets them probe and linger for a few moments and then, reluctantly, pulls herself away, turns and faces him. 'I thought we were finished with all that,' Claudia says lightly.

'So did I. Obviously I was wrong.' The robe has slipped open and he can see the glistening breasts, the solid thighs. Claudia lets him look and smiles to herself. But when he reaches out for her, she pulls away again.

'What's wrong?' he asks, puzzled.

Claudia allows her own lust to turn into anger. 'What's wrong? If you don't know, then you're the fool, Marcel LeLeannic.'

He puts his hand on her breast, ignoring the outburst. 'Oh come, Claudette,' he wheedles, calling her by the French version of her name that he used when they were lovers. 'Stop playing games with me. We were great in bed once; don't tell me you didn't enjoy it as much as I did.'

She looks at his hand scornfully. 'But we stopped,' she says. 'Or rather you did.'

'Only because we were getting too intense,' he replies, moving his hand slowly around and around the full breast. 'It was interfering with our music. You know nothing must do that.' He lowers his head and puts his lips to her other breast.

172

Claudia stands quietly, unmoving, for a few moments. Marcel is gently sucking on her nipple, but as well as flooding her with erotic stimulation, there is something else. The odd flush of hormones heating her body is not just lust this time. It is the same urge trembling inside her as it did once or twice before, when Steffie talked about her baby. It's that maternal stuff, Claudia recognizes, the same feelings that she had experienced before, thinking it merely compassion for Steffie.

This is not compassion; this is something much more primitive. Marcel has begun on her other breast, and Claudia succumbs to the primal need inside her, one which she realizes now has been building up for some time. She murmurs, 'I'll make love to you again only if you'll give me a baby.'

Marcel stands upright, takes his mouth off her breast and drops his hands from her body. Claudia mourns the warmth, the pressure, but remains adamant. 'A baby, Marcel. Yours and mine.'

Marcel collapses on the balcony chair, laughs shakily. 'You must be crazy. I don't want a baby. Nor do you.'

'How do you know what I want? When have you asked me lately?'

'But you're an *artiste,* a pianist. You have a career.'

Claudia looks at him disdainfully, not bothering to reply to this nonsense. 'No baby,' he repeats firmly.

'Women can have babies and still be musicians, Marcel. Look at your Alina. She has a daughter.'

Marcel seizes on this. 'Ah, Alina. I hoped you'd remember her. I'm in love with *her*, not you, Claudia. How can you marry a man who doesn't love you?'

'You can be a cruel bastard, can't you, Marcel.' Claudia says this reflectively, as if she were commenting on the state of the weather. 'But you don't really

173

love Alina. You haven't a clue what love is.'

Marcel stands up, goes to the balcony and looks out at the storm gathering above the forest. Another shaft of lightning rifts the sky. Marcel would like to make love to Claudia right here on the balcony, while the storm crashes and roars and lights up the sky above them. 'Claudette, *chérie,* you know I love you; you're my dearest friend, my companion, my partner in music,' he murmurs winsomely. 'Why can't we fuck each other too?'

'We've tried that. It doesn't work. I won't do it again without a commitment from you. A baby is that commitment.'

'*Mon dieu*, you've been talking to that silly Steffie for too long. She's turned your head. Or is it my mother, going on about my giving her grandchildren?'

Claudia thinks of the look that passed between her and Bernadette earlier that evening. It was as charged as any bolt of lightning; it was as if all the longing of the older woman for Marcel's child had been poured into her. Or rather, Claudia realizes, Bernadette's longing had made her recognize her own dormant desire.

'Perhaps it is these things,' she says now.

'Well, forget it,' Marcel says shortly.

'Look, I'm not asking for you to marry me. Or love me. Or even support me, though you make a hell of a lot more money than I do, you jammy bastard.'

'That's because I'm magic, I'm enchanted.' Marcel grins mischievously. He is beginning to enjoy this. 'Do you think you're the only sorcerer, with your oils and herbs and healing?'

'Ah, Marcel.' Claudia looks at him fondly. 'What a child she would be.'

'She?'

'A girl first, then a boy.'

174

Marcel throws back his head and roars with laughter. 'You're loony, *folle*, mad. Enough joking, dear Claudette, my angel, *mon bijou*, my sweet treasure, let's go to bed now.'

Claudia's eyes remain on his face as she opens her robe provocatively, ostensibly to shake the tie loose, then slowly covers herself. 'How little you know me, Marcel,' she murmurs as she walks past him off the balcony and into her bedroom.

He follows her inside, takes a step towards her. He knows that she wants him as much as he does her, but she says, 'No, Marcel. I mean it. Go now, please.'

Marcel knows when not to push it. Frustrated and not a little confused, for he had always assumed Claudia was pliable where he was concerned, he swears softly and leaves the room.

When he has gone, Claudia takes off her robe and gets into bed. Her eyes stay open in the dark and sure enough, soon there is the sound of the recorder in the garden, under her balcony, trying to entice her, enchant her, lure her into the thundery night.

It is a battle of wills and goes on for a long time. The thunder comes closer, louder, the lightning more frequent, but it doesn't rain and the air remains hot, sultry. Claudia throws off the thin blanket. The music invades her body like probing fingers, but she refuses to be seduced. Finally, after a long, long time, the sound stops, and the night is quiet. The storm has not materialized, not fully, and the stars are out again.

Claudia lies on her bed, bathed in starlight, wide awake. She wants Marcel, wants him now, wants him here in her bed making love to her.

But she wants more than that. She is content to wait, to have it all. It never occurs to her that she might end up with nothing.

The next day there is a telephone call from Ireland. It is Troy, asking them all to return to Heron's Cove for a concert. 'You have one every month,' Steffie says. 'This must be something special.'

'It is. Very. I'd like you here for support. Ivo, too, of course. And Marcel and Claudia, as both friends and musicians – their presence will encourage her. She is so nervous, she's making herself ill.'

Steffie says, 'Alina. You're talking about Alina. She's giving the concert.'

'Yes, yes, of course. Please come, Steffie. And bring the others.'

Steffie shakes her head soundlessly over the pleading in her brother's voice. 'You haven't told me when it is, this concert.'

'In a week's time. But if you could come earlier . . . Alina is so terribly frightened, Steffie. You could help distract her. And I know she's fond of Marcel.'

'And he of her, certainly he'll come. And Ivo needs to get out of his slump. I hope you can conjure up some storms for him, Troy, if he goes back to Ireland.'

'As a matter of fact, I've just heard the week's forecast on the radio. Thundery and rainy. Good for the concert; if it's too warm and sunny, the summer people want to be on the beach or hiking the hills.'

They hang up and Steffie goes to find the others. Marcel is, of course, eager to go, to see Alina, be present at the concert. He has dismissed last night as a trick of the moon, a temporary bewitchment, though he is disconcerted this sunny morning to find he still itches for Claudia. She is sitting at the breakfast table resplendent in her black satin robe and strong bare feet, and he cannot help but remember how it had opened last night, how soft her skin was to the touch of his fingers.

Seeing Alina will cure him of this ridiculous hankering after Claudia, he thinks. Besides, it is time he went back to Ireland to sort out Alina, he has decided. This ridiculous attachment to Troy has gone on long enough; she must be made to see some sense, go back to Dublin where she belongs.

Claudia, drinking black coffee and smoking a herbal cigarette, knows exactly what Marcel is thinking. It doesn't bother her. She saw how he looked at her a moment ago, knows that last night was more than a temporary derangement. She knows, too, that it is necessary to go to Ireland. There are things that must be exorcized, before her baby can be conceived.

Ivo joins them, euphoric after last night's storm, and agrees to go to Ireland with them when he hears Troy's weather predictions. They are all looking forward to moving on now, and talk about Heron's Cove with enthusiasm as they drink Marcel's strong black coffee. The doors to the garden are open, and the heady scent of roses already tinges the warm air. From a willow tree a thrush sings.

Steffie feels a momentary pang at leaving all this. Britanny has healed her, Britanny and the soft mystical forest and, most importantly, the ministrations of Claudia, who has helped Steffie believe again in both herself and the baby she had despaired of finding. She knows that somewhere there is a child waiting for her, perhaps one not even born yet, but Claudia's magic has taught her patience. She can wait, and wait in Ireland as patiently as she can here.

Claudia is looking fondly at her. 'There are some wonderful plants in the hills behind Heron's Cove, Steffie, I noticed them last time. Many will be in flower now. You can help me find them. The exercise and

177

fresh air will be good for us both.' She pats her stomach, a small gesture that only Marcel notices.

'You're outrageous,' he whispers in her ear. But he cannot help but admire her tenacity.

It is misty and wet in Ireland when they arrive. Heron's Cove seems cold and dismal after Marcel's cosy home, after the hot sunshine of their last week in Brittany. Troy seems fretful and distracted, and Alina pale and harassed. Though outwardly still composed, she is clearly stressed. Her violet eyes look both tragic and terrified, and she has to make an effort to stop her hands from trembling.

Claudia finds herself alone with Alina, early on their first morning in Ireland. It is not even six o'clock, but both women have been awake for hours. Claudia has been prowling the house for an hour, unable to sleep, after dreaming all night of babies.

Unlike Steffie, Claudia has never wanted children. An only child herself, born of an older mother and father who had despaired of having children, she found family life in the small village in Western Ukraine lonely and cloying. Her parents smothered her with an excess of nervous timid love; her numerous cousins were too old to be much use as companions. From early days she was desperate to leave home, to embark upon her career as a pianist. Even when she first met Marcel, and began to love him, the thought of having his child never occurred to her.

She wonders now why it did not. Once begun, the tremors that had been set off by Steffie have reached earthquake proportions, causing her sleepless nights and days of pure longing. Perhaps, Claudia thinks suddenly, it was my own medicines that set off this craving? Perhaps the fertility herbs, the invocation of ancient rites that I used so carelessly with Steffie, were too potent to play around with. The thought makes her slightly uneasy.

Alina startles her in the midst of all this contemplation, walking into the kitchen like a ghost, in a long pale yellow dressing gown made of some gauzy material. 'I couldn't sleep,' she says, making herself a cup of tea and offering Claudia one.

'The concert. It's keeping you awake.'

Alina nods. 'Yes. So much depends on it.'

Claudia accepts tea, drinks it black with a spoonful of honey and lights one of her special cigarettes which permeates the room with the scent of exotic herbs. She says, 'There will be mostly friends here. No music critics. The other members of the audience will be here because they love music. Many know of your accident; they'll be on your side.'

'I'll be my own critic,' Alina says harshly. 'I shall know exactly how well or badly I play.'

Claudia, a musician herself, cannot contradict this.

'There's something else. There's Troy. He believes so strongly in me. I can't bear the thought of letting him down.' The anguish in her face is a living thing, twisting her mouth into unnatural shapes, crumpling her forehead with lines of pain. On her neck the silver slash of her scar gleams like a sword.

Claudia leans over the table and takes her hand, presses it comfortingly. 'Let me help you. There's nothing wrong with your playing; I heard you rehearse yesterday and you were perfect. You need to compose yourself now.'

'Oh God, don't I know it, but how? I've totally lost the ability to focus myself before a concert. I know I'm a wreck, look at the circles under my eyes, and I've lost weight again. I'm terrified, Claudia. Frightened to

179

death. If I bungle this, I'll never have the confidence to try again.'

Quickly Claudia turns over in her mind the remedies she has brought with her, for relaxation, composure. There is rock rose, Star of Bethlehem, cherry plum. Some basil, which does wonders at clarifying the mind and aiding concentration. Alina is clearly in a state of trauma and needs all the help she can get. 'Come upstairs with me,' Claudia says, already standing up. 'Let's see what we can do.'

That night Marcel comes into Claudia's room, surprising her in bed, and tries to persuade her once again to make love. 'Ah, Claudette, I don't understand you,' he groans when she refuses, as she had in France.

'What about your precious Alina?' Claudia cannot resist asking. 'How can you make love to me in the same house as your Irish princess?'

Marcel is rather sheepish about this, for in truth he doesn't know either. All he knows is that he wants Claudia desperately. 'My relationship with Alina is on a different plane,' he says loftily as he tries to bury his face in her belly. Claudia lets him graze for a few moments, then pulls away and says again, 'No.'

What amazes Claudia, is how she is able to resist Marcel. He has always been her soulmate, her match, her partner not just in music, but in love and desire, even when he withdrew these things from her after their initial fling. But she wants something else now, even more than she wants Marcel: she wants his baby.

After several days of aromatherapy massage and rich herbal drinks, with a bit of yoga deep breathing thrown in (Claudia is determined to try everything)

Alina is transformed. 'I'm so relaxed,' she enthuses one morning at breakfast. 'So much calmer. Claudia is incredible; she's either a born healer or a witch doctor. Either way, it works.'

Marcel, listening, looks at Claudia and shakes his head, marvelling. She returns his look with a complacent smile.

'Perhaps we could all do with one of your herbal baths, your massages,' Troy says ingenuously, not realizing that he is the only one of the present company who has not, at some time or another, experienced those firm healing fingers on his skin and spine.

For the next few days, Claudia takes Alina under her wing. She is allowed only a certain amount of hours for rehearsing, for socializing, and the rest must be spent in relaxing, sleeping, being massaged and oiled, and exercising.

'My God, you are too much,' Marcel says to Claudia on one of the rare occasions that they are alone together since their arrival in Ireland. 'I can't get near Alina. But I suppose that was the idea.'

'No, to be honest.' Claudia is thoughtful. 'Hard as it may be to believe, I wanted to help the poor woman. She was in a terrible state.'

'Your hormones are screwing up, darling,' Marcel snickers. 'First a baby, now all this compassion . . .'

'I think the compassion came first, actually,' Claudia reflects.

Marcel, seeing that he cannot goad her, stops being so flippant and says, plaintively, 'Claudette, let's go home to bed, you can give me one of your massages. One of your sensual ones, not the brisk professional pre-concert rubs.' Though they are in a public place, he leans over and kisses her on the mouth with both tenderness and passion. Claudia is not unmoved.

'No, Marcel,' she sighs finally. 'Not until I can have my baby.'

Marcel groans. 'Look, what kind of a man do you think I am? How can I impregnate you and then go merrily on as if nothing happened? Don't you think I'd get attached to the thing too?'

'Of course you would. You're really not as hateful as you make yourself out to be, Marcel.'

They are sitting in a tiny teashop in Dingle town, taking refuge from the drizzling rain that has not stopped since they arrived. It is mid-morning, and the others back at Heron's Cove are only now beginning to stir. Claudia had errands to do, purchases to make, and wanted an early start before the town filled with tourists. Marcel, claustrophobic without his forest, restless and unable to sleep, decided to come along.

He broods into his hot chocolate. 'I see what all this is, it's a ploy to get me committed to you, via a child. I'll be damned if I'll do it, Claudia. Even for the pleasure of going to bed with you.'

She shrugs. 'Suit yourself, Marcel. I just want to have your baby, whether or not you choose to be committed to either one of us.'

Marcel sulks all the way back to Heron's Cove. Claudia, driving Troy's car, ignores him, enjoying the splendid scenery despite the drizzle. The hills remind her of the Carpathian Mountains she left behind in Ukraine. She wonders what plants and wild flowers grow there and decides she must explore. June is a good time, and her practised eye takes it all in. The blackthorn is extremely late this year; when they arrived in Ireland the blossom was everywhere, making the fields seemed fenced with snow. Here in County Kerry Claudia has admired the prolific yellow flag, a strong handsome flower of the iris family, and noted wild cotton on the mountain behind the house. She thinks she has spotted a type of sorrel, as well as wild thyme. All this needs investigating, she decides. She will leave Marcel to his moods and go out into the hills.

Steffie, bored with the interminable rain, with her endless waiting, sees Claudia preparing to leave and asks if she can come along.

'It's very wet,' Claudia warns.

'I know. I was going to go up the mountain earlier with Ivo, but it was pelting down. He's in one of his black depressions because there hasn't been a thunderstorm. The rain has eased a bit since then, I think it'll clear.'

'I've had enough of all these brooding men,' Claudia says. 'Even your brother Troy, normally so cool, so detached, is twitchy with nerves. Let's get out of here for a few hours.'

Alina is practising in the music room. Troy is outside, looking for his swans who have not been around today. 'Don't let her practise for too long,' Claudia warns as she leaves the house with Steffie. 'Another half-hour, then up to bed for a nap. Make her a camomile tea before her rest.'

Troy awkwardly clutches her hand. 'I don't know how to thank you. For Alina. She is so transformed.'

He is desperate that her comeback is a success. But the irony of it is, he knows that if she succeeds, she will have no reason to stay at Heron's Cove. His mind can't get itself around that conundrum.

Listening at the door for a moment, to the sounds of the harpsichord, Troy, satisfied that Alina is all right, begins to roam away from the house and around the cove down to the sea, looking for his swans. He thinks Alina is safe, believes he need not stand guard for the next half-hour.

He has forgotten about Marcel. Marcel is, at this moment, entering the music room, carrying his recorder. At an appropriate time, he puts his recorder to his lips and begins to play, accompanying Alina. Startled, she looks up at him, but continues her music.

Marcel plays with all the charisma he can muster. If Claudia can take over this woman with her charms and magic, then so can he with his own.

The piece ends. Alina looks up at Marcel and smiles uncertainly. Marcel goes to her and reaches out his hand.

Chapter Nine

The day brightens as Claudia and Steffie walk along the narrow river at the base of the mountain. The sun comes out for the first time in days, and as they walk they shed clothes: head scarves, waterproofs, jumpers. 'I found field scabious on a bank not far from the house the other day,' Claudia says. 'Good for skin complaints,' she tells Steffie.

Claudia seems to walk with a permanent stoop out here in the hills, so interested is she in every plant she spots. She stops often, crouching excitedly, beckoning Steffie to look. 'Greater butterwort, see that? Called bog violet. Look at the colour, simply beautiful.' She doesn't pick those, nor the foxgloves. 'Poisonous, of course,' she says. 'I wouldn't fool with it, though of course the drug digitalin is made from the leaves, used to treat heart disease.'

'I'm surprised you haven't added it to your collection,' Steffie teases her. 'Become a heart specialist.'

'There are some things even I don't trifle with,' Claudia says grimly. 'In the old days they used to use foxgloves as a remedy for weak hearts; they must have killed off hundreds. You have to be careful with medicinal plants, Steffie; you must know what you are doing.'

They climb the slope of the mountain, and after almost an hour's walking, come to a barren rocky bit which they climb over. On the other side is a vast lake, hidden, still, dark. 'Oh, this is wonderful!' Claudia exclaims. 'Shall we stop and rest a bit on these flat rocks above the water? I've brought nectarines and some of my special wine.' She rummages through her rucksack.

The women recline on the rocks, sipping Claudia's wine, that is not really wine, from white enamel mugs. The sun is welcome, warm on their bodies and Steffie rolls up her jeans, exposing pale freckled legs. Claudia, in billowing thin cotton trousers the colour of claret, worn with sturdy Polish walking sandals, does the same with her larger browner legs.

After a time Steffie says, 'I dreamed of that other baby again last night. The one I left behind. I haven't done that since we've been back in Ireland.'

Claudia, her damp thick hair standing on end as it dries in the sun from the soaking it got in the morning rain, says softly, 'Try to forget her, Steffie. You can't torment yourself with guilt because you couldn't take her. Think of the baby that's coming to you. Your own baby.'

Steffie sighs. 'God, I hope it's soon. I can't describe it to you, Claudia, this desperate craving I have, it's like hunger or thirst; I feel I won't survive until it's satisfied.'

'I know what you mean.'

Claudia says this nonchalantly, almost indifferently, but Steffie picks up something deeper in her tone. 'Do you want children?' she asks curiously. 'One day, perhaps?'

Do I want to breathe? Claudia thinks. Do I want to live? 'Yes,' she replies. 'One day.'

Steffie is looking at her expectantly.

Someday Claudia will tell her how *her* passion for a baby triggered off Claudia's, made her whole body ache for Marcel's infant, made her strong arms feel

186

useless because she was not holding a child. But not yet, not yet. There are some dreams a person must keep to herself, at least for a while, at least until they become a reality. So she closes her eyes to Steffie's curious gaze and says nothing, looking as inscrutable as the dark-brown lake.

Steffie does not probe. They lie wordlessly in the sun, until Claudia checks her watch and cries, 'Oh, look at the time! Marcel wanted to try out a new bit of music before dinner; I promised I'd rehearse with him.'

'And I promised Troy I'd do some errands. We'd better get going.'

They set off in great haste for about an hour. The sky has darkened again but the rain holds off. 'How different the hills looked in sunlight,' Steffie says.

They walk another half-hour. Finally, stopping at an outcrop of rock to get their bearings, they look at each other uncertainly. 'I don't recognize this,' Claudia says.

'We should be approaching Heron's Cove by now. We've been walking quite fast, no dawdling like we did on the way up.'

Claudia looks down the way they came, or thought they came, and just sees more hills. They have lost sight of the coast.

With growing trepidation, they change direction. As the afternoon chills with the sun behind a wall of charcoal grey, they put on the clothes they have discarded. Suddenly Steffie shouts to Claudia who is behind her, 'Look, there's somebody just over there, on the next slope, see? I think it's a man; he looks like he's digging or something. Hurry, we can find out where the hell we are.'

Their relief is so great that they practically run up the hill where a man in boots, jeans and a loose grey T-shirt, is cutting turf from the mountain.

'Jack, good God, I don't believe it's you!'

'Steffie! Sweet Jesus, what are you doing on this mountain? And Claudia, too, hello there.'

'What are *you* doing on this mountain, Jack Murphy?' Steffie laughs with relief.

Jack is leaning on his slean, a turf-cutting implement: a long trench spade with a right-angled blade. 'What am I doing here?' he grins. 'Well now, I own this mountain, would you believe. Well, me and the other neighbouring farmers. We've got turf rights and grazing rights.'

'Is that peat to burn?' Claudia asks, wondering if she could make use of it in her remedies.

'It surely is that, but here we call it turf. It keeps our fires going.'

Steffie and Claudia admire the long bricks of turf stacked up and drying on the mountainside. 'I didn't know you were back,' Jack says.

'We came for the next concert. Alina's. We've not been back long.'

Jack appraises Steffie candidly. 'Sorry about the baby. I heard it didn't work out.'

'Yeah, well.' Steffie shrugs and changes the subject. 'We're seriously lost, Jack. We're trying to find our way back to Heron's Cove.'

'To be sure you *are* lost,' he says, shaking his head. 'And will you not know better than to come up these mountains without being prepared? You've gone miles.'

'We hadn't intended to walk so far,' Claudia says.

'You're nearer my place than you are to Heron's Cove. My farm's just over the hill and down in the valley there.' He sweeps his arm in the direction they've been walking.

He sees their look of dismay and says, 'Look, now,

I've just about finished here for today. My van's not far, walk down with me and I'll drive you home.'

Claudia and Steffie accept with alacrity. Jack hoists his slean over his shoulder and they trudge down the mountain to a dirt track where the van is parked. 'I'd never have thought you could get a car up that rutted path,' Steffie says.

Jack wants to stop by his farm first. 'Will you be stopping for a cup of tea?' Though they will be late getting back to Heron's Cove, Steffie and Claudia feel it would be rude not to accept. Steffie says, 'I'd like to thank your mother for the lovely bread if she's around.'

Jack's mother is in the kitchen straightening out a cupboard. The neat farmhouse is clean and comfortable. Next to it is a ruin of a stone house that was obviously the original dwelling, which was abandoned when Jack's grandfather earned enough to build a newer accommodation.

Sitting at the kitchen table eating bread and jam is a boy who looks uncannily like Jack. 'My son, Tom,' he says after he has introduced his mother, Lil, who welcomes them warmly.

Tom is bright, chatty and eager to tell his father what he's been doing while Jack was cutting turf. Both Jack and Lil listen to him fondly. Finally he winds down and runs outside to find his grandfather to bring him in for a cup of tea.

Steffie says, 'I didn't know you had a son. You never said.' She looks at Jack with new interest.

'Didn't your brother mention we met in Ballycaveen? He and Alina saw Tom then.'

'No, Troy didn't say.' Steffie inwardly despairs again of musicians, so wrapped up in their own rarefied world they forget to mention such things as a chance meeting with Jack and a son she never knew he had.

Jack says, 'I don't see him as often as I like. He lives with his mother in Donegal.'

'Oh, that's hard for you.'

'Tom's mother was – is – my wife. Though I suppose we'll be getting a divorce soon enough now, with the referendum through. We've been separated four years.' He looks out the window at Tom, who waves as he runs past. Steffie sees the longing in Jack's face as his eyes follow the boy out of sight. She recognizes that look, empathizes.

Lil, busy making tea, slicing fresh bread and offering cake, overhears Jack's last remark and frowns. She is a short stocky woman with a weather-worn face and kind eyes. Jack turns in time to see the frown and says quietly to her, 'There's no help for it, you know. We've not been good together for years.'

'But sure you're married, Jack. In the eyes of God and the Church.'

The arrival of Jack's father, Paudie, creates a diversion. He too is short and stocky, with wild curly hair like Jack's, only slightly speckled with grey. Paudie is garrulous and jovial. 'Hello and welcome,' he says. 'Will ye be having tea with us? I see you will, and I would say Lil has it all in hand. Will ye be staying long in Ireland now? Jack, those chairs are hard for the ladies, pull these two over to the table. Which of ye two is the musician, now?'

The talk is lively, noisy and fun, with Paudie and Lil keenly interested in the visitors. Claudia soon discovers Lil knows about plants and herbs, and plies her with questions. Paudie is interested in the music he's heard about at Heron's Cove and asks Steffie all about it. 'You must come to a concert one day,' she tells him.

'I would say in winter, when things are quieter on

the farm. There's music enough here to satisfy me until the nights come in.'

Finally Jack says, 'I promised I'd get these two ladies back to Heron's Cove; we'd best be off now I think.'

Tom chooses to stay and help Paudie with the milking rather than go with Jack for the ride. Steffie and Claudia leave with many invitations to return soon.

At Heron's Cove Claudia thanks Jack for the lift and rushes into the house. Steffie is about to follow her, but Jack puts his hand on her arm. 'Steffie, I'm sorry about the baby. Your brother told me you never came home with one.'

'No. It . . . it wasn't right.' Jack looks at her questioningly. She stammers on, 'There was something wrong with her, I don't know what, but something terribly wrong. I . . . refused to take her.'

'And surely you were right,' Jack exclaims firmly. 'Jesus and Mary, I see my wife trying to raise Tom, and even with me around to take him at times and to send money, still it's a tough job. She'd never cope if Tom were ill. I just pray he'll never be that.'

Steffie says, after a moment, 'Would you like to be with your wife?'

'Sure, for Tom's sake, yes. But we were too young. There's nothing between us now, only Tom. But he'd be enough for me. She won't have it. She has another man in her life now, wants a divorce.'

Steffie says nothing to this; there is nothing to say. But she doesn't move. The discovery that Jack has a child, that he cares about this child the way she already cares for her unknown baby, has altered him in her mind, as if she has unearthed another dimension in him.

191

Jack goes on, 'My family is outraged at the thought of divorce. You probably noticed. I don't like it, but what can you do.' He sighs and runs his hand through his hair. 'I need to move out, get me a place of my own. When I save enough money I'd like to rebuild the old farmhouse. Dad thinks I'm crazy and so does Mam. They say I'll have the big house when they die or retire, whichever comes first, Dad says. I don't want them to do either for a long time yet, and I need something now. They're great with Tom, don't know what I'd do without them, but we need some space on our own.'

He sounds so wistful that Steffie says, 'Do come to Alina's concert. Stay afterwards for a late supper. Bring Tom.'

'He's away in the morning. The wife and her new boyfriend are picking him up.' His face clouds, looking older, sadder, damaged somehow. Like that poor baby, Steffie thinks. I wonder where she is, whether she is alive or dead.

She reaches out for Jack and touches his arm. 'I look forward to seeing you at Heron's Cove,' she says. 'I'm sorry Tom can't come.' They say goodbye. Steffie watches the blue van drive away and out of sight.

Inside Heron's Cove there is total pandemonium. Alina is crying silently in the corner, looking wrecked. Claudia is shouting and swearing at Marcel in French and English and bits of every language she has picked up, as well as in her native Ukrainian. Marcel stands letting it all wash over him, shrugging his shoulders in an infuriating insouciant Gallic gesture. Ivo, apparently oblivious, is banging out 'Für Elise' – the only piece he ever learned how to play as a child – on the piano. Troy is alternating between comforting Alina and striding over to Marcel to join Claudia in berating him angrily.

Steffie is taken aback to see her normally cool and collected brother in such a state. She intercepts him in a vituperative attack on Marcel and says, 'What the hell is going on? What's wrong with Alina?'

'That fucking Frenchman,' Troy shouts. 'I left him alone in the house with Alina for twenty minutes, and he's caused havoc.'

'Don't blame him,' Alina says, wiping the tears with the back of her hand. 'It was necessary.'

'Not now. Not the day before the concert. Ivo, can you stop that bloody playing?' Ivo takes no notice.

'Just calm down,' Steffie says. 'Tell me what happened.'

Alina, pulling herself together, says, with dignity. 'She's right, Troy, you must calm down. Nothing has happened that wouldn't have occurred sooner or later.'

'But not now. Not before the concert.'

'Please, go. Make me some tea, anything, I need to pull myself together. No, leave me for a moment, Troy. I'll tell Steffie everything. Marcel, you go too, please.'

Troy reluctantly leaves the music room and goes out through the kitchen to the patio, where he tries to steady himself by watching the heron standing in its favourite spot on the shore. The swans are nowhere to be seen, but Troy sees a cormorant at the end of the cove. He holds his mind on the seabirds, trying to still it.

Claudia and Steffie hover around Alina, who is crying again, silently: awful tears which twist her face in an unnatural grimace. 'Für Elise' drones on; as usual, Ivo is in some space far from the real world. The women take no notice of him as Alina is finally able to speak.

'I have phoned David, my husband. He is coming to the concert and then afterwards taking me home.'

'It's all Marcel's fault, the sneaky shit,' Claudia says. 'I wish I had picked some of that foxglove,' she adds ominously.

Despite the situation, Steffie can't help smiling at this. 'Thank goodness you didn't, Claudia. You calm down too and clue me in on what's happened.'

Claudia calls Marcel a few vile names and says, 'He's so jealous of Troy that he wants Alina out of here as soon as possible.'

Steffie doesn't understand this. 'Alina . . . and Marcel? Is there something I've missed?'

Alina sniffs and says, 'No, no, it's nothing.'

Claudia explains. 'Marcel has had this platonic infatuation for her for years. All very harmless up until now. He doesn't really want her – sorry, Alina.'

This makes Alina smile, to their relief. 'It's all right, I know that quite well. He'd run a mile if I ever even hinted I was tempted by him.'

'But he hates the thought of anyone else, such as Troy, having her. David is all right, of course, he's her husband, he has a right to her.'

'Like any other object he might own, I suppose,' Alina says crossly. 'A vase, a violin, a wife . . .'

'So what did Marcel do exactly?' Steffie asks.

'Nothing much, really,' Alina says. 'Everyone's blaming him and it's not his fault. He just talked to me. Convinced me that it was wrong not to invite David – and Kate too, of course, my daughter – to the concert, my first since the accident.'

Steffie says, practically, 'Is that what *you* want, Alina? Do you want them here?'

'Kate would be fine, I'd very much like to have her here. She'd love it no matter how poorly I played; she's totally uncritical. But I can't very well tell her about it without telling David.'

'You've not told her?' Claudia is surprised. 'You are often talking to her on the phone.'

'I know, and I've hated keeping it from her, but it wouldn't be fair asking her to keep it from her father. I'd never ask her to take sides.'

'And David?'

Tears well up again in Alina's eyes. 'Marcel convinced me that it would be cruel, wicked, not to tell him about my post-accident début. And he's right; David is my husband, he must know, and if he wants to come, what can I say?'

'But you don't want him,' Steffie concludes.

'Isn't it obvious?' Claudia groans. 'Look at her, she can't stop crying.' She shakes her head, then shouts, 'Ivo, that's enough!'

Ivo is still playing, the same piece over and over, as if he were the one practising for a musical début. He takes no notice of Claudia or the scene on the other side of the music room. Steffie wonders distractedly if he is all *there*, banging the piano like a wind-up toy that won't run down. She makes a mental note to talk to him after this crisis with Alina is over.

'No, I don't want David here,' Alina wails, getting herself into a state neither woman has seen her in before. 'But of course he insists; he wouldn't miss it for the world. The great David Montgomery, at his wife's side during her brilliant comeback concert, making musical history. Or if the scenario is different, the great David Montgomery at his wife's side picking up the pieces as she fails in her first concert after her horrific accident. I really don't think he'd mind either way. The publicity would be as good for one as for the other.'

There is a shocked silence for a few moments after

195

this outburst. Claudia thinks, I will never be able to listen to that damned 'Für Elise' again without thinking of this. She goes to the piano, slams the lid on Ivo's fingers, and goes back to Alina. Ivo sits for a few seconds staring at his hands in a vague puzzled way and then wanders outside.

'I'm sorry,' Alina says. 'I shouldn't have said that. I'm being unkind.' She begins to cry again.

Troy, looking distraught, comes in with a tray of tea. 'Look, Alina, I'll phone David, tell him he simply cannot come. He will have to understand and accept the truth, that you're just too nervous to play in front of him.'

Alina looks up at Troy. Her face is a ruin: swollen, pocked with dark circles and shadows. He realizes he has never loved anyone so much.

Alina, seeing his troubled face, tries to pull herself together. 'I'm being ridiculous, I know, but David is always so critical. And he thinks I shouldn't even try to perform again – for my own good, of course.'

Claudia snorts.

'He thinks my nerves have gone, as well as my hands. He's only trying to protect me from failure.'

Claudia, knowing from Troy that this is not exactly the whole truth, that the biggest obstacle to Alina's comeback was her husband, says with irony, 'Your loyalty is admirable, Alina.' She wants to say more, but restrains herself.

'I'll telephone David right now,' Troy announces. 'Explain why it is best he doesn't come.'

'No.' Alina stops him. 'It's all arranged. He and Kate are driving down together the afternoon of the concert. Kate is so excited, so thrilled for me. I want her here now, and she wouldn't be able to come without David.'

'But afterwards,' Troy asks softly. 'After the concert. Do you have to go?' His face is ravaged with distress.

For a moment it is as if the two are alone in the room, in the house, in the world. Then Alina, her face mirroring his, says, 'I promised. Ages ago. I told David I'd go back either when I knew I could play professionally again, or if I failed. I'll know tomorrow.'

Troy nods. He is still holding the tea tray, having frozen in place when he saw Alina still in tears. Now he puts it down and wordlessly leaves the room.

'Come on,' Claudia says gently to Alina. 'I'm taking you upstairs, putting you to bed. A massage first, then some special tea, and I or Steffie will bring you a light supper on a tray. You'll be all right you know. I promise.' She leads Alina out of the music room.

Steffie, alone, wanders outside to find Troy, but he has disappeared into his workshop. She spots Marcel aimlessly walking up and down the dirt track that goes around the cove as far as the pier. Beyond the pier, at the end of the cove, Ivo is sitting on a massive outcrop of rock staring motionless into the horizon. Steffie heads for Ivo but is intercepted by Marcel. 'Is she better now? Alina?'

'I'm not sure. Claudia is with her.'

'Ah, good, good. That witch will sort her out.'

Steffie says, with some annoyance, 'Claudia is quite angry with you.'

Marcel opens his eyes wide, all innocence. 'I didn't phone David, Alina did. She agreed it was necessary.'

'Only because you worked on her feelings as a wife and mother.'

'And what's wrong with that?'

'Oh, get real, Marcel.' Steffie turns from Marcel and flops down at the edge of the small, rather rickety, wooden pier. Marcel sits next to her. The swans swim out towards them, hoping for titbits. By now it is evening and no-one has made any suggestions for dinner. Steffie decides she'll help herself to bread and cheese in the kitchen; no-one will feel convivial tonight. She thinks briefly of Jack and wishes he were here, adding some normality to Heron's Cove.

Marcel is justifying his actions to Steffie, or trying to. Steffie interrupts impatiently, 'Alina's first and only thoughts for the next two days should be for herself as a musician. Her daughter is an adult, her husband, a pain, from what I've heard. I think it's dreadful that you interfered. If she had really wanted her family here, or felt she should invite them, she'd have done it ages ago.'

Marcel now looks troubled. 'I didn't realize she'd be so upset, go to pieces like she did. She was quite fine about it, quite rational, until she finally got hold of David, just before you and Claudia got back from your walk. She came off the phone and dissolved in tears. Then everyone else came in and began screeching at me,' he finishes petulantly.

The male swan ruffles his wings impatiently at them, annoyed that they are not feeding him. Marcel feels that the swans are getting at him too. Steffie says, 'Oh, grow up, Marcel. Look around you. She's upset not just about the concert, though God knows that would be enough, but about Troy. David insisted, on the phone, that she keep her promise and go back with him.'

'Well? She knew she was going back eventually. She and Troy, it is nothing: friends, *amour platonique*. There is no liaison. Why is everyone so upset?'

'Because everyone, you dumb fool of a Frenchman, knows how it really is between them. They're crazy about each other, even though they won't admit it to each other. Knowing those two, I'd be surprised if they even admitted it to themselves.'

Marcel is seriously flustered. Nothing has gone to plan; everything has backfired. He had hoped to be rewarded for bringing Alina back with her family; he had also, of course, had a more selfish desire to see her safely out of Troy's reach, but he certainly had not intended to cause such havoc. And he truly is distressed about Alina. He was sincere when he told Steffie he had no idea she'd get so overwrought.

'Look, I didn't mean—'

'Oh be quiet, Marcel, I've had enough of you, enough of musicians right now. All that goddamn sensitive creativity crap, and you've got a thicker skin than anyone else I know. Troy, too, not doing anything about the fact that he's at last found the only woman in the world who seems able to put up with him. And Alina, going back to a marriage that seems without love on either side. Claudia's the only sensible one amongst you.'

Marcel looks worriedly out to sea, but it's not the dark clouds building up again on the horizon that trouble him. 'Claudette . . . Claudia, I mean. She's very angry?'

'She'll probably poison you with foxglove leaves if Alina blows her concert. Claudia feels personally responsible for its success.'

Marcel shudders. He feels wretched, and guilty as hell. He adores Alina, and will feel terrible if she goes to pieces before the concert. He's begun to like and respect Troy, who will certainly order him out of Heron's Cove for ever if all goes wrong. And Steffie too will have no more to do with him, nor will, he fears, Alina.

Oddly, other than Alina's performance itself, none of

199

this matters. Except one thing: Claudia's disdain. He has gone too far this time, he realizes, and wonders if she will ever forgive him.

That there is a serious chance that she won't, upsets him more than anything else that has happened today.

Fed up with Marcel, Steffie leaves him staring miserably at the swans and goes off to join Ivo. By now the wind has freshened, driving the black clouds towards shore like a conductor leading an orchestra through a tumultuous passage. The wind is high, eerie over the sea, and for a moment Steffie thinks the clouds are making stormy music of their own.

'There, Steffie!' Ivo shouts. 'I just saw it, a flash of lightning, over the sea.' He stands up and begins taking out camera and lens, from his bag.

'It's far away still, Ivo,' Steffie sits on the rock and pulls Ivo back down. 'I can't even hear the thunder yet.'

Ivo reluctantly sits down again. 'I can feel it, Stef. In the air, around me. It's coming.' He can hardly stay still, he is so exhilarated.

His mood is catching. 'It *is* exciting, an approaching storm,' Steffie agrees. The wind whips her hair around her face and makes Ivo shout with joy. He looks younger, happier, than he has for days, out here in the wind and in the damp air that is beginning to smell like rain. Steffie feels a sudden swift kinship with her brother: with his mood, his intensity in the face of the storm.

'You feel it too, Stef?' Ivo is absurdly pleased. 'The anticipation, the mixture of joy and excitement, the fear? There's always slight fear at the beginning, you know. Each storm is different; each is, in some way, dangerous.'

'It's like my waiting for my baby. I'm bursting with happiness, but terrified too. It's like I'm about to confront what life is all about, and I jump between dread and excitement, wondering if I'll be able to live up to it.'

Ivo turns his face from the sea to look at Steffie. 'That's it! That's it exactly.' They stare at each other with both awe and delight, suddenly totally understanding each other. They have not been so close since childhood.

The storm is nearer now, the moisture in the air is thicker, nearly rain but not quite. Ivo stands up, unable to remain seated. He throws his arms out to the wild sky in his usual gesture to the storm gods: it is of abandon, but also an embrace. There is nothing sad about Ivo now.

Steffie stands and also throws her arms wide to the sea, feeling one with Ivo in the wind and dark. For a few seconds they both stand there, arms outstretched, until the sky is suddenly illuminated with a golden streak.

'It's here, Steffie. See that flash of lightning? Oh, it's going to be a winner!' Ivo goes to his camera and begins to shoot.

Steffie shivers, feeling cold and frightened. She has never liked to be out in lightning. Ivo says, 'You'd better go in. It's going to be fierce.'

'No. I'm staying.'

He looks away from his camera in surprise. 'Are you sure?'

She nods. It's time she shared more of Ivo's life, as she hopes he will of hers from now on. Ivo turns back to the sea and begins to photograph the lightning that is now smearing the clouds with eerie shades of yellow and orange.

It lasts nearly an hour. Steffie huddles in the shelter of the rock, terrified, so terrified that later she will recall she never noticed when the rain began, never realized she was getting soaked. But she knows she cannot go back inside, not now; she owes this to Ivo. She will stick it out, for him and for herself, for their lost childhood, their lost selves.

Ivo takes photograph after photograph. Steffie overcomes her fear to peer out from her inadequate shelter of granite and earth to watch him, fascinated by his exultation, his affinity with the storm. This is a different Ivo, an Ivo strong and confident, powerful and secure. She understands for the first time why he needs the lightning.

When the storm finally dies down, Ivo crouches on the ground for a few moments, facing the sea. At last he turns to Steffie, who is huddled against the rock, wet and chilled. 'Come on,' he says gently, 'let's go home.'

'Home? Where's that?'

He smiles. 'Heron's Cove is as good as any, for now. Let's get inside, get dry.'

They walk back together, arms around each other, as the sea simmers after the storm and the sun begins tentatively to break its way through between the last lingering clouds.

From her bedroom window at Heron's Cove, Claudia watches the storm. She has just left Alina, who seems slightly calmer, but not enough, not nearly enough if she is to give a concert in less than forty-eight hours.

Unable to settle, Claudia goes down to the empty music room, sits at the harpsichord, and disconsolately stares at the keyboard. If Alina's dreadful husband can't be stopped from going to the concert, then someone must prevent the negative impact his presence obviously makes on her. If only . . .

Claudia's hands crash on the keyboard in a jubilant chord. That's it, she thinks; that will do it. She remembers her grandmother: old potions, remedies, handed down for hundreds of years, some since medieval times. She remembers the women in the village of her own country: their legends, their stories; their wisdom and healing. Their magic, too, if one believes in these things.

Call it magic, or just giving a gentle push in the right direction; whatever. Leaving the music room, Claudia goes upstairs to her own room with a sense of purpose, to plan and prepare for the next day.

Chapter Ten

The next day Claudia takes command of the household and issues orders, which everyone meekly follows. Troy is banished to his workshop, where he tries to find solace in the texture of walnut and mahogany, using his hands to calm his spirit. Marcel is despatched to the town with a long list, for the wine and cheeses that Troy always serves after a concert. The music room, and the rest of the house, is scrupulously cleaned by the woman from the village whom Troy employs for this purpose, and when they are finished, Steffie and Ivo take out the folding chairs from the shed and dust them off, put them in rows in front of the harpsichord, moving the armchairs and sofa at the far end so that it faces the instrument rather than the fireplace.

Claudia is everywhere, polishing elegant silver candle-holders, arranging flowers, candles, glasses; very much the mistress of the house even though this is only her second visit to Heron's Cove. 'If we get everything done today, we can relax tomorrow, the day of the concert, and make sure Alina relaxes,' she orders imperiously.

When the music room is prepared, Alina comes in to have a look. The men have been peremptorily ordered out of the house by Claudia, to give Alina some peace and quiet in which to rehearse for an hour. Troy retreats once again to his workshop, Ivo to his dark-room, and Marcel to take an aimless walk along the coast.

Alina gives an involuntary cry when she sees the music room, all the empty chairs standing in rows, waiting to be filled by people coming to hear her play. Panic begins to roll over her like Ivo's thunder, and she starts to shake.

'You'll be fine.' Claudia, suddenly at her side, pats her arm reassuringly. 'Trust me.' She wishes she felt as confident as she sounds.

Alina stands at the harpsichord, runs her fingers lightly over the keyboard and finds that they are steady. This surprises her after yesterday's trauma. She had been devastated by David's voice: abrupt, cool, detached, belying his words. 'I want you home, Alina. Where you belong.' He sounded, she thought, like a keeper, a minder, rather than a loving husband.

'Of course I'm going back, when I've proved myself as a musician,' she had replied.

'Or when you're tired of your affair with Troy.'

'Dear God. David, I told you ages ago, when you insinuated the same thing, that the relationship between me and Troy is strictly professional.'

'What's the difference if you're sleeping with him or not?' he had shouted at her in a loss of temper. 'People will *think* you are, and I'll be the laughing stock of all my colleagues. Holed up with him for months, do you think everyone is not going to talk? They'll say I can't hold on to my wife, can't control her.'

His reasoning appalled her, and the realization that tomorrow night she will go home with him depresses her. She has, since her accident, faced the fact that she loves David only as Kate's father. She has in truth always known this. But it was her choice to stay with him, as she has chosen now to go back.

There is Troy. Wandering around the music room, left alone by the others so that she can adjust herself to the familiar room prepared now for her comeback début, Alina allows herself to think of Troy. That she loves him, there is no doubt. That he loves her, she is less sure, though she thinks that perhaps he is beginning to. She would not encourage him in this love, even if she were free of David. What could she give him? Since her accident, she has become a woman without a body, without physical needs, wants, desires. She eats, but food no longer interests her much and she has to be reminded, usually by Troy, to keep refuelling herself. Her hands, of course, are very much alive and part of her, but only as a means to express the music that refuses to be quiet within her. Her emotions are still intact; she knows this because of the intensity of her feelings for Troy.

As for the rest of her, it is as if her body died in the car crash, as if she were no longer a physical being. She does not worry about this because she knows David is relieved, knows neither of them need pretend on that score any longer. David can discreetly have his other women, Alina her music, and the two will live harmoniously together in their separate, civilized, existence.

How bleak it all sounds. Determined not to think about it now, Alina sits down at the harpsichord and begins to play. She goes through her concert pieces, ending with the Scarlatti, which she plays to perfection. When she finishes, there is a burst of applause.

'Alina, that was terrific,' Steffie says. 'We came in only in time for the Scarlatti, but it was perfect.'

'Brilliant playing,' Claudia adds. 'Do it just like that tomorrow night, and a star will be reborn.' As long as David doesn't rattle you, she thinks. As long as you don't despair when he walks into this room tomorrow night.

The three women chat companionably for a few

minutes. How different we all are, Steffie thinks. When we first met, we were wary, uncertain whether we'd even like each other. Now we are as easy and comfortable together as old, old friends.

Steffie remembers her date with Jack that evening. He had rung earlier, asking her out for a meal, and, remembering how he had looked as he watched his son, she agreed to go. 'I'd better go upstairs and get ready,' she says. 'See you later.'

'What about the rest of us?' Alina asks. 'Shall we go out to eat tonight? There's food in, but I don't think anyone feels like cooking.'

'No, you must listen to me,' Claudia says. 'I want you to have an evening alone, before the concert. You don't need to listen to Ivo obsessing about thunderstorms, or Marcel grovelling at your feet trying to ease his guilt over the way he upset you. I shall take the two of them out for a long leisurely meal, then to a pub or two for some local music. Troy can stay behind to keep an eye on you.'

Alina is hesitant. It would be good to have one last evening together with Troy; they have hardly been alone since the others arrived. On the other hand, she is afraid it will be painful, will distress her again before the concert. She looks at Claudia indecisively.

'Everything is prepared for tomorrow, and we shall all relax, forget about the concert,' Claudia goes on. 'Tonight, it will be good for you to be with Troy. He's a calm person; it'll rub off on you. And I've got a treat for you in the fridge, a meal all ready to be eaten. A special wine, too. One of my herbal concoctions, an ancient remedy passed down from my grandmother. I think you'll like it.'

'I musn't drink tonight,' Alina says. 'I must be clear-headed tomorrow.'

207

'This is special wine, it is hardly alcohol, more a remedy. It will help you sleep and aid your concentration tomorrow. We don't want you falling apart when your husband arrives.'

'Whatever you say.'

'Good. Come with me, I'll fetch it for you.'

Troy comes in from his workshop, sees Alina leaving the room and unguardedly looks at her with such disconsolate longing that Claudia, glancing back and catching his eyes, takes a sharp breath. 'Please,' she whispers to some vague unknown goddess, 'please let it work.'

Jack and Steffie are drinking coffee in a small seafood restaurant in Dingle town overlooking the harbour. It has turned hot, muggy, and the harbour is filled with visitors ambling in shorts and T-shirts and cameras, enjoying an after-dinner stroll before vanishing into pubs for the rest of the evening. It is still quite light; tomorrow will be the longest day.

'That was delicious,' Steffie says, refusing dessert. 'I adore crab.'

A waitress with merry eyes flirts a bit with Jack as she asks if they want more coffee.

'How the ladies love you,' Steffie teases. 'Have you been back to see that young woman in the pub in Tralee?'

'You mean the day you picked me up?' Jack smiles. 'I'm irresistible, so?' He laughs. 'Sure, and it's my Irish blarney, don't you know?'

'How did you get on with the English girls, when you lived in London? I suspect your blarney got you nowhere, Jack Murphy.'

Jack's mood changes at once. He says, sombrely, 'I never had a chance to find out. I wasn't in London long before I met the Donegal girl I married. We met on the Hammersmith Line, at the Shepherd's Bush stop. She was visiting friends, had lost her way. I lived right next door to those friends. Small world, as the cliché goes.'

Jack tells her something of his marriage: the years struggling at odd jobs in London, the aborted attempt at college, which failed because of lack of funds. 'I did a year,' Jack says, 'then had to drop out. My wife had trained as a nurse, so she got a job while I stayed home and looked after Tom. Those were good days, before it all began to go dismally wrong.'

'When did you come back home?'

'When we split up. I was missing Ireland anyway, and Dad was needing me on the farm. Mary went back to Donegal.'

He is silent for a moment. 'I think I wanted Tom much more than Mary did. I had hoped we'd have a daughter, too, one day.'

The crowded restaurant is emptying out, their waitress clearing debris from the deep-red tablecloths.

'I envy you,' Jack says. 'You have it all ahead of you: your child. My time with my boy is behind me. All I have are weekends and holidays.' The bitterness makes his voice harsh, strident.

When they leave the restaurant, they pass a pub bellowing out laughter and music. 'Will we go on in and have a drink?' Jack suggests. 'I've been a bit melancholy and I apologize. It's talking about Tom, you see. I so rarely do.'

They stay late, but still they are the first ones back at Heron's Cove. It is after midnight and the house is dark, quiet. Only one dim light burns through the heavy curtains in Alina's bedroom. Troy's room opposite is dark.

Jack has come in for a last cup of coffee, which they

take to the original drawing room of the house, since the music room has been turned back into a concert hall. The room is spacious and overly decorated; it has not been touched since Troy moved in. The furniture is ornate and fussy, now lumpy and frayed. The patterned carpet is bravely gaudy but threadbare, and the gilt curtains, heavily brocaded, are spotted with age. The room has a meretricious air about it, of slightly trashy gentility. 'A strange room for a maiden aunt,' Jack says.

They sit gingerly on a velvet Victorian settee which looks more decorative than functional, and envelops them in a musty aroma which makes Steffie sneeze. 'Oh dear,' she says, 'and I thought this seat was the best of the lot. Troy really will have to do something about this room.'

Jack is scarcely listening. He has put his coffee down on a scarred oak side table and is facing Steffie. He reaches out to her, kisses her. She responds, as she knew she would. Since yesterday, when she met Tom, learned Jack was a father, saw how he looked at his son with both love and yearning, Steffie's feelings for the Irishman have altered. No longer is he merely the attractive, amusing younger man who openly fancies her, who she enjoys flirting with, but something more: someone she can bond with. Steffie has been touched, moved by his fatherhood; in her eyes, it has given him depth, dimension.

Besides, it's a long time since she has been seriously kissed like this. Her last relationship with a man, with Al, ended over a year ago. Since then, there has only been her brief dalliance with Marcel.

This, though, is totally different; Steffie is feeling things for Jack she never felt for Marcel. But just in time she realizes this is crazy.

210

'Steady on,' she says rather shakily, moving away from him.

'Why?' he murmurs, reeling her back in again.

There is a clamour in the kitchen; Marcel, Claudia and Ivo have returned. In minutes they have breezed into the drawing room, talking and laughing.

'*Mon dieu*, I'm glad I'm not playing tomorrow night,' Marcel says. 'My head is spinning. Claudia just would not come home; we've been in one pub after another. I never knew she had such a fascination for Irish stout.'

Claudia smiles enigmatically; she has as a matter of fact drunk very little, being in charge of the driving.

'A wild evening,' Ivo agrees rather unsteadily. 'I think I'll go out on the pier. I need some fresh air.'

'Don't fall in,' Steffie says worriedly. 'Are you all right?'

'I'm fine, Stef. You've got to stop worrying about me, you know. You'll have another baby to fuss about soon.' He flashes her a cheeky grin and goes outside.

Marcel has settled in an armchair, looking at Jack and Steffie with interest. He wonders if he should be miffed that Jack seems to be succeeding where he failed, but decides it's not worth it. He lost interest in Steffie ages ago, and anyway, he's so delighted that Claudia seems to have forgiven him for getting Alina to phone David that he can't be bothered to be cross at anything.

Claudia says, 'Where are Troy and Alina?'

'Troy must be asleep, his room is dark,' Steffie replies. 'Alina's bedroom light was on when we came in so she's probably stewing about tomorrow night.'

Claudia nods her head. 'I think I'll go to bed too. Tomorrow will be a long day.'

'Must you? Stay and talk,' Marcel says. 'Just a minute ago you were so sociable you wanted to stay out half

211

the night; now that we're home you abandon me.'

'Sorry, darling,' Claudia says breezily, and kissing him on both cheeks, she says good night to the others and goes.

Marcel contemplates going after her, but doesn't move. Jack is looking both annoyed and impatient, which wickedly influences Marcel's decision to stay. Steffie, rather relieved that she does not have to decide then and there what to do about Jack, says to him, 'I suppose we should all turn in. It will be a long day tomorrow.'

She walks Jack to his van, where he kisses her again. 'Tomorrow night?' he asks. 'After the concert?'

'You're rushing me,' she warns, though she nonetheless does not hurry out of his arms.

They finally part, and Steffie goes upstairs and decides to speak to Alina before going into her own bedroom. But the light is now out and there is no sound from within, so she tiptoes past.

Claudia waits in her room until she hears Marcel go into the bathroom, then to his own room, before creeping out and through the music room into the main part of the house where the others sleep. Troy's door is tightly shut and no light shines under it. Claudia hesitates, then knocks, taking a chance. She knocks again, slightly louder. Finally she silently opens the door and peers inside. It takes several seconds for her eyes to adjust to the darkness, but soon she can see for herself: Troy's bed is empty. It is still neatly made, unrumpled; he has obviously not been in it tonight.

Letting out the breath she has been holding, Claudia leaves the room as soundlessly as she entered. She returns to her own quarters with relief and a smug feeling of satisfaction.

In Alina's bedroom, she and Troy listen quietly to the sounds of the occupants of the house settling for the night. Troy had wisely put out the light after Steffie and Jack came in, though he did so reluctantly. He wanted to look at the woman in bed with him; he wanted to marvel; he was frightened that she was just a ghost, the fantasy he has not allowed himself to have. He needs to keep looking at her, afraid that if he doesn't she'll disappear.

When the house is finally still, Troy switches on the bedside light once again. Alina is smiling at him.

'Oh my dearest love,' he says, burying his head in the warmth of her naked body.

Neither Alina nor Troy had any idea the evening was going to end like this. Troy, desperate, had anticipated a calm farewell scene: calm, because he had no intention of agitating Alina before the concert, and a farewell because he knew he would not have time to see her alone the next day.

Alina had anticipated much the same thing. She had begun to dread the evening ahead when Claudia came into her room, saying, 'We're off in a minute. Marcel and Ivo and me. Steffie and Jack have already gone.'

'Have a nice evening.'

Claudia looked at her critically. Alina's face was pale, her hair in its usual plait, but hanging down her back rather than up in a coil. She was wearing a creamy long skirt and a plain silk T-shirt. 'You look like someone right out of Wagner,' Claudia said without thinking.

'Troy said something similar once. Isolde, he called me. I wonder if he remembered that she was the Irish princess doomed to fall in love with the wrong man, the man not her husband.'

213

'Like you?' Claudia asked gently.

Alina didn't answer and Claudia didn't push it.

'I've brought you my wine. As I promised.'

'Are you sure I should drink, with the performance tomorrow?'

'Like I told you earlier, this is a special concoction. Healing. Not an ordinary wine at all, nor like any of my other wines.'

'All right. Thank you.'

'Here, have a glass now.'

Claudia poured Alina a small wineglass of the brew. 'Hmm, pleasant, nice,' Alina said as she took a sip, then another.

At that moment Troy knocked, then walked in. 'Ah, there you both are. Marcel and Ivo are hungry, Claudia, and anxious to go out and find some food. They asked me to hurry you up.'

'I'm ready. But before I go, you must also taste my wine.' She produced another small glass, filled it and handed it to Troy. 'You two must finish the wine between you. It will be good for you both, I promise you.'

Blowing a kiss she breezed out, her many chains of sea-green beads crashing on her bosom like waves, her long velvet dress trailing robelike behind her.

'Is Dingle town ready for Claudia?' Alina said fondly.

'She'll wow them,' Troy smiled.

And then they were alone in the house together.

They have been alone before, of course, but tonight somehow all is different. There is an immediacy about the moment, created by the knowledge that it is their last time together. The coming night, still distant this summer's day, is already weaving a spell with its pale white moon pencilled against the still-blue sky. Soon there will be stars, and the ripening of the moon to a golden orange, and perhaps a soft sea or hill mist. The approaching midsummer magic is all there.

Alina and Troy make no move to go downstairs, to eat the cold seafood supper Claudia has prepared for them. They stand at the open window in Alina's bedroom, sipping the wine. The mountains are exceptionally clear in the evening light, their outline etched against the sky as if drawn with a sharp pencil. As they watch, the colour deepens and light shadows begin to creep over the landscape, darkening as the sun begins to go down.

Troy pours them each another glass of wine. The first one soothed his agitation, dissipated the despair he has been indulging himself in all day. He has always known Alina would one day leave Heron's Cove; now that that day has arrived, he cannot handle it. But with this brew that Claudia has concocted, whatever it is, he feels stronger, more optimistic, though nothing has changed.

Alina too feels different. Claudia's strange wine seems to be filling her bloodstream with tiny prickles of heat. The wine smells odd too: musky, sweet, not unpleasant. Troy, inhaling it as well, feels slightly faint.

Time seems to alter as they stand there silently, not needing to speak. They drink the wine, watch the day slowly fade, a star or two beginning to appear. Yet still they do not move; they hardly speak except for the odd word, the occasional sentence.

Finally Troy says, 'You know I love you. I don't want you to go, but I understand that you must.'

Alina is not surprised at his words; she finds she has been expecting them. She drinks the dregs of the wine in her glass and says calmly, 'I'm not at all sure at this moment why I'm going. For, of course, I love you too.' She finds she is trembling. She is feeling terribly confused, her senses giving her messages she is not sure she can handle.

Troy groans like a man in pain and takes her in his arms. She tries to tell him why it is no good, that though she loves him, she has become sexless, frigid, physically incapable of responding to any man since her accident.

He continues kissing her face, her neck, her breasts, not hearing what she is saying. She knows she should push him away so that he will listen, but his hands are covering her body as he uncovers the layer of clothes from her skin. She is no longer quite sure she wants to tell him anything, except to please not stop whatever it is he is doing.

Only when they become in danger of falling out of the window do they stumble onto Alina's bed. There they make love, and it is Alina who is urging Troy on, unable to get enough of him, wanting more of him, all of him, now, quickly, until at last she shudders, moans softly, and is suddenly very, very still.

Troy says, uncertainly, 'Are you all right?' and is frightened out of his wits when Alina begins to cry, loudly, harshly.

'Oh, love,' Troy gasps, full of remorse. 'What have I done, I'm sorry, I didn't mean, I didn't intend . . . I took advantage, you're overwrought. Oh God, I'll never forgive myself.'

Alina gulps between her tears, 'You don't understand. I'm so happy. I thought . . . never thought . . . Oh Troy, oh love!'

It takes some time for Alina to explain, and Troy to understand what she is saying, and by that time they

216

are making love again, more slowly this time, wanting to savour every sweet moment of it. Alina cries silently off and on throughout, which is somewhat disconcerting for Troy, but he understands that her emotions are wrecked, fragile, just like her body was after the accident. After a time her tears dry, and her face is so transformed with happiness that he feels like crying himself.

Lovemaking was never like this, Troy thinks with wonder as the short night turns into day and the seagulls begin to call to each other outside the still-open window.

At about five in the morning, in the full midsummer light, Troy looks at Alina and says, fearfully, 'We could have missed this. Let it pass us by. If we hadn't happened to be alone tonight, you'd have gone tomorrow. Or rather today.' A sudden thought seizes him. 'Perhaps you really are gone. Perhaps you are in Dublin and I'm alone in Heron's Cove, dreaming this.'

Alina kisses him firmly to assure him he is not dreaming. For a few moments he lies back and enjoys it, then sits bolt upright. 'You're *not* going, are you? I mean, I just assumed . . . that is, you couldn't . . . Oh God, am I being presumptuous to think that this might make you stay?'

Alina lays her head on Troy's naked belly. Her hair ripples over his body like a field of barley. 'What do you think? What do you really think?' she asks dreamily.

All these questions, Troy thinks. Me, now Alina. Yet I don't mind. I want to ask, want to know, want her to ask anything of me.

'I think we're under a spell,' he says. 'I think you are trapped here. For ever, as they say in the stories.'

'Do you mind?' The golden hair swishes against his belly as she lifts her head to look at him.

'Mind?' he says, slightly delirious. 'Mind?'

She is convinced. 'Oh, Troy, how lucky we were that we stayed in tonight. That I didn't just say goodbye and thank you, and leave. I'd have done it, you know. If this hadn't happened.'

'And I'd have let you go. How fortunate we were, what luck that we didn't lose each other.' They cling to each other, appalled at how different their lives would have been had they missed this.

Chapter Eleven

Steffie begins to worry about Troy about eleven the next morning. Troy is, of course, still in bed with Alina, though no-one yet knows this. 'He's never slept in this late,' Steffie says to Claudia. 'He's an early riser. I expected him to be up at dawn, fussing about tonight. I think I'll go see if he's OK.'

'No!' Claudia is adamant. 'Let him sleep.'

'What if he's ill?'

'Relax, Steffie. I promise you he's not ill.' Claudia looks smug.

'And what about Alina? It's late for her, too, though I suppose she's resting as long as possible.'

Claudia says nothing, merely smiles enigmatically. They are on the terrace, relaxing after checking that everything is in order for tonight's concert. The chandelier in the music room is sparkling in the morning sunshine; the harpsichord is tuned, polished, gleaming.

Ivo walks in with a basket of turf which he puts by the fireplace at the far end of the room. 'Shouldn't need this, but in case the evening gets chilly . . .'

'It's supposed to be like this all day, warm and sunny,' Steffie says.

'I know,' Ivo responds gloomily.

'It's just as well,' Claudia says briskly. 'It wouldn't do Alina any good to have you walk out in the middle of her concert because you've heard a rumble of thunder in the distance.'

Ivo looks at Claudia regretfully. She positively glows

with energy this morning, and he wishes he could plug into it. She is the only woman he has ever known that might have deflected the lightning and given him the high that neither sex nor love have given him in the past.

But really, he thinks as he watches her, would anything ever give him the buzz that a storm does? He decides not. There is no line between himself and the lightning he photographs: they are one. There is no room for a woman there, not even one like Claudia.

Anyway, he has Steffie back now, the Steffie who loved him, mothered him, in those lost days of childhood. It's enough. Steffie, he decides, is the perfect mother: caring, understanding, yet letting him go to do what he needs to do, never nagging him to keep clean or warm or safe. If she's the same with her baby, the child will be lucky indeed.

Marcel joins them on the terrace. 'Anything else to be done for tonight? I've been to the village, told them not to sell any more tickets. People will be standing as it is.'

He is on his best behaviour today, aware that the others, and especially Claudia, will be watching him to make sure he does not upset Alina again. He will be glad when this wretched concert is over. They can all leave Heron's Cove and go back where they belong: Alina to Dublin and her family, Steffie to America, and he himself to Brittany, to his forest, there to forget all these confounded difficult women and devote himself to his music and his woodland.

And Claudia? She is looking at him thoughtfully. She can go back to Paris and leave me in peace, he thinks, scowling at her.

'Don't look so fierce at me,' she says with a mischievous grin. 'You'll miss me when I'm not around.'

He's startled enough to say, without thinking, 'Do

you know, you wicked witch, I believe I will.' And he realizes he means it.

At that moment Troy walks in. He is dressed in old jeans and a ragged jumper with holes in the elbow, as if he grabbed the first thing to hand. He has showered and shaved, for there are nicks in his cheeks and his hair is damp, but he looks thrown together, slightly askew. Yet his dishevelled state belies some inner contentment tinged with excitement, for his eyes are unnaturally bright, his face luminous in the late morning sunshine.

'Troy, I've been worried about you,' Steffie cries. 'Are you all right? You look strange.'

'Yes, yes, fine, wonderful. What a glorious day. What sunlight. Such an omen for tonight.'

'Alina's not up yet. Claudia, should we bring her coffee?' Steffie worries.

Troy says, 'She's up. I'm making her tea. And breakfast.'

'I'll take it up,' Marcel volunteers.

'No, no, I will,' Troy says hastily.

Steffie is still concerned. 'Did she sleep last night? I was afraid she'd be too frightened about the concert.'

Before Troy can answer, Alina appears beside him, dressed in the soft grey shirt that Troy had worn last night. It comes down nearly to her knees. Her legs, her pale feet, are bare, her hair hangs long and loose over her shoulders. 'I'm not frightened. Not any more.' She places her hand in Troy's and the two beam radiantly and idiotically at each other.

There is no doubt in anyone's mind what has taken place. Claudia is smiling widely, not at all surprised, and Marcel, shocked, stares at her. He is sure that she has had something to do with this.

But Alina is speaking, and for a few moments he can

barely believe what he is hearing. 'I'm not going back with David tonight,' she is saying. 'I'm staying here. With Troy. For good.

'I'm starving,' she blithely continues, oblivious to the stunned speechlessness of the others, who are still reeling at this piece of news. 'I suppose it's too late for breakfast.'

'I was going to bring you up a tray,' Troy smiles at her. Roses and honeysuckle, he thinks wildly, and mead, and honey made from the purest heather. He has gone slightly mad and rather enjoys the feeling.

Alina begins hacking off great slices of bread from a fresh loaf Jack brought over earlier, along with flowers for Alina. 'Ah, bliss,' she says with her mouth full. 'I feel I haven't eaten in days.'

When neither Troy nor Alina add any more information to their headline news, but absorb themselves in bread and butter, coffee, throwing a crust now and then to the swans, Steffie says, somewhat uncertainly, 'Well, I guess congratulations are in order, huh?' She prods Ivo and glowers at Marcel.

Claudia, who has been beaming throughout all this, is already embracing them both. She turns to wink at Marcel, confirming his realization of her complicity. Surprisingly, he's not at all cross with her, but actually nods at her with grudging admiration, mixed with a small amount of uneasiness. He's not sure if he's comfortable with other people's witchcraft.

Marcel makes an effort, smiles at Alina and Troy, and says, 'Good for you both. Congratulations.' Ivo joins in the well wishes, as Claudia disappears into the music room to savour the glorious news with a wild gypsy polka on the harpsichord.

Marcel follows her. He interrupts her playing to say, 'You did this. Alina and Troy.'

'Nonsense, Marcel. I set the scene, gave them a few props, and they did it themselves.'

She doesn't really believe this, nor does Marcel. 'I'm never letting you near me again,' he mutters. 'You're not going to bewitch *me*.'

Claudia throws back her head and laughs. Her throat is smooth and golden, and her thick hair, grown longer and wilder this summer, stands away from her head like brambles. 'You've always been the magician, haven't you, Marcel,' she says, when her laughter stops. 'You've charmed with your music. You can't bear knowing that other people have their own magic.'

Her laughter is contagious. Marcel, despite himself, begins to grin, then to chuckle. He has a great longing to kiss that golden throat.

'You're too much, Claudette, *mon bijou*. Too much, *ma chérie*.'

'But not for you, Marcel, surely?'

He succumbs to the kiss, and suddenly Alina seems unimportant, insignificant.

Steffie walks in. 'God, this is contagious,' she blurts out. 'Troy and Alina are clutching each other over the soda bread, and now you.' She doesn't mention that she and Jack were doing exactly the same thing that morning when Jack brought the bread. 'Midsummer's Eve isn't until tonight, so we can't say we've been enchanted.'

But they are, or seem to be. And indeed the next few hours seem to pass in some kind of dream. The six of them linger on the terrace, enjoying the sunshine, picking at cold food throughout the day. Even Ivo relaxes, only occasionally scanning the skies for a sign of turbulence. But there isn't any today. The atmosphere both in the air and in themselves is tranquil. Alina seems the most serene of them all.

But it cannot last. Suddenly it is late afternoon and the air is filled with tension, as before a storm. Claudia runs around arranging all the flowers that have arrived for Alina off and on all day: from well-wishing neighbours, from friends and colleagues in Dublin and elsewhere. News of the concert has spread; there are many people who will be silently cheering for Alina. The thought gives her a tremor of nerves.

Steffie has to ask. 'David is still coming?'

Alina nods. 'I want Kate here. I will talk to them both after the concert. Thank goodness they won't arrive until just before it begins.' Cold fear slices into her gut.

Claudia orders her a hot herbal bath and a rest alone in her room. Even Troy is not allowed near her. The two women disappear upstairs, where Claudia is to give Alina one last quick massage. Steffie follows them, to shower and change.

'I hope she'll be all right,' Marcel murmurs. He is beginning to worry now about how Alina will react when she spots David in the audience, as surely she must. Guilt rattles him again for his part in this complication.

Troy doesn't answer. He knows the ability is there, but he, too, is concerned about David, afraid that all that negativity he dumped on her will surface when she sees him again.

'If she doesn't lose her nerve, she'll be brilliant,' Troy says finally.

Marcel nods. He finds he is quite nervous himself for Alina. He wants her to succeed, wants her to be happy. If that means leaving David, living with Troy, then that's all right too.

Surprised at such generosity of spirit in himself, he says to Troy, 'I think we need a drink, no? Shall we open one of the bottles of red wine I brought from France? Perhaps the Beaujolais?'

Troy agrees, for he too needs a drink. He's been wary of Marcel ever since he got Alina in such a state. But when Marcel impetuously drinks a toast to Alina and Troy, to a happy future together, Troy begins to relax.

'Come, join us,' they call to Ivo, who is sitting watching the tide recede from the cove, leaving murky wet sand in its wake.

Ivo does. When Claudia and Steffie, sparkling and festive, appear from upstairs, the three are in a jaunty state indeed. Even Ivo seems to have jollied up for the evening. 'Hey,' Steffie exclaims, 'you guys aren't even dressed yet.'

The men let themselves be bullied into moving. Troy, suddenly sober, is filled with panic. Ahead of them this evening is Alina's post-accident début, which could make or break her as a concert musician. There is David and the ensuing confrontation; there is Kate, who will have to be told about Alina and Troy. 'Do you think,' he says to Claudia, in a rather pathetic voice quite unlike himself, 'do you think you can make me one of your calming teas?'

'I think you need it,' Claudia says briskly. She marches him off to take him in hand.

There is a loud burst of applause as Troy, having made the introduction, leads Alina into the music room. Alina stops, acknowledges the packed house with a slight bow. The applause is thunderous.

Alina's husband and daughter are standing at the back. They arrived too late to get a seat, which pleases David because he can stand in a conspicuous position and be recognized not only by Alina, but by the members of the audience when they turn around and shuffle in their seats between pieces. He is indeed a commanding figure, very much a presence with his abundant brown hair standing stiff from his high imposing forehead, a dramatic streak of silver going through it like a comet. He has a perfectly tanned face, and magnetic eyes that command all other eyes to look at him.

Their daughter Kate is just happy to be here. All she wants is to see her mother, know she is all right. She feels sick with apprehension for Alina

Alina glances at the audience and, of course, her eyes fall immediately on David and Kate. She gives her daughter a slight but warm smile. Kate grins in return. Her skin and hair are fair like her mother's, but she is shorter and stockier, like David. Alina notices that Kate's hair has been cut short, spikey, and that she is wearing a beaded waistcoat. She looks both cocky and healthy, and her cheery grin steadies Alina's trembling nerves.

David also looks well, but he does not smile at her. He is dressed in a smart pale linen suit, an outrageous tie, and his distinguished hair has grown longer; his forehead seems broader. He is standing as if he were on stage, as if he were about to conduct his orchestra. As he looks at Alina she sees the eyes of a music critic, a teacher, a colleague given to professional jealousy and possessiveness when her success surpasses, rather than enhances, his. She realizes that this is what he has been for her all their married years. It is time now to have something more.

She looks away from David to Troy, who has seated himself on the end of the front row. He is looking at her like a friend, like a lover. He too is a musician, a professional, but now he is the man who loves her, who is letting the love spill from his eyes and spray over her like sweet summer mist.

Alina, seated at the harpsichord, the room hushed and expectant, feels the rapid beating of her heart, notes the quivering of her fingers. This is it, she thinks, and total panic engulfs her. Then she begins to play and the trembling stops, the panic evaporates. As she loses herself in the music, everything disappears: Troy, David, Kate, the memory of her accident, her failed marriage. There is only this harmony, and herself at the centre, herself whole and complete at last.

Troy, witnessing this, murmurs silently, 'Thank God.' He doesn't even notice that there are tears in his eyes. He sees nothing but Alina, knows with joyous certainty that she has, at last, come through.

The audience takes a long time to disperse. There is wine to drink and various cheeses to nibble, and many congratulations to be made to Alina. Everyone wants to talk to her, everyone wants to share her light, the strong beam of success.

Finally they go, all but the residents of Heron's Cove, plus Jack, who cannot seem to leave Steffie, and Kate and David, waiting to take Alina home.

Alina speaks with Kate first, while David is being introduced to Marcel and Claudia. Alina takes her daughter to the old drawing room, which is empty. The debris of the evening, dirty wineglasses and plates with crumbs, lie strewn about carelessly. 'They'll have some cleaning up to do tomorrow,' Kate says lightly.

'*We* will,' Alina says. 'Troy and myself. I'm staying on, Kate. I'm not going back to your father.' She knows this is blunt, but cannot do better. The quicker it is said, the less painful, she feels.

Kate runs her fingers through her stubble of hair. Alina continues gently. 'I love Troy, and he loves me, though it wasn't this way when I arrived here. You know why I came, I've told you all that. You know, too, how your father said I'd never play again, but Troy insisted I would. We didn't mean to fall in love. But even if we hadn't, I'm not sure if I would have stayed with David. There have been great divides between us for years.'

Still Kate doesn't speak. When she finally does, her words surprise Alina. 'I'm so proud of you, Mum. You were just brilliant tonight. We were wrong, Dad and me. We honestly believed you were finished as a performer.'

'I suspect the doctors thought it too,' Alina says, moved. 'It doesn't matter now.'

'It does. If it was us instead of Troy who had the faith in you, would you have come home with us?'

Alina could weep, and nearly does so. 'It's more than that, Kate. It goes back years, like I said. The house in Dublin isn't my home any longer, it's here, in Heron's Cove. And you know it's your home too, if you want it to be. You can live here with us whenever you like, when you're not at college.'

Kate, who has surreptitiously wiped away a tear, sniffs and says, 'I shouldn't be surprised, I suppose. I've known for years you and Dad weren't that crazy about each other. And Troy's OK; he's good for you, I can see that, I always have.' Another tear trickles down her cheek. 'Don't know why I'm blubbing.' She tries to smile but doesn't quite make it.

How hard it is, Alina thinks, holding her daughter and waiting until the tears stop. She's an adult, she'll have her own home soon, she understands why I am doing this. Yet at this moment she is only a child whose parents are splitting up.

The moment is acknowledged by them both, and passes, though not without leaving its scars. Kate, brightening, says, 'So now for my news, I've been saving it till I saw you. I'm moving out of the Dublin house next week, I'm renting a place with three other students. I was afraid you'd be upset, me moving out just as you were coming home. But I had to do it anyway.'

Alina allows herself a small smile. 'I felt the same. I was afraid *you'd* be upset, at home all summer and my staying here, then not going back with you tonight. But like you, I had to do it anyway.'

Kate, with the sophistication of her nineteen years, says, 'I do understand about you and Troy, you know. When you stayed on here, I knew you must be having an affair.'

Alina starts to protest, then decides it isn't necessary.

'Sure I was upset at first. But then I met someone myself a few weeks ago. I was going to tell you on the phone, but it seemed so special that I decided to wait until I saw you again. We're going out together now. He's one of the friends moving into the house I'm renting. So you see, I understand.' This is said with not a little condescension, which delights Alina no end.

'Bring him here,' she says. 'Bring him to Heron's Cove.'

At that moment David walks in. 'There you are. It's time we left, it's getting late. Where are your cases, Alina? We won't drive back to Dublin tonight, it's too late. I've booked a hotel I know in Killarney; we'll drive there at once and set off early tomorrow morning.'

Kate and Alina exchange looks and Kate hastens out of the room. 'Sit down, David,' Alina says.

David shakes his head. 'We'd better go. Or are you waiting for me to tell you about your performance? I suppose that's understandable. It was flawless, Alina.

You've done what I frankly never thought possible.'

'Thank you,' Alina says faintly.

'I suppose you'll go on performing. I hope your nerves can take it. You know you've become over-emotional since the accident. Nervy. I'm still not at all sure you should be doing this. You'll give yourself a nervous breakdown.'

'Thank you,' Alina says again. David doesn't notice the sarcasm.

'I suppose I should thank Troy. Being a harpsi-chordist himself, he was able to coach you in a way I couldn't. And, of course, you had that beautiful new instrument to play on. I really think it's one of Troy's finest, even better than the one you bought from him several years ago. I've offered to buy this one for you, but he was evasive.'

Alina is touched by this. It makes it harder for her to say, 'David, I'm not going back with you.'

For a moment he looks confused. David is an orchestra leader; he is the one who orders, commands, has others doing his will. It is as if a second violinist is saying to him, 'No, I *won't* play that passage more slowly.'

Pulling himself together he says, 'Nonsense. You're my wife. I want you back.'

'Do you, David? Why?'

He is thrown by this. As usual when this happens, he becomes aggressive. 'Alina, your accident has obviously unhinged you. And this enforced isolation, surely it was the last thing you needed after the months in hospital, the weeks convalescing at home. Now please collect your things. I told the hotel we'd be there shortly after midnight and we are already running late.'

Alina says calmly, 'You haven't answered my ques-tion. Why do you want me back?'

David is about to lose his temper, but decides it would only be counter-productive in getting Alina out of this house. 'Because we've always been together,' he says with exasperation. 'We've worked together and no doubt will again, if you're sure you can take the stress. It would be disruptive to change things. We've not had problems before; we've led fairly separate lives, I've given you space – isn't that what women want these days?'

He does not mention love, of course. He has not mentioned love for a long time. Alina sits silently, unnerving David further. He rushes on, 'What will people think, for pity's sake? Your parents, they're old, they're good Catholics, they don't even know what you're up to here; they think you're convalescing still. They'll be horrified.'

'They'll cope.'

'Our colleagues then. It'll be a scandal, Alina. You're too frail to face a scandal like this.'

'Oh, David, stop that,' Alina says wearily.

'Kate will hate you.'

'I wondered when you'd get around to Kate. I've already talked to her. She doesn't.'

David, frustrated, slams his fist into his hand. 'Damn you, Alina. Are you punishing me because I didn't encourage you to make a comeback? I explained that to you, I thought you understood, it was for your own good.'

'How dare you decide what is for my own good? Did you ever listen to *me*? Did you ever listen to what *I* wanted?'

David looks at her, and the look is one of hatred. 'So this *is* a punishment.'

'Of course not. Oddly enough, I believe you did want to protect me from failure. What hurt was that you

231

didn't know me enough, or want to know me, to understand that the failure would have been if I *didn't* try.'

'It's the other thing, then. The reason you're leaving me. You're punishing me because, later, I couldn't face touching you, wanted separate beds, separate rooms. I thought you were too fragile, too ill, too delicate. Once again, I was trying to protect you, and you do *this*.' He makes a grand theatrical gesture, embracing Alina, the house, Troy somewhere inside waiting for this scene to be over.

Alina shakes her head sadly. 'I wish you'd stop going on so about punishment. The old Catholicism dies hard, doesn't it. I know why you couldn't face me, didn't want to make love to me after the accident. I was too much of a reminder of your own mortality.'

'That's rubbish.'

'I don't think so. In our profession, it's not hard to begin to believe in one's own immortality. The music we make is as close to the gods as you can get, and the adulation of the audience can be heady. As a conductor, you get not only the audience but the whole orchestra to command, so it's even more difficult to remember how ordinary you really are.'

David contradicts this vehemently. He doesn't think he is ordinary at all, so Alina's argument has no logic to him.

She finally interrupts. 'It doesn't matter, David. Though it hurt me at the time, when you so blatantly let me know you no longer wanted me, I blamed myself, thought the accident had changed me, made me cold, frigid, as well as physically undesirable. And that in turn made me shrink from you. Neither of us helped the other.'

David finds this an unpleasant turn in the argument,

232

so he goes back to more solid ground. 'If you won't think of Kate or me, think of the scandal. It will look odd, your leaving me when you've only just recovered from your accident; it will start rumours, people will talk.'

Alina looks at him wearily. The compassion she had felt for him drains away and she just wants him to be gone. This is not the end of our marriage, she thinks; it ended years ago, only neither of us would recognize it. She wants David to acknowledge it now and be gone from Heron's Cove.

'I'm no longer afraid of scandal, of what people will say and think,' she says with some asperity. 'I wish I hadn't been so afraid years ago, when I was pregnant with Kate. I wouldn't have married you then.'

David is shocked by this. Up until now he has been standing, but he slumps in an armchair opposite Alina and says, bewilderedly, 'You wouldn't have married me?'

Again Alina is touched by his confusion. She says, more gently this time, 'No, and if you're honest, you will admit to yourself that you wouldn't have married me either. You were more frightened of the scandal, the repercussions, than I was. You were my tutor, David, twelve years older than me. I was only eighteen. If we hadn't married, you would have been thrown out of your job; seducing a student and getting her pregnant.' She sighs. 'What a farce it all was. All that covering up. I should have been brave enough to have just gone away and had the baby on my own, raised it myself.'

'Fine words now,' David says scornfully.

'I suppose.' Her voice is so forlorn that David is moved to ask, 'Was it that bad then? All those years of marriage to me?'

She thinks for a moment, then says, 'No, we had good times. But so few together. We were both so intent on getting our careers established.'

David leans back in the chair and closes his eyes. When he opens them he seems calmer, resigned. 'How much does Troy have to do with all this?' he asks.

Alina hesitates. She wants to be honest, but she doesn't want to hurt him more than necessary. 'If I hadn't come here with Troy, our marriage might have jogged on, for a while anyway,' she says slowly. 'But it wouldn't have been good for either of us. You've left me too, David. You left me long before I found Troy. You left me for your other, more exciting, more dramatic life, which gradually became your only one. Kate and I were on the fringes.'

David realizes that this is true. He stands up slowly. 'I'll be in touch,' he says, his voice drained of emotion. 'We'll need to speak, to arrange things.'

Alina stands up and faces him. 'No acrimony?'

He forces himself to smile. 'Why should there be? As you said, the marriage ended long ago.'

He goes, and she allows herself a few tears for the ending, for the finish of a story that was not all bad, not all the time. Kate comes in, embraces her and cries a bit too. But they part in harmony, Alina promising to visit Kate's new rented house as soon as she has settled.

'Good luck, Mum,' Kate says as she leaves. 'And tell Troy . . . well, I don't know what to tell him, it's too soon. And I can't talk to him tonight, not yet.'

'It's OK, Kate. He's not expecting you to. Nor am I.'

'Tell him to look after you.'

Alina smiles. 'I can look after myself now. That's what Troy has done for me. But I'll tell him, Kate.'

*   *   *

Troy finds her still sitting in the drawing room, unable to face the others just yet. 'Are you all right?' he asks.

She's not, of course. Not yet, though tonight she has at last wholly recovered from her accident. Her hands are completely healed; her nerves steady; her body totally recovered.

Yet there are other wounds now, which will take time to mend. One doesn't slice nearly twenty years of marriage, no matter how unsatisfying, from one's life without some blood and scarring.

Troy understands this, and lets her grieve. 'You will recover from this, too,' he says softly.

She is grateful for his patience. They sit amongst the debris of Alina's comeback party silently, both celebrating and mourning at the same time.

Chapter Twelve

Everyone, except Ivo, wilts in the next few days. The weather is muggy and hot, with sporadic thunderstorms. Only Ivo is sparky; the others drift about in a somnolent state, unable to set their minds to anything after the nervous tension generated by the concert. Troy and Alina wander around in a trance of their own, dazed at being together, groggy with a surfeit of lovemaking.

'I'm distracting you from your work, your harpsichords,' Alina says every morning in bed as they linger, listening to the morning noises, loath to get up.

'This is high summer. Most people are on holiday. I will be, too, for once. I was a workaholic until I met you, remember.'

'I must get busy.' But she doesn't move, because Troy is stroking her hair which hangs loosely across her breast. 'I must phone my agent, tell him I'm ready for work again. There was a recording coming up before my accident, I must see if that's still on. And my students in Dublin, I have a select few that I coach — perhaps they will come here? I know it's too far for a day, but we could have weekend workshops, Troy. Along with the concerts . . .'

'There is plenty of time,' he murmurs. And his hands assure her it is so.

Marcel and Claudia have made no move to return to France. Marcel cannot leave Claudia alone, but she lets him near enough to smell the scent of her fragrant oils and spicy perfumes, and no nearer. If he tries to get closer, she is unyielding. Her patience, or stubbornness as he calls it, both maddens and intrigues him.

Steffie also seems unable to get a grip on herself. She feels she must get to Peru to see Luis in person, though he tells her that there is no need; there are no suitable babies available for adoption at the moment.

Jack is at Heron's Cove every evening, when his farming work is done for the day. 'I'm the only honest working person amongst you lot,' he says, grinning, but quite serious, to the protestations of the others. Steffie cites her weekly column that she must keep up, and the series of articles on Britanny she wrote for the monthly magazine in New York. 'And besides,' she tells a sceptical Jack, 'I'm entitled to a break, too, you know. I work like a maniac back in Miami.'

'We all work,' Marcel chimes in indignantly. 'Claudia and I have been rehearsing for most of the summer. We have a strenuous tour lined up for autumn and winter. Troy makes his harpsichords, Alina practises constantly – what do you call this if not work?'

'But that's *fun*,' Jack protests. 'I practise my fiddle, I play in pubs most evenings, or used to before I started hanging around here, but that's not *work*, so!'

'And what about Ivo?' Steffie demands. 'He runs himself ragged photographing storms.'

But Jack scoffs. He doesn't believe that what any of them do is really work.

Then, finally, as if by some collective unconscious decision, they all resurface in the real world again, though Jack would not call it that. The real world is his farm, the cows put out to grass after milking, the smell of them after rain, the turf on his mountain waiting to

237

be cut and brought home. But he is fascinated by this other world, where music is a serious profession rather than something to lift your soul after the toils of the day, where lunatics chase after lightning, where witches brew potions, where Celtic princesses go falling in love with men who bewitch them with the tinkling notes of a harpsichord.

Troy has asked Marcel and Claudia to give the July concert, for the cellist he had booked suddenly cancelled. Marcel is quite willing, which surprises Claudia, for he hates being away from his beloved forest for too long a time. But he has changed his mind about going; there is something about Ireland that he is drawn to. It is because the country reminds him of his own Brittany, his own Celtic origins, and he is beginning to feel at home here.

He and Claudia start to rehearse again. Steffie also returns to work; dragging out her laptop computer, she begins to work on a series of travel features on County Kerry, and then further afield on West Cork. Jack, deciding he needs a holiday, drives Steffie around the countryside in his clanging old van, encouraged by Lil and Paudie who alternate between hope and despair at this new interest of their son's.

'But he's married,' Lil says when despair takes over. 'In the eyes of God he's still married. A sin, is what it is, Paudie.'

'Sure but what God would deny the boy a bit of happiness, Lil? His wife doesn't want him. Would you say he should live like a priest the rest of his days?'

'Ah, Blessed Mother in Heaven forgive me, but surely it breaks my heart either way. Still,' she admits, 't'would do him good to have another child. And me as well, God help me.' Her face gleams at the thought of another grandchild.

It is Paudie's turn to lapse into despair. 'Don't forget the woman's an American. She'll take both the child and our son away from us.'

'Isn't she English? Hard to tell, the way she speaks. So she will, Paudie, so she will, whatever foreign parts she's from. And she's older, now.'

'And would you be forgetting your sister Brid, now then? She had a child at forty-five and her husband no more than thirty, and ten years on they're happy as the heifers on the first day of spring.'

Variations on this theme take place almost every evening when Jack is out with Steffie. Sometimes Paudie takes the optimistic view, sometimes Lil; most nights they bounce from court to court like a tennis ball.

Their friends and relatives join in the speculation. On Paudie's sixtieth birthday, they are all at the farm to celebrate. It is a surprise party, organized by Lil. Jack's brothers are all there from England, and Jack has invited Steffie.

'She's a bit of all right,' one of them says to the others in the kitchen that night, when the party is well underway. 'Nice legs. I like the miniskirt.'

'God, you're a yob,' says Brendan, the oldest. 'She's got a nice sense of humour, I like that.'

'To be sure, Jack seems light-hearted tonight, the first time I've seen him so since he and Mary split. The woman must be good for him.'

'But is she toying with him now, Michael? She's only here temporarily. She's some high-profile journalist, so it seems.'

'And he's crazy about her, Sean. You can see that a mile off.'

They talk and they worry. They are all off again tomorrow, back to London and their wives and girlfriends and work, but they're family, they care.

Steffie likes the brothers. She feels at ease with the whole family, enjoys the party: the spontaneous jokes and roars of laughter, the talk of politics and history, the noise of it, the merriment of it.

At around midnight Brendan, in response to a comment by one of the guests, bursts into the chorus of a song, which sounds to Steffie like: 'Whack fol the do, fol the diddely idle ay,' which makes no sense, but everyone seems to know it. Brendan sings a verse, and the others join the chorus. The song is long, and by the end Steffie too joins in: 'With me whack fol the do, fol the didely idle ay.' She realizes it is the joy of the singing that matters, not the meaning of the words.

All the guests are crowded in the living room now. Though the evening is warm, it's damp, and a turf fire smoulders in a tiled fireplace. When the song is over, Michael calls to one of the guests, 'Come now, Therese, give us a tune.'

A slim woman in a short black dress makes a look of mock horror, rolls her eyes, then, not moving from the armchair where she is seated, she sings in a lovely soprano voice. Steffie recognizes it as an old Greek song, sad and haunting, lovers parting and not meeting until the wild rose blooms again. The words are lyrical, the tune evocative, and everyone listens appreciatively.

One after another, the guests sing. Some are Irish songs; there is one in Gaelic sung by an older woman, a nursery song that she says she hasn't sung since she was fifteen and crooning it to her younger sisters. There is a murmur of recognition as she sings.

Steffie is surprised at the quality of the music, of the rich remarkable voices of the singers. The songs vary: one man clicks his fingers and sings, 'Sixteen Tons' and everyone joins in the chorus; another one begins 'Galway Bay' and again the others join the refrain.

After an hour or so, with no-one showing any signs of wanting to go home, though it is one o'clock, Paudie says, 'Lil, will you be singing my favourite now?' He looks at her softly.

Lil, curled on the sofa next to him, sits up and nods. There is a silence in the room. In a sweet clear voice she begins to sing 'Danny Boy'.

Paudie's eyes are closed. His boys aren't far, only in London, and there's no famine, and there's peace, of a kind, so the boys can come and go safely. And Jack's right here on the farm, God bless him, and God bless all of them for leaving work and family and getting here for his sixtieth. Yet the words of the song bring out the sadness in him, and he knows he'd like the boys back, more than anything. Thanks be to God he has Jack, and surely it would kill Lil if he up and went to America with that Steffie. To be sure she wouldn't settle in Ireland, now, though she likes it well enough. But sure she's a town girl, whatever she thinks. Born and bred in cities, and what would Jack be doing in a city? He was unhappy in London, never liked it. Paudie would like to see Jack settled on the farm, and yes, with a woman who would give him more children, whatever the priests say, whatever Lil thinks about mortal sin, with Jack being bound to Mary for ever in the eyes of the Church. The Church can just look the other way for once.

Lil has finished the last sweet refrain of 'Danny Boy'. There is a small moment of silence. Paudie says gruffly, for the music has brought on the filling behind the eyes, as it always does, 'T'was beautiful, Lil. As always.'

Steffie, sitting with Jack on the opposite side of the

room, is not unmoved by the song and leans her head against his shoulder. All the eyes of the brothers note this gesture, wink and prod each other.

Steffie would be amazed at all the speculation going on about her. So far as she is concerned she is Jack's friend, nothing more. She's too wrapped up in her coming baby to analyse the fondness she is beginning to feel for him.

As the days pass, Steffie tries to immerse herself in work, so that the waiting goes more quickly. Her writing is on a roll, which helps; she is busy on numerous articles about the area. Finally she exhausts the immediate vicinity for ideas and decides to go further afield. Years ago she wrote a series on the Burren, the limestone plateau that occupies most of North Clare and culminates in the dramatic cliffs of Moher at the edge of the sea. She has been asked by the same magazine to follow it up and she needs a few days to do this.

And so Steffie, and Jack who has offered to go with her, book into a small hotel in the village of Bally-vaughn on the edge of Galway Bay. 'Two single rooms,' Steffie announces to the receptionist.

Jack is disappointed, but not unhopeful. He knows Steffie is softening towards him, as eager to have his company as he is hers. It's only a matter of time, he feels. What exactly he wants of her he has not yet examined closely. To go to bed with her, of course. But there is something more, something that has been growing steadfastly since the time of their first meeting, when he gave her a lift from Tralee to Dingle. He likes her spirit, he decides. The carefree way she was hitch-hiking to Heron's Cove, the ease with which she talked to him that day they met. He likes the way she's herself with everyone, from the visiting musicians at her brother's place, to his own parents on the farm.

Most especially, he warms to her passionate longing for motherhood. Though he doesn't quite understand why she wants to go so far afield to adopt, he can relate to her need for a child of her own to cherish, nurture, protect and care for. He felt that way for Tom before the boy was born, feels it now still so intensely that he is bereft for days when the boy leaves to go back to his mother's.

'What are you thinking?' Steffie asks as they walk around the bay one last time before going back to their rooms. 'You've been quiet for the past half-hour.'

'Tom. I'm thinking of Tom.'

That's another thing he's beginning to love about Steffie, he realizes. The way she understands this, never tries to distract him, lets him just get on with his thoughts.

It's quite late and they are tired after a busy day. They have walked all over the Burren, looking for the rare and exotic plants which have colonized the limestone, plants which are normally found in places as diverse as the Arctic and the Mediterranean. Steffie, on her second visit, lectured Jack. 'No botanist has really come up with a satisfactory answer for all these wonderful plants in what appears to be such barren land. They think the Gulf Stream contributes, and the warm rain, the lack of frost. The name, you know, comes from the Gaelic word, "bolreann". It means rock land.'

'I know.' Jack had grinned. 'Are ye forgetting I speak the Irish?'

Steffie had asked him more words, and repeated them after him, trying to learn some of the language. He liked this about her, how she was always asking questions about Ireland, wanted to get at the root of it. He knew it was partly her job as a travel writer, but he could sense it went deeper. Her father after all was half Irish. Though Jack lived in England for many years, Ireland – its land, its history, its people – is important to him. He's glad Steffie does not treat it lightly.

Steffie took photographs with a camera borrowed from Ivo. They walked along spectacular cliffs, climbed over ancient dolmens and stone forts on the stormy terrace hills.

'We deserve this, I'm beat,' Steffie had said that evening, settling in Monks, the pub overlooking the bay. The place was heaving with tourists listening to the musicians: a man with a banjo, and a fiddler and an accordionist. Jack had brought his own fiddle, just in case they needed a spare. The musicians knew him and asked him to join them.

'Sure you don't mind sitting on your own?' Jack said.

But Steffie hadn't minded. The music was good, the atmosphere friendly; she was content to be part of it.

And now the evening is nearly over. She and Jack are strolling around the bay a second time, reluctant to go in. Steffie says, 'What a fun day. All of it, Jack. I'm glad you came along with me.'

'Steffie—'

'Where did you learn to play like that? You're a real pro.'

'Paudie, mostly. You know Patrick's, the pub I usually play in, in Dingle town? Paudie used to take me there when I was barely able to walk. He played the fiddle like a demon when he was young. Still does, sometimes. Still comes to Patrick's for a jar and a fiddle when he's not too tired.'

Jack lapses into another silence. Steffie knows he is

thinking of Tom, how he would have liked to have enough time with his son to teach him to play, take him to Patrick's to saturate him with music like his father did with him.

She lets him be, leaves him with his thoughts while her own drift up to the stars that are large and glittering over the bay. She will take her daughter to the Burren one day, she decides, to the fine pub in Doolin where they stopped this afternoon, where the musicians come from miles around and the music is some of the best in Ireland. She will walk her daughter along the dramatic cliffs of Mohar and watch the twilight on the calm sea, as she and Jack did this evening, and she will take her to this very bay where earlier they saw seals dozing in sunlight.

Her daughter will like Ireland. Perhaps one day she will even play her recorder in Patrick's, and Troy and Ivo will watch fondly, avuncularly, while she, Steffie, will weep with pride.

Steffie smiles to herself at her whimsy, but she would like that: to see the two worlds meet, Troy and Marcel and Alina and Claudia's world of classical music, of concert halls; and Jack and Paudie's world of fiddling in pubs, of great traditional folk music passed down from generation to generation. Perhaps her daughter will be that link, she daydreams.

'And what are *you* thinking?' It is Jack's turn to ask.

She tells him, somewhat shyly, but he is touched, finds it endearing.

He is so moved he has to kiss her. She in turn is so gratified that he doesn't laugh at her dreams that she must kiss him back. The kiss goes on and on, tongues touching, bodies pressing.

'Such a glorious evening, t'anks be to God,' cries a voice a metre or so away, and Jack and Steffie jump quickly apart. It's a fisherman, checking out something on his boat moored in the darkness. They exchange pleasantries, then Steffie and Jack, shamefacedly, walk hand in hand back to the hotel.

'Stay with me tonight,' Jack pleads. It is not the first time he has asked.

Steffie is torn. She would like to, but she says, 'I've told you before. I'm not into flings. And this can't be any kind of a meaningful relationship. I'm about to become a mother, I won't have time for this sort of thing. And soon I'll be back in the States, and we'll probably never see each other again.'

'Jesus, you sound so bloody American. Meaningful relationship, what is that crap?'

Steffie takes umbrage. 'I suppose you haven't a clue. What with your many women – I'll never forget that poor barmaid in Tralee, wondering when you'll be back.'

'Oh, and you haven't had men in your life? And were those relationships so meaningful? If they were, why aren't you with them now?'

Steffie is flustered. 'They didn't work. Not every relationship does.'

'So why not start one with me? We're one step ahead; we already know it won't work, you've said it again and again. Think of all the time and trouble we'll save ourselves.'

'You are so cynical.' Steffie is enraged. 'At least I started my other relationships hoping that they'd have a chance to work, become something—'

'Meaningful?' Jack interrupts with chilly sarcasm.

'Something that is not entirely without hope. Like it would be with you and me.'

Jack shakes his head, exasperated. 'Jesus and Mary. It's *you* who is the cynic. Why can't we simply enjoy

246

each other, for however long we can? Why do we have to worry where we'll be six months, a year from now, when we both very simply would like to go to bed together here and now?'

'That's where we'll never agree.' They are at the door of Steffie's room and she takes out her key, unlocks it and opens the door. 'You see, I don't think going to bed with someone is simple at all. I think it's terribly complicated.'

She walks inside, says good night curtly, and shuts the door before he can say anything else.

'Bloody women,' Jack mutters. He goes out of the hotel, restless and irritable. Walking along the bay he comes across the fisherman again, leaving his boat and heading home. 'No luck?' he asks jovially.

'None at all,' Jack growls.

The fisherman raises his hand in sympathy and walks away. Jack is left at the water's edge, sulking. The moon over Galway Bay moves him not in the slightest.

'I'm going nuts,' Steffie announces to Claudia a few days later.

'So what's new,' Claudia replies.

Steffie plops disgruntledly into the chair next to Claudia, who is seated at the piano. She had been practising, but stopped when Steffie walked in, obviously wanting to talk. Steffie says, 'Oh, God, I know I'm such a bore these days, but this waiting is getting to me.'

'What about your work? I thought that was keeping you occupied.'

'I've finished my series on the Burren, and I can't think about anything else now.'

'What about Jack? Concentrate on him for a bit.'

Claudia strikes a few flashy chords for emphasis. 'Some passion is what you need.'

'Keep lethargy at bay, huh?' Steffie grins.

Claudia shrugs and strikes another chord. 'That boy will make you forget the baby for a time. I think he's quite in love with you.'

'Claudia, don't start. He's not in love with me, he just wants to go to bed with me, and I suppose he's fond of me too. And I adore *him*, but I don't *want* to be distracted from my baby. I mean, it's more than that. I wouldn't be distracted, whatever Jack and I got up to. It would only be a diversion, and that's not fair for him.'

'That's up to him to decide, no?'

'No. I've got no emotion left, Claudia. Not for anything but that baby. It's wearing me out. God, I'm exhausted by motherhood already and I haven't even got a child yet.'

Claudia plays some lighter gentler chords. She knows exactly what Steffie means. She too has begun to dream about children, has begun to imagine herself sitting quietly on a tidy nest somewhere surrounded by little chicks. For someone who never wanted anything but a career as a pianist, this is unsettling. She feels faintly disoriented all the time, like a rather dim duck flapping about looking for mislaid eggs.

'Physician, heal thyself,' she mutters as her fingers ripple along the keyboard.

'What?'

'Talking to myself. I think we both need a tonic, Steffie. A good dose of one of my cleansing herbs. Purge us of our obsessions.'

'But I don't want to be purged,' Steffie wails. 'I love thinking about my baby.'

'Poor Jack,' Claudia murmurs, and launches into

248

another of her favourite noisy flashy Hungarian rhapsodies.

Poor Jack is completely bewildered. Bewitched and bothered, too, it seems; he can't seem to keep away from Heron's Cove. He cannot understand Steffie, cannot comprehend why she won't have a gentle but passionate, intense though brief, love affair with him. He accepts the fact that though he is besotted with her, and she seems not uninterested in him, there can never be anything long lasting between them because of their polar lives, the fact that they are, as Steffie put it with a wry smile, geographically unsound. Yet there is *here*, and *now*, and still she keeps him at a distance, all because of that accursed baby.

Jack is, he realizes, sick with jealousy. The bond he felt at first with Steffie because of their shared longing for parenthood, is now knotted with conflicting emotions. He is jealous of a child who might not even be born yet, and who is unborn thousands of miles away in a Third World country he can't even begin to imagine. Because of this fantasy baby Steffie won't allow Jack into her life, a fact that leaves Jack whimpering helplessly. He alternates between brooding romantic despair and impotent fury. He who was once so sympathetic and understanding, can now hardly bear to hear Steffie mention the child.

'What's the matter with you?' Steffie asks one day. She had gone into Dingle to get groceries and called in to see Paudie and Lil, whose company she has begun to enjoy. Both are out fencing, but Jack is there, waiting for the vet to look at one of the heifers. They have only seen each other once or twice since their argument in Ballyvaughn, and the meetings weren't a riotous success. But Jack offers her tea, and Steffie accepts, and now they are sitting in the farmhouse kitchen talking.

'Nothing's the matter,' Jack says testily. 'It's just that you're always talking about that baby.'

Steffie is stung. 'Sorry,' she sniffs, offended. 'I listen to you talking about Tom enough.'

Jack is full of remorse, for this is quite true, but he cannot tell her he is seething with jealousy of her fantasy child. They part crossly.

'Will ye be leaving now?' Lil shouts as Steffie gets into Troy's car. She and Paudie have just returned from their far field, carrying stakes and wire. They are flushed, grubby, happy after a job well done. 'Stop for tea.'

'I did, with Jack,' Steffie calls out.

'You'll not say no to another cup, now,' Paudie says.

Steffie is torn between wanting to stop and not wanting to talk any longer to Jack. Luckily the vet comes so she can drive off without being rude.

'Dear Mary Mother of God, if those two haven't had words, sure I haven't eyes in my head,' Lil says to Paudie. 'Did ye see Jack's face?'

'Leave them be, Lil,' Paudie says, bouncing over to the optimistic court today. 'They'll sort it out.'

'Seeing Jack tonight?' Alina asks when Steffie gets back to Heron's Cove.

'No,' Steffie says shortly.

Alina is distressed. Like most lovers, she wants the whole world to be in love. 'You've not had a row?'

'He's terribly childish,' Steffie says dismissively. 'He's very young for thirty-one. I should have known better when I started up with him.'

But that night a repentant Jack is at the door of Heron's Cove, complete with a bunch of daisies he has

250

picked from Lil's garden. Ivo nearly knocks him over with his camera bag as they pass on the terrace. 'They're predicting mega storms tonight,' Ivo shouts. 'About time too. The past week has been dire.' A distant rumble of thunder makes them both look up, but the sky above is clear, innocent. Only in the distance, over the sea, is there a patch of darkness.

'Good luck,' Jack says. The two men look out towards the horizon. The approaching storm has made a mauve patch in the sky, deep and glowing. 'Man,' Ivo hisses. 'Man oh man, this is going to be a big one, I can feel it.'

For a moment Jack recognizes that look: the excitement, the radiance of Ivo's face as he stares at the sky. It's the way he looks at Tom, or at a quiet sunset in deep winter, the sun going down over the silent frosty mountain. 'Good luck,' he says again. 'I hope you get some winners.'

'Thanks.' Ivo's eyes gleam like the approaching storm. 'Tell Steffie where I've gone. Tell her not to worry.'

'I'll tell her. But she will, you know.'

Ivo smiles. 'She always has. That's why I love her, I guess.'

Later, Jack will remember those words. Later, much later, he will tell them to Steffie.

Steffie isn't surprised to see Jack. She is alone in the music room, playing the piano rather badly. She breaks off in embarrassment when Jack walks in. 'I don't dare touch the piano with all these musicians around, but everyone's out now, gone for a meal.' She doesn't add that she felt too listless to join them. All she can do these days is hang around the house, waiting for that call from Peru.

'What were you playing?'

Steffie smiles sadly. ' "Für Elise", the only thing Ivo or I ever learned in years of piano lessons. Troy was the only one of us with any musical ability.'

Jack feels a softening inside himself as he looks at her, and knows he wants more than just to go to bed with her. He thrusts the flowers in her lap and says contritely, 'I've been thinking about you all afternoon. You and your baby. Cutting turf up on the mountain. I've thought of how important a child is to you, just as Tom is to me.'

Steffie clutches the daisies with one hand and the back of Jack's neck with the other. 'Oh, I knew you couldn't have meant it, that you were fed up with my baby. I've seen you with Tom, I know what it means for you to be a father. I knew you understood how I feel, that it's the same even though my baby hasn't arrived.'

Jack puts his own hands around the small of her back, drawing her towards him and crushing the daisies pitilessly. 'I've come up with the answer. To everything,' he says, kissing her earlobe at the same time.

Steffie relaxes and lets herself enjoy it. 'What's the answer?' she asks softly, letting his kiss extend to her neck, her throat. Perhaps Jack is right, perhaps she is being ridiculous in not simply enjoying him, having an uncomplicated affair with him until it is time for her to collect her child.

'So what's the answer you've come up with?' Steffie murmurs again as Jack kisses her mouth, and then again and again. This time it is Steffie who is pulling him harder against her body, whose hands are beginning to creep underneath his shirt. She is, she decides, ready to be convinced.

It is Jack who pulls away. Stroking her fine ginger hair, slightly sparkly with some kind of electrical energy, he says, 'I want you to have my baby.'

A pause, as both Steffie and Jack hang suspended by his words. Then she says, 'What?'

'My baby. Our baby.' He attempts to resume mouth to mouth contact. But Steffie has shot off the piano bench, scattering stems and petals of hapless flowers all over the polished wooden floor.

'Jack, have you gone mad?' she says cautiously.

'I know it's a shock,' he says serenely. 'I know I've been the one talking about flings, summer affairs, that sort of thing. But today, on the mountain, I had a kind of revelation. You know, like St Paul wandering through the desert, or wherever it was he saw the light.'

'You told me you left the Church ages ago. That sounds suspiciously religious to me.'

'No, not religion. Sense, Steffie. Everything fell into place, like a song, the sweetest song in Ireland.' He is suddenly too shy to tell her that the real epiphany on that mountain was the realization that he was in love with her, that he wanted her around always.

Steffie says nervously, 'Jack, why don't we just go to bed? I've sort of come around to your thinking. We can live for the moment, *carpe diem*, that sort of thing.' She can't believe she is saying this.

But Jack is burning with the fervour of the converted. 'Listen to me, Stef. It all works. You are desperate to have a baby, I can understand that. You're over forty, you haven't much time—'

'I'm adopting, Jack,' Steffie says tersely. 'I have plenty of time.'

'And I'd love another child,' Jack plunges on, ignoring what she is saying. 'Tom lives far away, with his mother—'

253

'You're off your tree,' Steffie explodes. 'Do you think that if I had your baby, I'd just hand her over to you?'

'Did I say that? Pay attention, Steffie. I'm saying I want us to have that meaningful relationship – Jesus, I hate that phrase – you're always on about.'

'I'm not always on about it, I mentioned it once.'

'I want you to stay in Ireland and have our baby here. You said you can work anywhere in the world. You also said you settled in America the past few years only because it would be easier to adopt a baby as a single mother. Come on, Stef, you're European, not American. You don't even talk like an American. Well, not all of the time.'

Steffie stops pacing the floor and sits down again on the piano bench beside Jack. She absent-mindedly picks up one of the broken daisies and shreds it ruthlessly as she speaks. 'Jack, this is all very sudden, and very sweet of you. But it is certainly an extremely elaborate, and unnecessary, way of getting me to go to bed with you. I've been thinking too, and I guess you may be right. We're fond of each other, maybe even a little in love with each other. So why don't we have that fling, as you put it, and enjoy each other? No strings.'

Jack pats her hand fondly. 'You know you don't want that. Nor do I, now. You're going to have my baby, Steffie. And I'm not old-fashioned, you know. I've travelled too, I know how the world works these days. If you don't want to get married, that's fine. I'm nervous about marriage, too. If you want to stay in Heron's Cove with our baby, that's OK, as long as I can see him every day.'

And *you*, he's thinking, but he doesn't want to frighten her by saying too much. 'Of course,' he goes on, trying to keep it light, 'it would be much better if we set up house together. I could do up the old farm-house, you'd love it. A farm's a great place to raise a kid.'

'What about Lil and Paudie? To them, you're still married to Tom's mother, always will be.'

'They'll come around. They like you, Stef. And we get on so well—'

'This is a totally ridiculous conversation,' Steffie interrupts, coming to earth. 'I am not having your baby. I am adopting a child, as planned. I repeat, I am not having your baby.'

There is a long moment of silence. Then Jack says quietly, 'Why?'

She looks at him in exasperation. 'Look, how often have we seen each other, been together? Quite a lot, especially lately. Have I ever said that I wanted to bear a child myself? Have I ever mentioned wanting to be pregnant, wanting my own genes in my own baby?'

'No,' Jack innocently replies, 'but then you weren't involved with me. You didn't realize I'd want your baby.'

Steffie groans. 'Jack, let me make it very clear to you. I feel that there are far too many babies in this world, and that there is absolutely no need to go on making them when it isn't necessary. On the other hand, there are countless orphans needing a home to grow up in.'

'Every woman wants her own baby,' Jack says smugly.

'Wrong. Some women don't want babies period. I have no desire for pregnancy, especially at my age.'

'Don't give me that age crap. My Aunt Brid—'

'No, Jack. No.'

Jack's face begins to cloud, like the sky above Heron's Cove darkening now with the expected storm.

Once again thunder rumbles and rolls, lightning flickers and lights up the music room. 'Looks like the thunderstorms are back,' Steffie says distractedly. 'Ivo will be pleased.'

'What's wrong with me then?' Jack says loudly over the noise outside. 'Why don't you want my baby?'

'I've just told you. I've just explained all that.'

'You don't want a father for this child, that's it. You see yourself as one of these strong-willed independent women who can raise a child without a father.'

Steffie gets up again, walks to the other side of the music room and sits on an armchair there. She is getting weary of this, weary of Jack. She is thinking she has made a serious mistake getting involved with him, with anyone, at this stage in her life. She understands now why some women neglect their husbands after the birth of their child, and how the men can feel they have taken second place. There is no emotion left for anyone else, with a new baby.

This makes her patient with Jack, who after all is the one left out in this love affair. She says, 'On the contrary, I would like very much, one day, to have a father for my adopted child. When and if I meet someone who not only loves me, but is willing to take her on along with me, I would be happy to share the parenting. I'm not some kind of a masochist, you know. I realize how hard it's going to be, raising her on my own. But because I *am* on my own, I have no choice, if I want a child.'

'You have *me* now,' Jack says gruffly. 'But you don't want me.'

'Ah, Jack. How we misunderstand each other. I never said I didn't want you; I said I didn't want to give birth to either yours or anyone else's child. If you want another baby so much, are you willing to stick around me when I bring my adopted one home? Help share the upkeep? The responsibility?'

Jack is silent. The question stuns him. He is still young enough and hopeful enough to want a woman to bear a second child for him, a blood brother or sister for Tom. Perhaps if Tom were living with him, instead of being a visitor who came on holidays and the odd weekend, Jack could consider giving up his wish for another child one day. But the way things are now, he needs his dreams to keep going.

Whatever; he remains silent.

'You see?' Steffie says quietly between the growling of the thunder. 'That's the difference between you and me. You want your own child, made in your own image. I just want a child.'

Jack gets up slowly. 'I'd better go,' he says, but makes no move to do so.

'You don't really understand, do you?' Steffie says.

'Not really. The bottom line is that you don't want my baby.'

'Oh God.' She is losing patience with all this hurt male pride. 'And you see it as a rejection of yourself.'

He shrugs.

'I think we're at an impasse now. Let's just call it a night. We'll both see things more clearly in the morning.'

Jack takes heart at this. 'You're right. I've thrown this out at you, you need time to think it over.' He takes Steffie's last words as an injection of uncontaminated hope which has gone straight to his head. 'It's not such a crazy idea, you know. It would work so well, for both of us.'

'Jack—' Steffie begins warningly.

'Don't say another word, love. Think about it. We'll talk tomorrow.'

He kisses her quickly on the cheek and rushes out before she can reply. When he is gone, Steffie sits back in the armchair, exhausted. For a few moments, after she has absorbed the shock of what Jack has said, she lets herself think about actually having a baby, Jack's baby. She imagines herself pregnant, in labour; visualizes holding her own birth child for the first time. The thought is not unmoving.

And then, in a low-pitched roll of thunder, Steffie seems to hear a child's wail, and knows that it is her very own baby, calling to her, crying out not to be abandoned. A sudden rush of longing, starting deep in her belly and expanding through all the meridians of her body, makes her tremble with desire for this child she has never seen, who may or may not yet be born, but who is there, waiting for her, in some faraway place.

Steffie will not, cannot, turn her back on this baby.

'Please, Claudette,' Marcel whispers, much later that evening. 'Please, *ma chérie*, my sweet French pastry, my adorable Ukrainian witch.'

He is in Claudia's bedroom, having caught her standing naked at the window watching the storm raging over the cove and out at sea. Flashes of lightning illuminate her large strong body which is standing motionless, an imposing statue carved of some mystical golden wood. Marcel shivers as he stares at her.

'No, Marcel,' Claudia says, without even turning around to look at him. Another bolt of lightning strikes the sea and lights up the room again. Marcel thinks she has never looked so magnificent, nor so impassive, so untouchable.

'Shall I go?' Marcel says humbly. He has never felt humble around Claudia, or indeed anyone, before.

'Watch the storm with me,' she says magnanimously, bestowing the favour like a gift from a goddess. 'I've not seen such a one for years. It's been going on and on, and still doesn't seem to have reached a climax.'

Marcel moves closer and stands at the window, close to Claudia but not touching her. He is fully dressed, she completely naked but seemingly oblivious of the fact. It is unbearably erotic to Marcel.

They stand there silently for a long time, watching the thunderstorm. The flashes of light glow orange and mauve and rose and purple over the mountains, giving them an Olympian splendour, and the thunder crashes and raves like the wrath of the gods. Marcel, who has come into the room to persuade Claudia, once again, to make love with him, seems oddly cowed, subdued by the havoc in the skies. He feels sublime, other-worldly, standing at the open window with her watching this display of power and majesty. The rain gusts in at them but Claudia remains statuesque, oblivious to the wind and to the wet.

I belong here, Marcel thinks, with sudden insight. This is my home, my magic forest; this is where my music has led me after all these years. To this woman, to my Claudette. The thought is so profound that Marcel cries aloud, but the sound is lost in the explosion of thunder that must be, surely, the end of the world.

Alina and Troy, making love, feel the thunder vibrating in their bellies and the lightning illuminating their spirits. Troy sighs, 'This is so good.'

Alina is too lost in the moment, in the thunder and lightning and the fire in all her nerve endings, to answer. She is in some other dimension, transported.

259

If the world ends at this moment, she thinks fleetingly, it would not surprise me.

Steffie, alone in her bedroom overlooking the cove, watches the storm from her bed and hopes that her baby is safe and well. In every flash of light, in every vibration of thunder, she sees her daughter's face, hears her lusty cries. Steffie, as she watches and waits and listens, feels her soul merge with that of her baby's. It is almost time. Almost time.

It is almost time for Ivo, too. He has taken Troy's van and driven to the end of the Dingle peninsula, to Slea Head. He is on the headland, the high narrow promontory surrounded on three sides by a roaring sea. He drove through most of the torrential rain getting here, and though the lightning is at its fiercest, there is only a slight drizzle.

The storm has lingered for ages, and Ivo is blazing with joy, as if he has swallowed fire. He has taken photograph after photograph, and knows, just *knows*, there will be more than one winner amongst them.

The lightning has, in the past few minutes, moved in closer, and Ivo knows he should pack up his tripod and camera bag and get back to the shelter of the van, but with every flash the sky blazes with such extraordinary colour that even Ivo, who has seen so much of it before, knows this is something else. A luminous orange he has never seen before, streaks of ice blue, a violet purple: Ivo stands exulting, marvelling, unable to resist one last photo.

'Oh right! Oh man, oh boy, oh right, right!' he shouts aloud.

The sky roars in answer.

'Oh God you are beautiful. So beautiful.'

Another flash, perilously close, but Ivo is in the height of creative orgasm and is impervious.

'Oh man, you've outdone yourself,' Ivo shouts to the skies. 'This is bliss, this is heaven! Oh God, do I owe you one.'

There is a sudden hush in the sky, as if the gods were indeed mulling this over. Then there is an unearthly flash of fire and light, an unbearable scream of thunder, and Ivo, struck, is thrown into the churning sea below.

In the house at Heron's Cove, Marcel, drowning in the noise and the light and the figure of Claudia glistening in the illumination, is struck by a moment's fear, of panic. It is a premonition of death, of loss, of endings. He does not want expirations; he has been rejuvenated by the storm and wants beginnings, a fresh start. Some new magic, a new life. Turning to Claudia he says, over the chaos in the skies, 'It's time. It's time now.'

Claudia understands. She turns to him at last and smiles slightly. Her glorious body, big as the night, as the storm, takes his breath away. 'If you're sure,' she says. 'If you are really sure.'

Nodding, he takes her hand. But before they move over to the bed, they stand for a long time watching the storm blow itself out, the lightning become weaker, the thunder merely the grumble of an old man.

There is the first glimpse of a serene dawn when Marcel and Claudia finally lie down on the bed. A lone bird begins a tentative melody. Marcel has a sudden crazy impulse to get his recorder, join the bird, wake the whole household with a lyrical chorus. But Claudia is waiting, watching him with those bold eyes, and

Marcel decides, for perhaps the first time ever, that his recorder can wait.

'Are you ready for this?' Claudia asks with a smile.

Marcel knows what she means. Is he ready for the next stage, the next level of his existence. Is he ready for change, for love, for the kind of involvement that can bring not only joy and harmony, but also mind-blowing pain and discord?

'Who knows when any of us is ready?' he answers as honestly as he can. 'But at least I know what I'm getting into. At least I'm willing to take the chance.'

This satisfies her. Finally, and at long last, she reaches out to him and draws him to her.

Chapter Thirteen

Ivo's body is finally found four days later, washed ashore in an obscure cove not far from Heron's. It is the final shock for Steffie and Troy, for they had tenaciously clung to the frail and unreasonable hope that he might be found alive, despite the evidence of his jacket and equipment lying abandoned and sodden on the ground not far from the edge of the rocks.

'No, Ivo, no, please,' Steffie collapses when she is told. 'Oh baby, my little one,' she weeps.

The others, except for Troy, think she has been temporarily unhinged by grief and shock, confusing the damaged baby she left behind in Peru with her brother. But Steffie mourns the boy she had mothered, cherished, her first child, the one who awakened her parental instincts for the first time. 'Oh, Ivo, I tried to care for you, look after you,' Steffie cries wildly. 'Don't go, now that we've found each other again. Don't go, Ivo.'

But Ivo is gone, and Steffie weeps inconsolably. 'I failed, didn't I,' she says to Troy when she can speak. 'I couldn't stop him from being destroyed by the thing he loved most.'

'You didn't fail,' Troy comforts her, though he too is devastated. 'He died the way he would have wanted, outside in the middle of a storm. Doing what he loved.'

Alina says gently, 'You can't keep adults from doing what they have to, Steffie. You'll have to remember with your own child. It's a hard lesson for parents to learn.'

'Ivo was my child, my baby. I tried to protect him, but then I stopped, I lost him—'

'He grew up, you didn't lose him,' Alina says. 'All children do. You let him go, you had to, as you will with your own child.'

Steffie, tears on her face once again, says, 'He was never happy, never at peace with himself.'

'That's not true.' Claudia, who has been listening, says, 'He was when he died. He was always at peace, always joyful, in the midst of the lightning, when he was photographing it.'

Steffie, remembering the storm she sat through only recently with Ivo, concedes that this was true. Claudia continues, 'He wasn't whole unless he was part of every thunderstorm, Steffie, we could all see that. He was always trying to get closer and closer to the lightning, make it part of him. Photographing it was a way of doing it.'

'But it killed him,' Steffie whimpers.

'It's the price we pay sometimes, for pursuing what we love, what we crave, what we need.' Claudia embraces Steffie in her big strong arms and holds her tightly. Steffie weeps more, but is comforted. Marcel, watching, mutters words of solace. He is truly shaken by this, is himself mourning Ivo, whose life he has shared during this strange spring and summer. He has never lost a friend before, and he is shattered, vulnerable.

When the initial grief and shock abate slightly, Claudia and Alina pull themselves together, to lessen the burden for Steffie and Troy. There are things to do, Garda officials to talk to, people to notify, a funeral to arrange. Marcel, a useless organizer, surprises everyone by being inordinately helpful, being in the right place at the right time, easing things for the others. He is also a comfort to Steffie while the women are arranging things, and while Jack, who is at Heron's Cove constantly, is needed back at the farm. Marcel doesn't say much, but sits with Steffie, lets her cry, talk about Ivo, whatever she needs. Troy, of course, has Alina to do these things.

Marcel, awed by this proximity with death, and remembering his premonition on the night of the storm, rejoices that he chose life and birth and creation that very same night that Ivo died. Since then, he has exorcized death by clinging to Claudia, by wrapping her scents and oils and spells tightly around him, his own private talisman to ward off demons.

'Shall we go home?' Claudia asks Alina at one point, when everything that needed doing seems accomplished.

'No, please don't. I've postponed the concert, of course, but perhaps we can have it a few weeks later. The quicker Troy gets back to normal the better. If you have no other commitments, you could stay here until then. You can have full use of the music room, use the time to rehearse and plan your winter concerts. I'm afraid if you and Marcel go, Troy and Steffie would go into an awful decline.'

Claudia nods. 'Of course we'll stay, if you think it will do them good. Naturally we had planned to stay for the funeral. I can help you get rooms ready. There will be people coming from the States. When do Ivo's parents arrive?'

'Haven't you heard? They're not coming.'

'What?' Claudia is shocked. Her own parents would travel around the world five times to go to her funeral.

'The father has pleaded a bad attack of angina and says he can't travel. The mother says she is in bed with grief and shock and the doctors forbid her to go. They are opting out, of course. They want Steffie and Troy to cope, as they have coped with Ivo since the day he was born.'

So while Steffie and Troy grieve together, Marcel plays his recorder and Claudia the piano: requiems and funeral pieces, as befits the occasion. The music induces more tears in everyone, but it is comforting, cathartic. By the time the funeral is over, the mourners gone home, Steffie and Troy are slowly coming to terms with their brother's death.

'Thank God the parents didn't come,' Steffie says a few days later, discussing the funeral with Troy.

Troy was secretly hurt by their absence, for it confirmed what he always suspected, that none of them were that important in their parents' lives. He always knew this, of course, but this refusal to go to Ivo's funeral has appalled and shocked him.

'They'd have driven us around the bend,' Steffie goes on gently, knowing what Troy is thinking. She smiles wanly at him. 'Anyway, we've known for ages that we've been on our own. Ever since we were little.'

'Ivo was our responsibility from the beginning,' Troy says. 'We dealt with his life, and now with his death.'

'And we handled it,' Steffie reassures him. 'We couldn't have done more.'

Troy nods. 'He wasn't really able to live a normal life, was he. Photographing lightning was all he wanted or needed; there wasn't room for anything else.'

'But it was something. So many people don't even have that.'

'It eventually destroyed him.'

Or maybe our parents did, Steffie thinks, but doesn't say it.

She goes on. 'The storms were his life, Troy, his work. He knew the dangers, he chose them. Without it, he'd have died anyway; of apathy, bitterness, loneliness, whatever. People do, you know.'

Troy nods, giving way to tears again. 'There's only two of us now. Just two Ginger Nuts left.' He tries to say it lightly but fails.

Steffie cradles him in her arms. 'Just two Ginger Nuts, but not just two of us. Remember, you have Alina.'

And I have my baby, she thinks fervently. Wherever she is, I still have her. But for once thoughts of the baby do not console her, and with Troy, she weeps for Ivo.

Jack tries to comfort Steffie in the weeks after the funeral, and indeed, he has been a great support to her from the moment Ivo went missing. He has still not given up the idea of having a child with Steffie. Tom and his mother are away in England for the rest of the summer with her new boyfriend, and Jack misses his son inconsolably. He hopes that by having another child this loss will be more bearable. He hasn't learned yet that each child creates a special niche in the heart for itself, that it is foolhardy to think you can replace one with another.

Alina frets over Troy's grief and loves him more than ever in his sorrow. Before too long, her warmth, her harmony of spirit and his own deep love for her, melts his sadness and absorbs his loss. Almost guiltily, he becomes alive again, even joyous. His affair with Alina is still too new, too fragile, too blissful, to let mourning bog it down for long. And so Troy gradually lets the dead go and renews vows with the living.

Steffie, too, finds comfort. On the same day that

Claudia notices that her period is late in coming, Steffie gets a telephone call from Lima. It is Luis, telling her that there is a baby there for her. 'It's a girl, and already six weeks old,' Luis shouts down the telephone. 'The mother has relinquished her because she is too young, fourteen. She thought she would want to keep the baby, but after it was born she became ill, distressed, and wants no more to do with the child. The infant is yours if you want her.'

Luis goes on to say that this baby has been checked by many doctors, and is 100 per cent healthy. Steffie scarcely listens: she knows Luis would never dare try to deceive her with an ill child a second time. But it is not only that. This baby has been calling to her for weeks now, in the forest of Brociliande, in the hills of Ireland, in her own head and heart. This is her baby. She knows it beyond any doubt.

'Will you bring the child back here or take her home to America?' Claudia asks that evening, as the five of them sit on the balcony discussing Steffie's plans. She is leaving the next day for Peru.

'It's not as simple as that,' Steffie says. 'Once I decide to have the baby, there are a lot of formalities to go through. Papers to sign, legal stuff. Luis says I'll have to leave her for a month, maybe two or three, with foster parents, until the adoption is legalized.'

'So how long will you stay there?' Alina asks.

'Just a week or so. To see my baby and start procedures. Then it's home to wait again.'

Troy, who has been listening quietly, holds his hand out to Steffie. 'Come here again. While you are waiting. It will be easier for you than in Florida in a stifling heatwave.'

And without Ivo there, everyone thinks.

'Yes please,' Alina says. 'I'll have to be going back to Dublin again eventually, see Kate, talk to David, sort things out. I can go when you come back, so Troy doesn't mope.'

There is still Jack to see. Steffie borrows Troy's car and drives to Dingle town. She knows he will be at Patrick's tonight, making music.

Jack is there, playing his fiddle with two other musicians. They finish the piece and Jack takes a break, making room for her at their table. The pub is, as usual, crowded, the noise a babble of different languages and accents. It is hot and stifling. Summer has lunged into Ireland, bringing high temperatures, exquisitely clear blue skies, and a surfeit of tourists. No-one is complaining.

It takes a long time for Jack to get through the mob at the bar and bring back a Guinness for both of them. Steffie listens to the musicians singing a ballad about the First World War, about a young Irish boy who dies in the green fields of France. By the time the song is over, Steffie is in tears. She thinks of Ivo and his wasted life, then about her own baby, and for the first time sees the perils lying in store for her child. Wars, violence. Illness, pain. How will Steffie protect her, how *can* she protect her? Her own helplessness makes her tremble with dread. She can love her child, care for her, feed and shelter her, keep her from danger as best she can, but she can't shield her from life. Another lesson in motherhood, she thinks grimly. I'm learning fast, and I haven't even held my baby.

By the time Jack gets back with the drinks Steffie has dried her surreptitious tears and pulled herself together. He sets down the glasses and squeezes in next to her. He's delighted she's come, and delighted too that she seems more animated, less sorrowful, than she has been since Ivo's death. 'Ah Steffie, my love, you're looking pert and radiant tonight, so you are. How fitting that you should come looking for your dear Jack.'

'No blarney, not tonight,' Steffie says, and the seriousness of her voice makes Jack put down his drink, look carefully at her.

'I'm sorry,' he says instantly. 'You're still grieving for your brother and I'm making jokes.'

'No, no, that's not it.' Steffie takes a sip of her Guinness before she goes on.

Jack says, 'What's up, Steffie?'

'I'm off to Lima. To see my baby. To begin adoption procedures.'

Jack is stunned. In the aftermath of Ivo's death, he had thought Steffie was leaning on him more and more. He had been sure she was coming around, was contemplating having his baby instead of carrying on this wild-goose chase for an adopted child. 'You're going . . . for good?'

'No, actually, only for a week or so. I can't bring the baby home yet, and I don't particularly want to spend the rest of the summer in Florida. So I'm coming back to Heron's Cove until I can collect my baby. Then I'll bring her home to Miami.'

Relief floods Jack's bloodstream, flushing his face, causing him to exhale deeply. 'You'll be back,' he repeats inanely.

'Only briefly,' Steffie warns gently.

But it is enough for Jack. Anything could happen before Steffie actually goes home to Miami with an adopted baby; she will have time to change her mind a dozen times, and Jack will make sure that he is around to persuade her. He is not being totally selfish in wanting Steffie to give up the whole idea. This adoption business, in a country so unhinged and unsettled, is crazy, he believes, and bringing a child back from there would not be in Steffie's interests.

They do not have a chance to talk much longer, for friends of Jack's are joining them, talking to them, urging Jack to sing. 'Can you wait?' Jack asks. 'I've promised to play tonight, but I can get away in a hour or so. We'll leave here and find someplace to talk.'

'I can't, Jack. I need an early night; tomorrow will be a long day.' Troy is driving her to Shannon airport at six in the morning.

'Wish me luck, then?' Steffie asks as Jack walks her out to the car.

In reply he kisses her warmly, conveying all his emotions in the one embrace. Steffie, her mind on the baby, scarcely notices that he is even kissing her, let alone trying to convey anything. In less than twenty-four hours she will see her child. Nothing registers on her emotions but that.

'I think I'm pregnant,' Claudia says that night to Marcel.

'So soon? Impossible.'

'You changed your mind just at the right time.'

'You bewitched me,' Marcel says, enchanted with her and with his own manly prowess. 'You created that storm, drew me to your bedroom. Made me fall in love with you, just at the right moment for making babies.'

Claudia, wisely, says nothing, enjoying Marcel's admission that he loves her. If he thinks it is sorcery, so much the better. He'll know it is useless to try to get away, if it should ever cross his mind.

It is, of course, too early to tell for sure if she is pregnant, but Claudia is usually quite punctual in her hormonal cycle. Besides, she has a feeling. More than a feeling, an intuitive certainty.

Marcel is immeasurably pleased, and as usual when he is moved either in sorrow or joy, he turns to music. Taking out his favourite recorder, he warms it between his hands and begins to play. He starts with one of Claudia's favourites, 'The English Nightingale', and it is as if he has conjured a sweet singing bird to serenade her. Claudia, wrapped in her black robe, lies serenely on the bed, accepting the music, the homage. Marcel, in black jeans, a loose white linen shirt with no collar and flowing sleeves, moves from Van Eyck to Bassano, a French *chanson* and then a madrigal. He plays and plays, celebrating his darling Claudette, celebrating life and love, and birth and rebirth.

In the main part of the house, the music wafts faintly up through the open window in Troy's and Alina's bedroom, from the windows off the music room where Claudia and Marcel stay. It is soothing and somehow special, like the elusive song of a rare bird.

'Marcel – or a nightingale?' Alina says with a smile.

'Marcel turned into a nightingale,' Troy smiles back. 'Bewitched by Claudia.'

'Or to bewitch Claudia himself.'

'Either one.'

They lie in the dark with the windows open to the hot summer's night, the music of night birds. Stars glow above the cove and the air is still, calm. There has not been a storm since Ivo's death: no wind, no rain, no turbulence. It is as if the sky is at last at peace, having taken Ivo to its own.

Outside of Lima, Steffie follows Luis and the translator, Anita, into the orphanage. Anita is wearing a bright slinky red dress and high thin heels with open toes.

Her finger and toenails are painted the same colour as the dress.

Steffie's fingernails are bitten and ragged, victims of a last-minute attack of nerves last night in her hotel room. She looks pale and ill next to Anita's sensual animal health and Luis's well-fed sleekness.

They are escorted by the director into the same torpid green room, where he leaves them to fight over the one scruffy armchair. None of them make a move to sit. Steffie is unnerved that nothing has changed since her last visit, until she remembers it was only a couple of months, if that, since she was last here.

And yes, the same nurse with the dark wavy hair is bringing in a baby. The nurse is smiling, cooing in Spanish at the infant, whose tiny hands can be seen waving furiously towards the nurse's face. She says something in Spanish and Anita needlessly translates, 'This is your baby.'

Steffie holds out her arms and the nurse places the bundle in them. A wave of dizziness goes through her and she sits down awkwardly in the armchair. Then she looks at her daughter.

She is staring at Steffie, momentarily still. Her black eyes are ringed with lashes so thick and dark that Steffie is moved to touch them lightly with her little finger. The baby squirms, squeals and waves her fists. Then she resumes her staring.

Steffie feels as if this child is looking into her heart, searching her soul, and holds her breath, suddenly irrationally frightened that she will not pass some crucial test. While the baby looks and looks at Steffie's face, Steffie takes in the chubby arms and legs, the abundant black hair already curling on the scalp, the smooth light-brown skin, and falls hopelessly, irrevocably in love.

The baby begins to coo softly. Her face is still serious, still intent on Steffie's, but the sounds she is making seem favourable. Steffie begins to breathe again. 'Ah, baby,' she whispers as tears begin flowing down her cheeks. 'My daughter.' She puts a finger near the baby's tiny palm and the hand clutches it tightly, strongly. Steffie shakes it gently, making a deal, exchanging her heart for the responsibility of this child.

'I want to call her Maria,' Steffie says, and Anita translates to the nurse and to the director. Everyone approves. It is an appropriate name for a child of South America.

Steffie sits with her baby for the rest of the day. Luis urges her to go to the hotel, to rest, recover herself, before starting on all the legal work that must be done before she can go home. He tells her that they must visit the foster family who will look after Maria until she can be taken home, and arrange fees, finances. So much to do before Steffie can go home.

But she refuses to budge. She spends the whole day at the orphange, cradling her baby, feeding her, changing her, playing with her. By the time night comes and she is persuasively shown the door, Steffie feels that she has known Maria all her entire short life.

That night, back in the hotel, Steffie cannot sleep. She feels as if she has moved out of her body into some timeless eternal dimension, that she has fused with the earth, the stars, the universe itself. She feels both ancient and brand new, as if she has lived for ever, yet at the same time, that she is experiencing the very first day of her life.

And in everything, in the long night, her distorted visions, her snatches of dreams, she sees Maria's dear

274

face, feels the grip of her tiny strong fingers and understands that she has come home at last.

When Steffie leaves Peru, having left Maria behind with a jovial kindly foster family where she will obviously be well loved and looked after, Steffie is nonetheless distraught. She cries all the way back to Ireland, missing Maria unbearably. The child is now legally hers and she will be allowed to take her out of the country in six weeks' time, when she will come back to sign the final papers. But even so the parting is wretched, for Steffie, if not for Maria, who, a contented child, seems as happy being fed by her new foster mother as by Steffie.

This little agony, insignificant because the loss is only temporary, makes Steffie think of Maria's birth mother, what exhaustion of body and of spirit she must have felt to give up her child. Steffie, emotionally overwrought, weeps for her, too, weeps for all the women who long for a child and do not have one, as well as for those who give birth but cannot hold on.

And so it is that when Steffie finally arrives at the airport, she looks wrecked and battered, eyes swollen, face blotchy and distraught.

It has all gone wrong again, Jack thinks as he greets her. He is a decent enough man to be upset for her.

'Where's Troy?' Steffie asks. 'He said on the phone that he'd pick me up. I told him I'd find my own way to Heron's Cove, but he insisted.'

'He forgot, of course, that today is Marcel and Claudia's concert. I rang yesterday, to see if there was news of you, and Troy was busy organizing last-minute details. So I volunteered to fetch you.'

'I appreciate it,' Steffie says. 'God, I am so tired.'

In Jack's van, Steffie promptly falls asleep before

they can even begin to talk. Jack leaves her to rest, until she suddenly wakes and feels parched, wants to stop. They pull in at the next small town and find a café, buy pots of tea, sandwiches and cakes.

Steffie eats hungrily and in silence. Jack respectfully lets her be. He knows that she will tell him all about it when she is ready.

At last she finishes and looks around her. The place is full of holidaymakers in shorts and sunhats, sitting at tables laden with calorific goodies. The clatter of voices is lifting and happy. The dry sunny weather has held and the visitors are uniformly jovial.

Steffie says, 'This is where we began, you and me. In your van on the way to Heron's Cove. How long ago it seems, yet it was only last spring. If I hadn't been let off in Tralee by that priest who gave me my first lift, I'd never have met you.'

Jack smiles, liking this kind of talk. 'Sure it's fate, now,' he says, taking her hand across the cake crumbs. 'Steffie, look, I'm sorry about the baby. I really am. But maybe now you'll consider you and me—'

Steffie frowns and draws her hand away. 'Sorry? Well, I am too, at leaving her, but it's only for six weeks. God, it was a traumatic time, Jack. And parting with my baby, with Maria, was pure hell.'

'You . . . you have a baby?' Jack looks bewildered.

Steffie's tired face suddenly becomes luminiscent, like the sky at Heron's Cove before a storm. The transformation from ugly exhaustion to beatific radiance kills Jack's hopes once and for all. 'Tell me about her,' he says resignedly. 'Tell me all about it.'

Steffie does. All the way back to the Dingle peninsula, Steffie talks about Maria, about her time in Peru.

'And you'll be taking her back to the States, then?' Jack asks.

'Oh, yes,' Steffie replies, thus destroying any hope that Jack might have had of her wanting, in the near future, a baby brother for Maria, one with an Irish father. But suddenly all thoughts of babies, either his or hers, fly from his mind as he is hit with the realization that he'll be losing Steffie.

'I was hoping', he barely manages to say, 'that you'd stay on here. I thought you liked Ireland.'

'I do, Jack, but I have to go.' She sees his face and takes his hand. 'I'm sorry, but I must be realistic. My base is there, my home is there.'

'I thought you lot didn't have a home, you and Troy . . .' He falters. He was about to say, 'And Ivo.' Her hand on his is breaking his heart.

'Jack, I've got to make a home now. For Maria.'

'Why can't it be here?'

'I've got to be realistic, Jack. It's not going to be easy, and a cosmopolitan city like Miami will be best for us, at least for a time. Unmarried mothers are not uncommon there, nor are inter-racial adoptions. There is a strong multicultural community and a high Latin American population. Maria won't feel strange, out of place. I've already joined a support group, single women like me who have adopted babies from other cultures. She'll have children like herself she can grow up with. Can you imagine my raising her here? She'd always be an outsider, an oddity, no matter how kind people were.'

She squeezes his hand, in love and sympathy. She is not unmoved at leaving Jack, saying no to what she knows he is offering. She could love him if they had a chance. She does a bit already. 'Don't look so bereft, Jack,' she says softly, though she looks that way herself. 'You have a son, remember? Get that ruin next to the farmhouse done up, make a proper home for

Tom, for yourself. And for those other babies you want, and for the good Irish wife who will be their mother.'

Jack smiles wryly. 'The girl in Tralee?' he says lightly, trying to make a joke.

'You could do worse,' Steffie smiles back. 'She had a sweet face.'

They look at each other and their smiles fade. Privately, each indulges in a brief vision of what might have been, before reluctantly dropping hands and moving out of the café, back to the car and the long journey home.

At Heron's Cove, it is as if nothing has changed. The music room is filled with flowers and fresh candles, and the chandelier from Venice sparkles and flashes reflected sunlight on the walls and the people. Claudia and Marcel are warming up before the concert, while Alina and Troy are setting out wine bottles and various cheeses for the usual supper afterwards.

Jack leaves Steffie at the door. 'You're coming back for the concert, surely?' Steffie asks.

Jack was, but now he thinks not. He needs time; he's feeling too raw to be social. 'I'll give it a miss tonight.'

'Will you come around in a few days?'

'I'm not sure. I've taken a week off from the farm; we've got a couple of cousins staying who can help out.' He doesn't say that he had intended spending this time with Steffie, but she understands.

'What will you do, then?' she asks, knowing he needs to get away from her for a while to recover. She has no doubt that the recovery will be swift and permanent. Jack is young, personable, basically hopeful, and he knows what he wants, now.

'I might go to London, see my brothers and friends

278

there. I've got Tom's address; he and his mother are in Kent with the boyfriend. With a bit of luck she'll let me have him for a few days, take him camping or something.'

'Great idea. He'll love that. He seems a good boy. You'll have more like him one day, I'm sure of it.' She hugs him fondly, and they cling for a few moments. When they break apart, Steffie says, more uncertainly, 'Will I see you again, Jack? When you're home from England? Before I collect Maria and go back to the States?'

Jack doesn't know if he can handle this. But he sees in Steffie's open face a desire for everything to be right now. Like any other lover, she wants nothing to mar her new-found happiness.

'Paudie and Lil would never forgive me if I didn't invite you back to the farm,' he says with forced cheerfulness. 'You can tell them all about the baby.'

Steffie grins with huge relief. 'I took lots of photos of her.'

'You can show me when I get back,' he says magnanimously. They hug again and then he is gone.

Back in the house, Steffie is surrounded. The others stop what they are doing and gather around her in the music room, listening with interest and attention to her account of her daughter Maria, of how she has at last become a mother. It is Steffie's moment, and for once the others forget their own needs and obsessions and listen to someone who has satisfied her own. Even Claudia keeps her secret, not wanting to deflect a particle of Steffie's news. Her own baby can wait until later.

As Steffie winds down her tale at last, a low murmur of thunder can be heard in the distance. 'The first one,'

Troy says. 'The first storm since Ivo died.'

They are all silent for a moment, listening for the next rumbling roll, which comes shortly after. 'Maybe it's Ivo,' Steffie says. 'Maybe he's telling me he's delighted to be an uncle.'

The storm comes to a head during the concert. In the middle of a Castello sonata there is a blinding flash of lightning, a riot of thunder, and all the lights go off.

'Ivo,' Steffie whispers. 'Thank you.'

The lights do not come back on. Marcel and Claudia, true performers, play on with hardly a break, though the summer evening is dark now with the storm. Luckily Alina had lit candles earlier, for atmosphere rather than for any functional purpose. Now, they come into their own, and as Marcel and Claudia continue playing, Troy unobtrusively lights more candles and places them as discreetly as possible near the musicians.

Steffie sits, listening to the music of the piano and recorder competing with the music of the clouds. Gradually the instruments emerge victorious over the roar of the storm, which is lessening now as it blows itself out.

Steffie looks around her. She sees Troy go back to his seat near Alina, watches how their hands reach for each other. She turns back to Marcel in time to see him perform a sparkling piece of virtuosity, and when it is over, glance at Claudia in triumphant satisfaction. *Couples*, she thinks wistfully. Wherever you look, the world is made up of couples.

In the midst of her new euphoria, Steffie is frightened. I'm alone, she thinks in a sudden terror. Just me on my own, looking after, having total responsibility for, a fiercely demanding, helpless, tiny human being.

The thought overwhelms her. Then something in the music, in her heart, reminds her of Maria's cry, and in the candlelight she can see her daughter's dear face, the brightness of her eyes. The panic goes. It will come back, she knows, at odd times, when she is tired, lonely, when Maria is ill or obstreperous. But it will go too, and that is what she must remember.

Marcel and Claudia finish to applause which rivals the thunder they have just heard in the skies. As they take their final bows, the electricity comes on, illuminating the music room with sudden light. The shadows are gone, along with the darkness.

Steffie, with the others, stands and applauds, not just for Marcel and Claudia, for the harmony they have created, but for light and life. It is a moment outside of time, precious. Still applauding, Steffie catches Claudia's eye, and the two women nod and acknowledge each other with an understanding smile. Then Claudia turns to Marcel, who kisses her hand, leads her back to the piano, and together they begin their spirited encore.

Chapter Fourteen

It is a balmy April day on the Okefenokee swamp in Georgia. Alligators sun themselves on fallen logs, looking like the bark of trees themselves. A mockingbird sings. In the still brown water, the reflection of the cypress trees throw back a mirror image, until Steffie, dazed with staring at the water, cannot tell which is reality, which the image.

The man handling the boat has cut off the motor as the boat reaches the short wooden pier. 'Pick y'all up in an hour?' he drawls.

'Please.' She grabs her rucksack and the hand of the small figure next to her in the boat. It is a little girl, no more than a couple of years old. She is wearing an oversized red life jacket and clutching a stuffed leprechaun, recently brought to her from her Uncle Troy and Aunt Alina in Ireland. It is a garish toy, outrageously commercial, and Maria loves it.

'Hungry, honey? I've brought some peanut butter and jelly sandwiches. We can eat right here on the pier.'

'Hmm, goodie.'

Steffie and her daughter settle at the edge of the low wooden platform, munch sandwiches and look for birds and alligators. Steffie knows that Maria is too young to take in much of the swamp, but she had a sudden urge, on this balmy spring day, to get out of Miami, to take Maria to some of the haunts of her own childhood.

Steffie has not been to the Okefenokee swamp since the last time she was here with Ivo. He had taken her that time on an assignment, when he was still photographing landscape and trees and water. Steffie hadn't been back since they were children, and fell in love with it all over again. She had vowed to return often, but her own quest had taken her down a different track.

'But I'm back now,' she says happily to an oblivious Maria. 'Oh, sweetheart, look at all those little fishes in the water.'

They throw bread crusts for the fishes as they finish their lunch, then stand up to explore. They are on Joe's Island, where Ivo photographed his last storm in the States. Steffie has the photographs hanging in her study, along with dozens of others of Ivo's.

It is a weekday and oddly empty. Together they stand in the quiet of the island, palmetto trees surrounding them, the air warm, blowzy with spring.

Maria, a self-contained child, lies down on her stomach in the sandy earth and watches black ants scurrying, a beetle dozing in the sun. Steffie allows herself time to think of Ivo, something she has been too busy to do often during the last two years. Being a single mother was far harder than she had ever anticipated, even in her most pessimistic outbursts of brooding.

'It's worth every minute though,' she says aloud, talking to Maria as she used to before Maria was even born.

Steffie wanders a few yards from her daughter, taking deep breaths, sniffing the air, looking at the sky, which is a clear beguiling blue. She is, she knows, looking for Ivo, as she does these days in every storm, every flash of lightning.

'You're not here,' she murmurs finally. He's not at Heron's Cove either, where she and Maria vacationed last summer, nor is he in the forest of Brociliande, where they visited Marcel and Claudia and their one-year-old daughter only a few months ago.

'But maybe you're everywhere,' Steffie says loudly, causing Maria to look up from her ants for a moment. As she says this, she knows this is true. In Brittany, in Ireland, here, wherever there is a storm, there Ivo will be, sizzling with the lightning, roaring with the thunder.

Satisfied, Steffie lets him rest and turns to the living. Taking Maria's hand, they explore the small island, stopping to watch a woodpecker hammering into a palm tree, a porcupine lumbering into the underbrush.

When the boat comes to collect them, Steffie and her daughter get into the boat and sit up front, where Maria looks for alligators slumbering on fallen logs, or floating in the still water. Steffie, one arm around her daughter, the other holding the side of the boat, looks straight ahead, towards home.

THE END

Still Life On Sand
Karen Hayes

To an artist's eye, the receding sea leaves the boats in the
harbour looking like abandoned water toys after the bath has
been drained. Living in the harbour community of St Ives,
sculptor Esme Cochran has watched both her sons fall in love
with that sea – Hugo with the surfing and Crispin with the
fishing. But here, in the company of the tides, the mists and
the extraordinary local light, other love affairs are also begun.

Affairs that divide husband from wife and artist from canvas
take place alongside budding youthful romances, whilst one
old sailor, Percy Prynne, is haunted by the tragic echoes of
the past and watches over Esme's own growing turmoil with
uncanny foreknowledge.

In this beautiful and perceptive story, in which the sounds of
the sea mingle with the smell of oil paint, Karen Hayes has
drawn an evocative and lasting picture of the lives and loves
of members of a small community.

0 552 99724 2

BLACK SWAN

Evermore
Penny Perrick

'I LOVED IT'
Libby Purves, *The Times*

For Jared Dauman, being rich means being able to wear his
heart on his Savile Row sleeve and nurture his obsession. For
Ellis Peregory, being conventional means not being able to
admit to his own desires. Both of them need something
to happen.

For Ellis that 'something' ideally equals inheriting the most
productive farmland in Wales – Hayden Castle and its estate.
Here, Angela Stearn – the 'killingly gorgeous' married
woman who draws others to her like a fire – attends a house
party and finds herself on the set of a grand opera. One where
all the cast have their own hidden connections, hopes and
desires. But they all join in the same chorus: 'Happiness can
seem about as likely as growing mangoes on the moon.'

Pantomime aristocrats, ex-lovers and would-be lovers, the
compulsive philanderer and the obligatory decoy female – all
meet and collide in the country house setting by the River
Wye. Theirs is a world where betrayal is signalled by an ill-
fitting bracelet from Tiffany's, where the secret of married life
seems to depend on perfect soft furnishings and where there
are precisely ninety-nine steps between heaven and hell.

'INTELLIGENT AND TENDER . . . [A] RICH MIXTURE OF
TOWN AND COUNTRY LIFE'
Mail on Sunday

0 552 99701 3

BLACK SWAN

Touch And Go
Elizabeth Berridge

'MISS BERRIDGE HAS AN EYE FOR THE BEAUTY OF HUMBLE
AND FAMILIAR THINGS . . . SHE HAS A QUIET, WICKED SENSE
OF HUMOUR'
Honor Tracy, *New Statesman*

When Emma Rowlands returned to Wales, to the village where she
had spent her childhood, she brought with her no more than some
favourite pieces of china, books, flowers, and her small pregnant cat.
Behind her she left a broken marriage and an eighteen-year-old
daughter who had fled to India to escape the marital fights.

As Emma, approaching thirty-nine, stood in the solid red brick house
on top of a Welsh hill, she felt a tiny sense of happiness displace her
apprehension. Years before, as a small child, the somewhat maverick
village doctor had asked her what reward she would like for being
brave, and she had asked for the shell house. Now, at a time of
uncertainty and despondency in her life, she discovered he had left
her not the toy house she had asked for, but his own home.

As – hesitantly – she began to renew old friendships and re-examine
her relationships with not only her daughter, but also her mother, a
widow who assuaged her loneliness by continual travel, so gradually
she began to interpret the meaning behind the gift of the house, and
with understanding came the chance to rebuild her own future.

'ONE OF THE BEST, BUT NOT ALWAYS ADEQUATELY
APPRECIATED, OF BRITISH NOVELISTS'
Martin Seymour-Smith, *Oxford Mail*

'ELIZABETH BERRIDGE HAS THE SHARPEST OF EYES. BUT
SOMETHING RATHER MORE IMPORTANT AS WELL . . . WHAT
HER PEOPLE DO AND FEEL AND REPRESENT MATTERS,
SEEMS MEMORABLE'
Isabel Quigley, *Financial Times*

0 552 99648 3

BLACK SWAN

A SELECTED LIST OF FINE WRITING AVAILABLE FROM BLACK SWAN

THE PRICES SHOWN BELOW WERE CORRECT AT THE TIME OF GOING TO PRESS. HOWEVER TRANSWORLD PUBLISHERS RESERVE THE RIGHT TO SHOW NEW RETAIL PRICES ON COVERS WHICH MAY DIFFER FROM THOSE PREVIOUSLY ADVERTISED IN THE TEXT OR ELSEWHERE.

99630	0	MUDDY WATERS	Judy Astley	£6.99
99618	1	BEHIND THE SCENES AT THE MUSEUM	Kate Atkinson	£6.99
99725	0	TALK BEFORE SLEEP	Elizabeth Berg	£6.99
99648	3	TOUCH AND GO	Elizabeth Berridge	£5.99
99687	4	THE PURVEYOR OF ENCHANTMENT	Marika Cobbold	£6.99
99686	6	BEACH MUSIC	Pat Conroy	£7.99
99715	3	BEACHCOMBING FOR A SHIPWRECKED GOD	Joe Coomer	£6.99
99622	X	THE GOLDEN YEAR	Elizabeth Falconer	£6.99
99589	4	RIVER OF HIDDEN DREAMS	Connie May Fowler	£5.99
99657	2	PERFECT MERINGUES	Laurie Graham	£5.99
99611	4	THE COURTYARD IN AUGUST	Janette Griffiths	£6.99
99685	8	THE BOOK OF RUTH	Jane Hamilton	£6.99
99724	2	STILL LIFE ON SAND	Karen Hayes	£6.99
99688	2	HOLY ASPIC	Joan Marysmith	£6.99
99701	3	EVERMORE	Penny Perrick	£6.99
99696	3	THE VISITATION	Sue Reidy	£5.99
99747	1	M FOR MOTHER	Marjorie Riddell	£6.99
99608	4	LAURIE AND CLAIRE	Kathleen Rowntree	£6.99
99671	8	THAT AWKWARD AGE	Mary Selby	£6.99
99650	5	A FRIEND OF THE FAMILY	Titia Sutherland	£6.99
99130	9	NOAH'S ARK	Barbara Trapido	£6.99
99700	5	NEXT OF KIN	Joanna Trollope	£6.99
99655	6	GOLDENGROVE UNLEAVING	Jill Paton Walsh	£6.99
99592	4	AN IMAGINATIVE EXPERIENCE	Mary Wesley	£5.99
99642	4	SWIMMING POOL SUNDAY	Madeleine Wickham	£6.99
99591	6	A MISLAID MAGIC	Joyce Windsor	£6.99

All Transworld titles are available by post from:

Book Service By Post, P.O. Box 29, Douglas, Isle of Man IM99 1BQ

Credit cards accepted. Please telephone 01624 675137,
fax 01624 670923 or Internet http://www.bookpost.co.uk
or e-mail: bookshop@enterprise.net for details

Free postage and packing in the UK. Overseas customers: allow £1 per book (paperbacks) and £3 per book (hardbacks).